SABRINA KANE

1   /lvania,
S   father
P   a farm
in   illness
e   d land.
W   wn the
ri   njo, he
is   e ways,
a   raits to
th   , make
fc   roubles
cc   er de-
sp   er late
h   rriage.
A   match
fc   . .

SABRINA KANE

WILL COOK

SAGEBRUSH
Large Print Westerns

First published in the United States by Dodd, Mead

First Isis Edition
published 2019
by arrangement with
Golden West Literary Agency

A catalogue record for this book is available
from the British Library.

ISBN 978–1–78541–567–8 (pb)

Published by
F. A. Thorpe (Publishing)
Anstey, Leicestershire

Set by Words & Graphics Ltd.
Anstey, Leicestershire
Printed and bound in Great Britain by
T. J. International Ltd., Padstow, Cornwall

This book is printed on acid-free paper

135433724

CHAPTER
ONE

Since Cadmus Kane's sickness had grown worse, Sabrina had been spending most of her waking hours in the wagon with him. His fever had been mounting steadily. Delirium now robbed him of his senses for long periods of time. To ease his suffering, Sabrina Kane bathed his forehead with a damp cloth, and in a small copper dish burned black gunpowder, yet the acrid fumes did little to clear the strangling phlegm in his throat.

A week of intemperate spring rain had made the Ohio River difficult to navigate and the three *voyageurs* cursed the continual drizzle as well as the fickle current. Their cargo was a dearborn wagon, three horses, the sick man and his wife, and Sabrina's father, an old man who tolerated the rain with a stolidness completely out of proportion to his discomfort.

The durham boat in which they were making this part of their journey was long and of shallow draught. A crude, slab-board house squatted in the center of the low deck and there the keelboatmen slept and cooked their meals. Convenience and comfort to passengers was limited to what they could provide for themselves. Sabrina was forced to sleep under the wagon since their belongings and her husband occupied all available space inside and he was too ill to be moved.

With the river running swiftly there was little need of the tow rope and the three *voyageurs* steadied the boat on course with stout poles and a makeshift oar off the stern. During the last two days of Cadmus Kane's illness a change had come over the rivermen and their talk had been confined to whispers among themselves. Now, as if by common consent, the durham boat was nosed toward the west shore. As it neared the bank one of the *voyageurs* leaped into the water, and with cordelle in hand, made the bow fast to a handy cottonwood tree.

Sabrina Kane felt the boat jar against the bank and for a moment could not believe they had stopped. Then her father, who had been standing near the front of the wagon, said, "Sabrina, come out here." Priam Thomas spoke in a tired, fatalistic voice, as though he had walked with trouble for so long a time that a little more wasn't going to make an appreciable difference.

Sabrina recognized that tone. She lifted her long skirts knee high and went over the tailgate. "What's wrong?" She looked at her father and he shook his head. Putting out her hand she pushed him aside in much the same manner as she had often pushed him before when something unpleasant had to be done immediately. She walked around the back of the wagon in time to meet the leader of the *voyageurs*. His name was Jacques Fountainbleau, half French, half Cree; a blend of the bad in both. He swept off his cap which was a Madras cotton handkerchief, brightly colored and tied on four corners. Fountainbleau's face was dark with whiskers. Several broken teeth peered through the curtain of his lips when he smiled.

He said, "M'sieu, Madame — how you say — get off here." He gestured toward the bank. His long *capot* swung aside when he moved his arms, exposing a flintlock pistol and a hatchet thrust into his sash.

Sabrina favored her father with a glance but in it was little hope that he would say or do anything. The habit of standing back and letting others take the initiative was too strong in Priam Thomas to be broken. She faced Fountainbleau boldly, and if she felt fear she hid it well. "We'll not get off here! You were paid eighty Spanish dollars to take us to Cairo in the Illinois country! Now put the boat back into the current!"

She was not a tall girl, but her erectness and her anger made her seem tall. Her face was an oval frame for dark brown eyes, a straight, finely chiseled nose, and full, expressive lips. She wore a long homespun dress that was damply clinging from exposure to the rain. Her brown hair was parted in the middle; the two soggy braids were secured at the ends by limp blue ribbons.

Jacques Fountainbleau's smile broadened and became disarming. He spread his hands in a helpless gesture, as though he were merely executing the will of God. "Madame, *mes voyageurs* fear the sickness. You get off, *maintenant*." He spoke with the finality of one who has definitely made up his mind.

"I said it wasn't any good comin' out here," Priam Thomas murmured. "You remember, I told Cadmus that before we left Pennsylvania."

Sabrina moved her hand impatiently and Priam Thomas stopped talking. From the covered dearborn wagon Cadmus Kane's hacking cough grew stronger, ending finally in a choked gurgle. Sabrina bit her lower lip, then tried another tack. "M'sieu Fountainbleau, my husband must have a doctor. Do you understand? *Le docteur!*" She looked pleadingly at each of the *voyageurs* and read the same verdict in their eyes.

Now she understood how things were; no doubt remained. And anger made her take a step toward the front of the wagon where Cadmus Kane's bullwhip hung coiled on the brake handle. Jacques Fountainbleau read her intent and snatched the whip, laughing. He stood with it in his hands, his eyes bright with amusement, "You would cut the skin from Fountainbleau, *non?* The mind is made up, Madame. You get off now!"

Priam Thomas had a rifle in the wagon. He remembered it and took a backward step, but one of the boatmen stepped with him. This movement was warning enough for Thomas. He said, "Didn't think it would work."

"Madame, there is no *docteur*," Fountainbleau said. "We go no further with you."

"His only chance to live is to get to Cairo," Sabrina said tightly. "It's this dampness. Putting him ashore in a jolting wagon is murder!"

On Fountainbleau's face there showed a growing impatience. He spoke a few words to his men and they stepped forward, untied the horses and began to harness them. Animals and wagons were alien to them

4

and they jabbered among themselves trying to sort out the tangled leather.

Priam Thomas said, "They don't care, Sabrina. People out here just don't care. I heard about it, but I never believed it. I do now. Kill off the weak; that's the law out here. Should have stayed in Pennsylvania."

Sabrina ignored his droning voice. She spoke to Fountainbleau. "M'sieu, I'd like to be with my husband now. Is that all right?"

Fountainbleau cocked his head to one side, smiling. "*Oui*, but first I take the rifle." He went past them and lifted the long flintlock from the wagonbed. "Now, Madame, you may join him. But the old one stays *ici*." He looked at Thomas, near sixty, stoop-shouldered and accustomed to defeat. He read no danger in this man, but the woman — name of a cow! She could cut flowers with a bullwhip and shoot like a man.

But Fountainbleau had the flintlock and the bullwhip. He spread his hands in a courtly manner. "*Oui*, Madame, join your husband while you can."

Sabrina climbed into the wagon, anger a flame border around her mind. Cadmus Kane stirred and reached for her hand, but she pulled away and forced open the lid of a large trunk. Placed between the folds of a heavy blanket was hidden Cadmus Kane's coach pistol and when she left the wagon, she had this in her hand.

She cocked it and pointed it carefully at Jacques Fountainbleau's stomach. "Stop those men! *Arretez!*"

The two *voyageurs* eyed the heavy-caliber pistol, then looked to Fountainbleau for advice. The steady-held muzzle and the determination in Sabrina Kane's eyes impressed them all.

"*Arretez,*" he said softly. The other two men stood motionless. He smiled again. "*Eh bien,* you would not shoot poor Fountainbleau, *non?* A lady does not do these things, Madame."

But this lady would and he knew it. Beneath the softness of her flesh there was steel and determination.

Sabrina Kane leaned against the wagon to keep from trembling. "Put the boat away from shore, M'sieu. *Arrechez, mes voyageurs!*"

The smile faded from Fountainbleau's face and his eyes narrowed slightly. The fact that he stood just out of arm's reach caused him a moment's regret. "Madame, I do not think you shoot poor Fountainbleau."

"If you don't cast off I will," Sabrina said.

Fountainbleau's shoulders rose and fell expressively. "*Eh bien!*" He turned as if to speak to his men, then whipped his cape around, slapping down on the heavy pistol. The gun went off in a clap of thunder, the heavy ball shaving splinters from the planked deck. Then he pushed her roughly against the wagon wheel, wrested the pistol from her hand and threw it into the Ohio.

Priam Thomas remembered his manhood and stepped into the fray, but one of the *voyageurs* struck him on the head with the pole and the old man sank to the wet deck. Thomas was not unconscious, but the fight was gone from him and he stayed there, on his hands and knees, while the *voyageurs* finished the hitching.

"If there's any law in Illinois," Sabrina said, "I'll have it on you." She saw that Fountainbleau was unmoved by the threat.

Thomas lifted his head and glared at the Frenchman. "You manhandled a woman; there's a price to be paid for that."

The glance Fountainbleau gave him was one of scorn. "From you, *M'sieu?* You are a chicken with little fuzzy feathers. I fear such a bird more than you." He took the bullwhip and the rifle and placed these in the back of the wagon. "Madame, please get on the seat." She had little choice and Fountainbleau handed her the reins.

One of the *voyageurs* led the team ashore and the horses strained against the harness as the wagon wheels cut deep in the mud. As soon as they were clear of the boat, the cordelle was cast off. Fountainbleau called, "Madame, you *are* in Illinois. *Bon jour*, Madame, M'sieu!" To the boatmen. "*Pousse au large, mes gens!*"

A shove of the poles sent the durham boat into the stream where the current caught it. From the high wagon seat, Sabrina shouted, "*Vous etes un pou! Un chou!*" Lice and cabbage!

Fountainbleau's face filled with rage and he popped his cheeks with his fingers. Then the boat moved around a bend and Sabrina Kane permitted her anger to give way to defeat. She hunched forward on the seat, fighting back her tears.

At the rear of the wagon, Priam Thomas leaned against the wheel and groaned. Sabrina got down and lifting her skirts, pushed through the wet grass toward him. Thomas was massaging a lump on the back of his head.

"Knew it would turn out like this," he said. "Never was in a rumpus in my life but what I didn't catch some sockdolager."

"You're not hurt," Sabrina said. At times like this she was bluntly practical, a facet of her personality that Priam Thomas found vexing. She was too independent in her ways, like a man was independent. A woman had her place, but if Sabrina Kane knew it, she disregarded it too often to suit most men.

She walked to the water's edge where the forest grew thick and foliage was a tangle. She noticed then that they were parked in the mouth of a landing. She could see where other wagon tires had cut into the low bank and some woodsman's axe had trimmed low-hanging limbs to keep them from tearing wagon tops.

Her father joined her. "Fountainbleau figures he kept his bargain. Must be a settlement around here somewhere." He sighed and turned back to the wagon for an axe. "Expect I ought to cut some firewood." His optimism made him add, "Once Cadmus dries out he'll feel fine." He began to push his way into the brush. Sabrina watched him for a moment and then reentered the wagon. The dreary daylight filtered by the forest made the wagon interior gloomy. Cadmus Kane lay on a pallet of straw, his young face pale and drawn, alive only in his fever-polished eyes.

Sabrina spoke gently. "Papa's starting a fire. You'll feel better when you're warm." Her hands fussed with the damp blankets. She was without medicine or medical knowledge and because of this deficiency felt a strong sense of guilt, a conviction that she was failing him when he needed her most. She could not remember feeling more helpless, and this feeling was made worse by the knowledge that her talk had brought them to this new and savage land.

"I'll never be warm again," Cadmus Kane said weakly. He took her hand and held it against his feverish face. "Sabrina, forgive me for leaving you alone."

"You'll get well," she said. His voice was full of surrender and this frightened her, yet she dared not show it. "We'll have the place we talked about. Together, Cadmus. Don't let the dreams die. Hang on to them!"

A severe fit of coughing seized him and when it subsided he lay weak and breathing heavily. Sabrina heard Priam Thomas return with an armload of wood and dump it by the trailside. She lifted the wagon cover and saw him pour a small amount of black powder on some punk, then strike steel against flint. He jerked back as it caught suddenly.

She hoisted her skirts and dismounted from the wagon. Her father looked at her. "He any better?"

"His cough's worse. He keeps choking all the time."

"Lung fever," Priam Thomas said dismally. "Saw my share of it thirty-five years ago with Washington's army." He shook his head as though he had already mentally dug Cadmus Kane's grave and was now getting ready to shovel the dirt in on top of him. "Once the fire's goin' you can make him some pap, not that he'll eat it." He fed wood to the growing fire. "I told him it was a fool thing, comin' out here. Even Able said he was a fool. Beats me all get out how two brothers can be so different. Now you take Able for instance —"

"You were talking about Cadmus," Sabrina said. "Stay on the subject or quit talking about it."

"Cadmus is a clerkish man," Priam Thomas said. "Never meant for farmin'. But you couldn't tell him anything. Stubborn as a mule. Never looked before he jumped. I've told him a dozen times that half the troubles in this world can be traced to sayin' yes too quick and not sayin' no soon enough."

"It's too late for blame," Sabrina said. "Advice is like castor oil, easy enough to give but dreadful to take."

"Ah," Thomas said, "there's no arguin' with a woman like you. I told you when you married him that a dog who'll follow anybody ain't worth a cent. He never could see a rainbow without chasin' it." Thomas snorted. "Able could've provided you with a home. He had a good place back in Pennsylvania. But you'd rather have a man full of foolish notions."

"It's done, Papa! Why talk about it?"

Priam Thomas didn't hear her. He had a way of closing his ears when someone disagreed with him. "If a man wants frontiers, there's Ohio an' Kentucky. Why, there's parts of Pennsylvania that's as wild as a boar hog." He shook his head. "Can't figure out what's happenin' to folks. 1811's a bad year for movin'. The government's nearly busted. We're goin' to rack an' ruin, I tell you." He looked at Sabrina and found that she had gone to the wagon and was dragging a canvas

10

from the bed. Thomas snorted. "Women! Never listen to a man, but they sure as shootin' enjoy tellin' a man where to get off. Might as well shut my mouth."

It took them an hour to erect a pole shelter, for Thomas was an unskilled man. Darkness was drawing near and the rain-gloom turned the forest to sooty shadows. They fought the wet canvas until it was stretched tight and tied down. The open end overlapped the fire and a backlog threw heat inside.

Cadmus Kane was delirious when they lifted him from the wagon and placed him on a pallet of folded blankets. "I'll tend him," Priam Thomas said. "Get dry, Sabrina. You've been wet for three days."

The rain had penetrated everything: blankets, extra clothing. Thomas turned his back to her as she stepped close to the fire, untied the drawstrings of her dress and peeled it off. She thrust two saplings into the ground and stretched the dress between them to dry. Her petticoats came next, three of them. She stood shivering in her shift and pantaloons, burning on one side while the other chilled. Turning often to distribute the heat, she unbraided her hair, fanning it with her fingers to dry it.

Darkness grew thicker until the shadows she threw against the shelter sides were like ink splashes. The firelight flickered, glistening against her skin. Her underclothes felt deliciously warm as she slipped into her dry petticoats and dress again.

"All right," she said and Thomas turned back to the fire while Sabrina got the cooking pot from the wagon. The dearborn wagon was not large and many things she had wanted to bring along had to be left behind. Her clothes and the treasured keepsakes accumulated during her brief year of marriage were packed in one large trunk.

From the pewter-lined food box she took ground corn and a piece of dried beef. Not much food remained. There was seed: barley, oats, timothy, corn. Seed and a dying man to plant it! Sabrina clasped her hands together and let the darkness muffle her soft weeping. For a minute her grief was difficult to control. Then she dried her eyes. When she stepped from the wagon and faced her father, her manner was composed again.

Crouching near the fire she mixed the corn meal and water, then shaved beef into the mush as it cooked. A little sorghum molasses sweetened the pap. Thomas said, "I'll hold him while you try feeding him." He moved behind Cadmus Kane, elevating his shoulders. Kane's head rolled weakly and his breathing was bubbly. Thomas whispered, "He's far gone, Sabrina. Another hour and he'll have the strangles." He spoke without emotion, predicting the obvious.

In desperation Sabrina tried to force food into Cadmus Kane's mouth, but he choked and let it dribble off his chin. Helpless tears dimmed her vision and she set the dish down quickly. Priam Thomas watched her for a moment, then said, "Girl, a man's got to go when his time comes. You're not the first woman to be left alone."

She wiped the back of her hand across her eyes before looking at him. "It's not being left alone I'm crying about. It's just that his dreams are dying with him and I know what they meant to him."

"He had a head full of gosh-awful nonsense," Priam Thomas said. "Now Able was the worker; he surely was. Had you married him you'd be —"

"I'd be sitting back in Pennsylvania!" she snapped. "Now shut up about Able. I've made my choice and I'm not regretting it. Cadmus and I have had a good year."

"It's all crazy; I never understood it," Thomas said. "I guess I've been a poor father. Toward the end, your mother was disappointed in me the same way you are. She wanted me to pull up and go some place new, but a man gets set in his ways. I expect that's why you took Cadmus over Able; Cadmus talked big and made a lot of plans. But they never come out! You got to admit that. They never come out. Not one of 'em."

"No," Sabrina said regretfully, "they never did." For a moment she was remembering Cadmus Kane and how he had never been discouraged by his many failures, never doubted that tomorrow would be better. And Able Kane, the strong one, a good hand at anything he turned his hand to; Cadmus had lived a lifetime in the shadow of his brother. Sabrina supposed this was a tragedy, but she could not visualize how it could have been different. Some men were born to be nobody, and she had known two: her father and her husband.

She said, "I think I loved him because he never lost faith. You gave up a long time ago, Papa. You might think it's wrong that he wanted to come out here, that I encouraged him. You think it's wrong that he got sick. You think that's the worst failure he ever had, the failure to live." She put her hand on her breast. "It hurts inside because he's dying. But it hurts more to know there was so much in his life he never finished. And he wanted to! He really wanted to!"

"You're strange," Priam Thomas said. "I don't guess I ever really knew you, Sabrina. Not even when you were little."

"No," she said, "you never did."

He sighed. "We'd best be startin' back in the mornin'. There'll be a raft to build; we'll have to leave the wagon. Be too hard pullin' against the current with a big load."

"We're not going back," she said firmly. "That's what you do best, Papa — turn back." Priam Thomas raised his head and looked at her sharply. "That's so," she went on. "That's the cap-stone on the whole of it; you keep turning back. You say that 1811 is a bad year. Maybe it is, but I can't wait for a good one to come along. Illinois country is new, and you'll come with me wherever I go because you're old and afraid of dying alone. Don't blame your failures on Cadmus, Papa. I'm his wife and whatever he dreamed, I believed in it. Do you expect me to go and admit they're nothing? I'm going to make them what he wanted."

For a full minute Priam Thomas stared at his daughter. Then he said, "A woman's got her place, but you ain't never learned it. You been to school, but danged if they ain't ruined you, all them crazy notions.

14

They made you hard, Sabrina. Hard an' stubborn as any man I ever saw."

"Am I?" She smiled. "What am I supposed to be, Papa? Some kitchen drudge? That's what Able Kane wanted, someone to cook for him and fix his clothes, but always with her mouth shut. Well I can't live like that! I'm alive and I have to share life with my man. You can't understand that, can you?"

"It ain't natural, Sabrina. A woman's got her place."

"I'm not a servant to any man," Sabrina said flatly. Her voice softened. "Get some sleep, Papa. I'm going to sit up with my husband."

Thomas didn't argue. Argument wasn't in him, not where his daughter was concerned. He had known no other woman like her, save her mother, but he had put a stop to her nonsense early in their married life. Now he wondered if he had, for his wife's independence had been passed on like a legacy.

He turned his back to the fire in much the same manner as he had learned to turn it to the world and trouble. Sabrina Kane watched him, loved him and at the same time pitied him because somewhere along the path of his life he had convinced himself of his complete worthlessness. While on the durham boat she had seen him stand in the rain for hours, enduring it without protest. He often told her that only a fool cursed the things he couldn't control, but she knew this was not the case; Priam Thomas had long ago ceased to care whether it rained or shone.

She spent the early part of the night applying hot cloths to Cadmus Kane's chest and throat, trying to

15

relieve the congestion that was slowly strangling him. Twice she got up to stretch her legs and add wood to the fire. He lay drawn and shallow, breathing on the pallet of folded blankets, his eyes closed. She believed that he was beyond hearing her, for she had been able to get only the most feeble response from him for over a half hour.

This all seemed such a waste to her, this man dying before he really had a chance to live. Yet she knew this was not true. Cadmus Kane was not the kind of a man who went ahead with a thing. Some men did, but he always seemed more content to stand on the sidelines and watch someone else. But she loved him, not in spite of his weaknesses but because of them. He had pampered her, allowed her to be herself, a free spirit. A strong man would never have done that. Able Kane would have scolded her for her foolish dreams and made her like the others, old and tired at thirty. Strong men did that to a woman, drove the laughter from them. But Cadmus Kane would never do that.

She felt a touch of shame, for she had given him nothing; she had merely taken from him the gift of freedom, and only then because he had been too good-natured to object.

Around midnight the rain stopped. Only the popping fire and the drip of water from the trees broke the vast silence. Cadmus Kane's breathing became an agonized sawing for wind. His eyes rolled in their sockets. Finally he stopped struggling and lay absolutely still. The last moment, when it came, was an anticlimax. Sabrina looked at his face, now relaxed and without care.

16

Somehow she had expected this moment to be different, this breath to be unlike all other breaths. But it had been unchanged.

Life simply ended with a sigh of relief.

She drew the blanket over his face and woke her father.

"It's all over, Papa."

"Huh?" Thomas sat up, pawing sleep from his eyes. "Why didn't you call me?"

"What for?" She turned away and began to cry silently. When he put his hand on her shoulder she moved away from it. Priam Thomas sighed and stood up.

"I'll dig a grave," he said and stumbled through the darkness for the wagon and a shovel.

CHAPTER
TWO

Morning brought cleared skies, the storm having passed on. When the sun came up it soon spread a bright heat over the forest. By nine o'clock steam began to rise like thick wood smoke. The woodland floor was an artist's palette of spring colors: pale trilliums, wild lupines, moss pinks and yellow wallflowers. The air was heavily scented, for the recent rains had awakened rich odors from the earth.

Priam Thomas had chosen a spot by the trailside, a small grassy glen. He finished digging the grave, then wrapped Cadmus Kane in the wagon canvas and lowered him gently. Sabrina stayed by the wagon until Thomas packed the earth into a rounded mound. He called to her and she came over, standing with bowed head while he read from the Bible. He was a little offended that she did not cry, but then he supposed she was like her mother shortly before she died; all the tears had been used up. Someday he would die and she would stand like that, head tipped forward, but there would be no tears. Looking back over the span of his life, Priam Thomas decided that he had caused her tears to be wasted on the little things and now when there was reason to weep, the well was dry.

Afterward Sabrina gathered a bouquet of the wildflowers to lay on the grave. Her father removed one of the seat boards from the wagon and with a piece of hot iron, burned into it:

CADMUS KANE OF PA.
BORN SEPT. 15, 1782
DIED APRIL 9, 1811
"MAY HIS DREAMS COME TRUE"

"Now I wish I hadn't spoke against him," Thomas said with genuine regret. "He had his faults, but he had a heap of good in him, too. Never had a hard word to say about any man." He turned and went back to the wagon, tossing the shovel inside. Reluctantly he began to break camp. Sabrina joined him a few minutes later, carried her cooking pot to the wagon and stowed it. Nestled under the wagon seat was a trunk containing the many things Cadmus Kane had given her. Foolish things really. Things he could not afford. But he was the kind of a man who never stopped to put a price on things; he only thought in terms of happiness, usually someone else's. Winters could be hard in Pennsylvania, and she would always remember one in particular. The year had been bad for everyone, first a late frost that killed most of the fruit trees, then insects eating everything until the land looked like a fire-stripped forest. Yet when Cadmus Kane had heard about a neighbor who had nothing, he had sorted through their last peck of potatoes, picked out the best, then sent them over via the circuit-riding preacher so the neighbor would never know where they came from. As long as Sabrina Kane lived she believed she would remember that, and Able Kane sitting there with his disapproving scowl. Able believed that a man first owed to himself, then to his neighbor, if there was anything left. And the way Able managed, there never was anything left.

The sounds of her father moving around reminded her that day dreaming was for the idle rich and she turned away from the wagon, pausing there, her head cocked to one side, listening.

"Papa, come here!"

The urgency in her voice startled Thomas and he thought first of Indians, for this was their land. The Shawnee, Chippewas, Winnebagoes, Ottowas, even the war-like Sioux, Sac and Fox and Iowas ranged this river to hunt and make war. He lifted his flintlock rifle from the wagon and checked the priming charge.

"What is it?" he asked.

"I hear singing!"

"Singing?" Thomas snorted. "Your mind's a wanderin'."

"Is it? Listen!"

He turned his head slightly. A look of dismay crossed his face. "I'll be hornswoggled! It is singin'! Comin' from up river!"

"I'm going to see," Sabrina said and started off before he could stop her.

"Damn it," Thomas said and followed her because he had to. He found her at the Ohio's edge, peering upstream. The singing was growing louder and the twangy plunk of a banjo was clearly discernible. From around the upper bend a raft hove into view — a big raft, solidly made of stout logs planked together. Two horses and two cows were tied near the stern. A shanty had been erected in the center and on the low roof a man sat, legs crossed, singing while he played his banjo, letting the river current carry him haphazardly downstream. While they watched, the current swung the raft around but the man didn't seem to mind the brief backward trip for another eddy soon caught him and turned him again. Nearer now, the words of his song were clear, some nonsensical French ditty about an old man named Michaud who fell out of a tree.

> Michaud est monte dans un prunier,
> Pour treiller des prunes.
> La branch a casse —
> Machaud a casse?
> Ou est-ce qu-il est?
> Il est en bas.
> Oh! Reveille, reveille, reveille,
> Oh! Reveille, Michaud est un haut!

The raft made another complete circle while the man convinced the listening wilderness that Michaud had picked himself from the ground unhurt. There was a reckless gaiety about him that seemed limitless. Sabrina felt that in his voice and in his playing.

Then he saw Sabrina and her father standing near the bushes. The distance was yet a hundred and twenty yards, but he put his banjo aside and picked up his long-barreled Kentucky rifle, holding it carelessly across his knees. Only Sabrina knew that he was not careless. He was an extremely alert man, having seen them at quite a distance. This man, she decided, had a vigilance that never slept. As the raft came on he must have recognized them as white, for he put the rifle aside, though still within handy reach. Hefting a long pole, he steered the raft out of the current toward shore. He was a very tall man, nearly six-foot four in his moccasins. He wore long fringed buckskins and an outlandish coonskin cap with a tail hanging halfway down his back. The pelt from which the cap had been made must have been the granddaddy of all coons and this man wore it as a badge, proclaiming to all who saw it that here was the "most" man, half-horse, half-alligator, a man with the fastest boat, the meanest dog, and the prettiest woman on the river. About him lay a wildness that spoke of unnamed places and remote mountain reaches.

Just before the raft touched the bank, he smiled, a brief flash of white teeth; then he was knee deep in the water, tie rope in one hand, long rifle in the other. He splashed ashore, whipped off his cap and said, "Well here I be, Benjamin Travis from The Dark an' Bloody Ground. Wake snakes, the day's a-wastin'!"

He was young in years, somewhere in his late twenties, but in his pale eyes were mirrored the nameless miles he had traveled and the things he had seen. Things he never talked about because they were beyond belief. His buckskins showed a thousand greasy hand wipings and he smelled strongly of Pawnee lodge

22

fires. His hair was pale; an inch-long stubble covered his cheeks. On his face there was no mark of worry or care. When he looked at Sabrina Kane, bright shards of appreciation danced in his eyes, yet she felt no danger in him.

Priam Thomas still held his flintlock ready. Benjamin Travis favored it with a brief glance, then said, "I'll be dod-fetched if I mean you folks any harm. Was I you, mister, I'd be careful I didn't fire that into the wrong flock."

Thomas lowered his rifle to show he meant peace. Benjamin Travis leaned on his, his hands cupped around the muzzle. He looked from one to the other. "Why all the sad faces? The sun's shinin', the birds is a-twitterin' in the trees, an' the river keeps on flowin'." He frowned. "Have a mite of trouble?"

"Tolerable bad," Priam Thomas said. He introduced himself and Sabrina. Travis offered his hand briefly, as a man will when he has little faith in handshaking. "My son-in-law died last night. We buried him this mornin'." He pointed to the fresh mound.

Travis glanced that way, then said, "Too bad." His tone convinced Sabrina that he meant it, but at the same time informed her that it was no concern of his.

This offended Priam Thomas. "Sure don't bother you much, does it?"

Benjamin Travis looked at him for a moment. "I didn't know the man." He pointed up-river. "Shawnees killed my older brother there seven years ago. You feel sad about it?"

Priam Thomas squirmed a little. "I was just talkin', that's all." He looked down at the tips of his muddy shoes.

Travis said, "Ma'am, where's the rest of your party?"

"We're alone," Sabrina said. "The *voyageurs* put us ashore here. They were afraid of my husband's sickness."

"Fella named Fountainbleau," Thomas said. "You know him?"

"I've met him," Travis said in a noncommittal voice. "He make trouble?"

Sabrina looked at her father but said nothing. Finally Thomas said, "He got rough with my girl. Forced us to get off here."

Travis' eyes grew grave. "A man don't do that to a woman. Man's troubles is settled by men. I guess you got a bit of business to settle with him was you to meet again."

"I have that," Thomas said stoutly. "I'd like to meet him again too."

"Likely you will," Travis said, "if you settle on the river. Anywhere, St. Louis, Prairie du Pont, Prairie du Rocher or Fort Dearborn, you'll meet him. He comes and goes, but stays most at Illinois Town. Works for the Sweet brothers. A couple of traders who run things around those parts." He paused to swat a fly that braved the expanse of his forehead. "Better keep that rifle handy, Mr. Thomas. Fountainbleau knows how hard it can go with a man for troublin' a woman, an' he'll figure you'll be lookin' for him. There won't be any talkin', just shootin' was you to meet unexpected like."

"Well now," Thomas said, then glanced at Sabrina and let the rest trail off.

Benjamin Travis scratched his whiskered face as he pushed Sabrina gently aside to move by. He looked the wagon over, walked around it several times, then stood back and shook his head. Sabrina and her father came up.

"Mr. Travis," she said. "What's the matter?"

"Seems funny that a man'd start out like this," he said. He looked inside the wagon, then grinned at her. "He didn't have much, did he? From the looks of his traps I'd say there was no buff'lo, an' no meat and he'd been livin' off his moccasins; that's poor fixin's, I can tell you."

"My husband's business is none of yours!" Sabrina snapped.

"That a fact?" Travis leaned against the wagon wheel. "He died an' left you settin' in the middle of nowhere. Lookin' at his traps, I'd say he took all the knick-knacks an' left the plow at home." He shook his head. "This ain't an easy country, Ma'am; I guess you're learnin' that."

Sabrina's pride forbid speech. The fact that he had guessed the truth about Cadmus Kane was galling. Never before had she suspected that his transparencies were so obvious.

Priam Thomas cleared his throat. "Since you know this country, we'd be much obliged if you told us where we are."

"There's Shawneetown ten or twelve miles through the woods," Travis said.

"Thank you," Sabrina said coolly. "We won't keep you any longer."

"I don't guess you're doin' that," Benjamin Travis said. He smiled to ease his positive manner, for he saw how irked she was becoming. "I meant to take this trail anyhow."

He was lying; Sabrina knew it. He had judged correctly the depths of her pride and offered this palliative with blunt deference. The moment was upon her to speak, to oust him, but she hesitated and the moment passed. Benjamin Travis said, "Three horses; that all you got?"

"We lost one on the river," Priam Thomas said.

"I'll hitch one of mine," he said. His glance passed to the crude headboard and he added, "Your husband have any folks, Ma'am?"

"A brother. I wish there was some way I could let Able know."

"If you got a speck o' paper'n ink, you could write him."

"Can I mail a letter from Shawneetown?"

"Well, yes," Travis said, "but it'd get there a heap quicker if you mailed it from here." He saw her puzzled expression and laughed. "Ma'am, you just write what you want and stick it on a branch so's it can be seen from the river. Folks is always passin' up an' down. They'll see it and carry it on for you."

"But — but how can I know they'll do that?" She waved her hands. "It seems so — so haphazard with something that important."

"You're new here," Travis reminded her, "or else you'd know there was two ways for a fella to get shot quick: stealin' an' puttin' his hand on a woman. You put your writin' on a stick an' this Able fella'll be readin' it in a month. Most all the news comes in that way. I got a bundle in my possibles now."

She went to the wagon to write her message. Travis turned to his raft, led the two cows ashore and tied them, then went aboard for his horses. Within a half hour he transferred his trappings to dry ground. Priam Thomas stood around, the epitome of uselessness. He eyed carefully the tools Travis carried. Four long lumberman's saws for falling timber. Smaller saws for ripping. Mortising chisels, hammers, clamps, several planes, spoke shaves, files; everything a man needed to build with.

Thomas said, "You in the lumber business, Mr. Travis?"

"I might be," Travis said and cut the raft loose, letting it drift downstream.

"Seems a shame to waste that raft," Thomas said.

"It ain't wasted," Travis said. "Someone will fish it out of the river an' take it upstream. Once he's where he wants to go, maybe Pittsburgh, he'll leave it on the shore an' someone else'll come downstream on it. A man's got to help his neighbor in this country, Mr. Thomas. If he don't, he won't live long."

Without invitation he loaded his possibles into Sabrina Kane's wagon, tied the two cows and extra horse behind, then began to hitch up. Sabrina finished her letter and stood aside, holding it in her hand. He took it from her, notched a stick with his huge knife and planted the letter in clear sight of the river.

Sabrina said, "You're sure someone will see it? It's small."

"Folks keep their eyes open out here," Travis said, "or they're soon minus their hair."

"Won't the Indians take it?" Thomas asked.

Travis shook his head. "They'll look to see what it is, but they won't take it. You want to send money back East, just hang the poke on a limb. It'll get there."

"Seems too good to be true, there bein' so many honest folks out here," Thomas said.

"Didn't say that," Travis corrected. "There's a heap of men who'll lie an' kill. They'll rob too, but they're standin' so's they face you; they won't steal behind your back."

Travis finished loading her personal belongings. Twice Sabrina tried to interrupt his work to tell him his help was unwanted, but he brushed her aside in a manner that told her that any suggestion she might make was beneath his consideration. This kind of treatment had always been galling, yet she supposed these so-called strong men were all alike, not giving a care for anyone but themselves.

Priam Thomas hovered near Benjamin Travis' elbow, talking. "Mighty glad you come along, Travis. I was worried about my little girl. A man's got his responsibilities toward his women. I guess you know that as well as I do."

When Travis moved, Thomas followed him, yet Travis seemed to have closed his ears. Sabrina watched him carefully, for this was her father's habit; closing his ears and mind to any idea not his own. Yet she saw a difference. Beneath Benjamin Travis' manner lay something inflexible as a stout axe handle. He was a man of unfathomable humor; he whistled softly while he worked. Occasionally he paused to look up at the trees and listen to the birds and when he did this he would laugh softly.

Thomas was talking again. "Guess you're no stranger to these woods. Been away a spell, have you?"

"Fort Lee," Travis said. "Want to reach me that hip strap?"

"Sure," Thomas said. "Never been to Fort Lee. We're Pennsylvania folks. New York State before that."

"That's too civilized for me," Travis admitted. "'Course there's some dreadful nice folks and a swod of pretty girls there."

"Dancin' and kissin's your style," Sabrina said suddenly. "If you married a woman, you'd boss her to death in five years."

Benjamin Travis turned slowly and looked at her, that dancing light in his eyes. "Matter of fact, Ma'am, that is my preference. I've seen a swod of good men ruined by a *good* woman. Knew a fella once at Fort Osage out on the Missouri River. Laughin' all the time, he was, until he went back East and found himself one of them foofaraw girls. Seen him four years later. Serious as a mouse in a wire trap." He gave a final tug on the harness strap and stepped back. "Best we get movin', Ma'am."

"I agree," Priam Thomas said. "Sabrina, come now."

She turned abruptly and walked to the grave. Thomas snorted and said softly, "A man's dead, he's dead. Grievin' won't bring him back."

"She knows that," Travis said in an offended voice and joined her. He read the dates on the headboard, then said, "Young. It was too bad."

"The world's full of bad things," Sabrina said sadly, "but he was blind to them; he saw only the good."

"He was better off than most then," Travis told her. He took her arm and tried to turn her back to the wagon, but she jerked away from him, tears suddenly welling up in her eyes.

"I don't want to leave him!" She almost shouted this. "I just don't want to go off, leaving him here where there's nothing, nobody!" She put her hands over her face and cried, and Travis said nothing, allowing her grief to work itself out. Finally she quieted and wiped her eyes. "It seems wrong, never seeing his grave again. Never putting flowers on it."

"You won't forget him," Travis said. "That's the important thing."

She nodded. Her eyes became slightly glazed as her mind swung back, remembering Cadmus Kane alive, laughing. Benjamin Travis, wise in the ways of grief, recognized the symptoms of approaching hysteria. He shook her roughly until her eyes came back in focus.

"You want to stay?" he said. "Is that what you want?"

"I — I can't bear to leave him like this!"

"Then you just stay," he said. "There's Indians along this river, Ma'am. Early this mornin' I passed a passel of Shawnees. Was they to find you here, they'd kill you for your hair."

The threat of Indians was cold water, shocking her back to sanity. She turned with him and went to the wagon. When she was settled in the seat, Travis handed the reins to Priam Thomas, saying, "You'd best drive, Mr. Thomas. She's a mite upset."

This angered her beyond reason; somehow she could never tolerate any man who reminded her of her weaknesses. She snatched the reins from her father's hands. "Mr. Travis, I can handle a team as well as any man!" She defied him with her eyes, dared him to contradict her.

"Well," he said, leaning against the wheel, "you're as full of sass as a weaned pup."

He showed her a will as strong as her own, perhaps stronger if she chose to contest it. She disliked him intensely; his kind of man was a symbol of subjugation. Yet he had a magnetism she could not completely ignore. Here was a man unlike any other she had ever known. The antagonism she felt toward Benjamin Travis was basic; he challenged the very pillars of her self reliance. His kind of man would have to break a woman in order to love her and long ago she had vowed never to let any man do that to her.

And Benjamin Travis sensed all this in his primitive way; she read the knowledge in his eyes, a mocking laughter that increased her anger. Then he moved back a step and slapped the horses into motion. They pulled mightily against the harness to break the wheels' suction in the mud. Travis moved out, walking

31

twenty-five yards ahead of the wagon, his long rifle held negligently in his arms.

Throughout the morning they traveled northwest at a leisurely walk. Benjamin Travis was like a small boy, exploring every squirrel nest he came to. Once he insisted that they stop so he could fill a copper jar with honey from a bee tree. Sabrina and her father stayed in the wagon while Travis dipped honey, unmindful of the furious bees who stung him.

The land was rolling and thickly forested. Several times they flushed deer from their beds and while crossing one marshy section, a flock of teal took to the air with a loud beating of wings.

In the early afternoon they reached Shawneetown, a scatter of low, log buildings clustered around a larger trading post. The muddy trail ran through the settlement and in front of the store, traffic had chopped the earth until the mud was hock deep. Heavy planks had been laid for pedestrians. Sabrina Kane halted the wagon by the trading store, and got down when a man emerged and stood on the porch. He was short and built like a barrel. His dark whiskers were braided into four strands, dangling in front of his homespun shirt. He saw Benjamin Travis near the head of the team and let out a ringing whoop, clapping both hands against his chest.

Travis looked around quickly, saw him and thrust his rifle into Sabrina's hands. He made two jumps through the mud, gained the porch and then both men were locked together, straining, their feet thumping the planks for purchase.

Someone shouted and a crowd gathered on the run. There were more than thirty families in Shawneetown, and they all seemed to appear from nowhere. A dozen Indians came from inside the trading post and watched the fight, their faces impassive above draping blankets.

Sabrina grabbed Priam Thomas by the arm. "Stop them! Don't just stand there!"

"Hush your mouth," Thomas warned quickly. "And put your danged bonnet on. Can't you act like a lady?"

He never took his eyes off Travis and the bull-bodied man.

They were see-sawing back and forth across the small porch, their breath whistling through their teeth. The heavy man had a twisting grip on Travis' arm and he threatened to break it. Suddenly Travis advanced a foot and with his body leverage threw the heavy man over his hip. The porch posts trembled as the impact shook the entire building.

Stepping back, Travis panted for wind, and sweat stood bold on his forehead. "Another time, Povy," Travis said. He bent down and offered Povy his hand, pulling him to his feet with one, grunting effort.

Jake Povy rubbed his backside and grinned. Benjamin Travis said, "Got some new folks for you, Jake." He led Povy off the porch to meet Sabrina Kane and her father.

She looked from one to the other, her eyes wide. "I — I thought you were mad at each other!"

"Shucks now," Jake Povy said, "when a couple of old alligators meet, they're entitled to a little sloshin' about." He offered his hand to Priam Thomas, and manlike disregarded Sabrina because she was a woman.

"Welcome to Shawneetown. This all the family you got?"

"My husband died last night," Sabrina said.

"Too bad," Povy said. He turned his attention back to Thomas. "You folks figure to stay hereabouts?"

"Likely no," Sabrina said before her father could speak. Povy frowned, a bit annoyed that this woman kept sticking her nose in men's affairs. Yet he didn't know what to do about it. Sabrina was saying, "It was my husband's wish to take land to the north along the Mississippi, but we'll be grateful for your protection, Mr. Povy. There's a band of Shawnees near the Ohio."

Povy failed to mask his surprise. "Shawnee's?" He looked at Benjamin Travis, then at Sabrina Kane. "Did Ben tell you this, Ma'am?"

"He did," Sabrina said and Povy began to laugh.

He clapped his hands to his round stomach and roared. The white settlers gathered around joined him and the Indians, thinking it was the thing to do, added their voices. Sabrina Kane failed to see the humor. She waited patiently until Jake Povy's merriment died to a few sobs and tear-streaked face, then said, "Mr. Povy, it seems to me that Indians are hardly a laughing matter."

Benjamin Travis looked uneasy. He shifted his feet and acted like a man who has pressing business elsewhere. Sabrina saw this and whatever suspicions she courted were immediately crystalized. "Mr. Povy," she said, "what kind of Indians are these?" She indicated those gathered on the porch.

34

"Shawnees, Ma'am." Povy suffered through the dying end of a chuckle. "The Shawnees are friendly, Ma'am. It's kind of a joke on new folks, tellin' 'em that there's Shawnees about. They go into the dangdest fits over it." Glancing at Benjamin Travis, he said, "Ben, was I you, I'd cut an' run. She looks hot enough to fry pitch out of a coonskin hat."

Sabrina Kane was glaring at Travis or looking through him; Jake Povy couldn't decide which. "Pa, are you going to do something?"

"Well, hell" — Thomas began.

"That's what I thought," Sabrina said and went to the wagon. She reached into the back and took out the coiled bullwhip.

"Now wait a minute!" Thomas yelled, moving toward her.

Povy's jaw dropped. Travis took a step backward, to get out of range. Sabrina whipped her arm back, trailing the whip, then made the cast as Travis ducked and her father collided with her, grappling for her arm.

The tip caught Travis' coonskin cap, making hair fly. The cap sailed off his head and landed on the porch. Thomas had the whip now and stood with it in his hands, not knowing what to do. Sabrina didn't try to take it away from him, but the anger remained in her eyes.

She said, "Mr. Travis, I'm sure you had a good laugh at my expense, with my husband hardly cold in the ground. I hope you enjoyed it because you'll never have another. From the moment you came ashore, it never mattered a hoot to you what happened to us, or how we felt. All right, we'll leave it that way. I hope I never have to lay eyes on you again."

"Ma'am," Travis began, but she turned abruptly away and closed him out as surely as if she had slammed a stout door in his face.

"Mr. Povy, could you provide a room?"

"You an' your pa go right inside," Povy said and stood there while they crossed the porch.

At the door Sabrina paused. "Mr. Travis, I'd advise you to take your animals and traps from our wagon. You'll forgive me if I don't thank you?"

She closed the door before he could answer.

The crowd began to break up and Jake Povy scratched his beard. "Ben," he said, "that woman will be the match for any man. It's happened before. Adam held the best hand so far, but he didn't play it right."

Travis cuffed mud with his boot and retrieved his coonskin cap. A patch of hair was missing and he fingered the spot. That could have been an eye instead of hair and she wasn't the kind of a woman who would have regretted it later.

"I was tryin' to help her," Travis said. "I thought she was goin' to bust down like women do. A man just goes along, feelin' good because the birds is a singin', then he runs into a woman and it goes to seed on him. I've been hearin' the owl hoot for a spell now, Povy; I'm half-crazy for buff'lo meat and mountain doin's."

"She's hoppin' mad," Povy said. He crossed the porch to the door. "Stayin'?"

"A day maybe," Travis said. "Got some messages for the folks south of here. After that I might make a trip to

Prairie du Pont and maybe Illinois Town. Got some unfinished business there with the Sweet brothers." He moved his feet aimlessly. "Jake, you talk pretty good. Fix it up with her, will you? I mean, she's lost her man and I guess she's a mite scared. Thomas ain't much good. He thinks it's whistlin' that makes the plow go. I'll leave a horse an' the two cows, Jake. She ain't got nothin' to start with. You explain it to her, will you?"

"You leave the animals," Jake Povy said. "I'll think on the other."

He went inside and closed the door.

CHAPTER
THREE

In the year 1801 when Jake Povy built his trading post, the land here had been virgin, the only occupants being a small band of Shawnees. Never in his wildest imagination did he foresee that in ten short years more than eight thousand souls would stop at Shawneetown on their journey to French Illinois.

The settlement lay in an eighty acre clearing hemmed by timber on four sides. The trading post itself was built of logs, cottonwood boles set upright in the ground and chinked with mud and beargrass. Built into a long U, the main room fronted on the road. Inside, Povy had joined together four walnut butt cuts and set them in the dirt floor. The top had then been adzed flat for a counter, over which he dispensed trade goods to visiting Indians and mugs of Bald Face, when he had it.

Eight small windows opened toward the front, but since glass was unobtainable, they were glazed with deer-hide, scraped paper-thin to admit the light. The left wing of the building housed Povy's quarters and a storeroom. The right wing was part grain shed, part catch-all.

It was to this section that Jake Povy conducted Sabrina Kane. He opened the door for her and let it sag on the leather hinges. "Not fancy," he said, indicating a bale of buffalo hides in one corner. The bed was a pallet of straw on the floor, covered by a bear skin. "Best I got," he added. "Your pa can sleep on the counter." He closed the door and shuffled down the passage-way.

Sabrina sighed and let her shoulders touch the rough wall. The room was small, the log walls mud plastered, then sized with lime until they were dingy gray. There was one window, high, covered with deerskin like all the others in the settlement. She sank down on the straw pallet and removed her shoes. The weak light through the window indicated there was not much left of the day. There were things to be unloaded from the wagon and she should be working, yet she felt a deep reluctance to leave the sanctuary of this room. Since her husband's illness, Sabrina had thought of little else beyond his comfort, forsaking her own. Now that he was gone, she could afford to think of herself. This was a luxury of which she had been long deprived.

There was a comforting feeling of security about four walls and a closed door. *I don't have to be strong here;* this was her thought. She remembered her own room when she was a little girl, an alcove in the cabin loft. At night, when the ladder had been pulled up, the world had retreated and all the hidden hurt of the day could come to the surface without apology or fear of anyone finding out. She felt that way now, so she lay face down on the bed and let her anxieties and regrets seep forth from life's vexing wounds. She slept until Jake Povy's knock awakened her.

The room was completely dark. Through the door Povy said, "Ma'am, there's vittals on the table."

"Thank you, Mr. Povy," Sabrina said. She sat up and with her elbows planted on her knees, put her face in her hands for a moment. The trouble with waking, she decided, was that life started again. And life could be a chore, just a succession of trials and disappointments.

When entering this room she had seen a candle on the floor. She groped until she found it. The candle base held tinder, flint and steel. She scraped them together for a light, mentally thanking Jake Povy for this kindness, understanding well that on any frontier candles were costly and were used sparingly. As a rule, people went to bed when the sun went down and got up when it peeked over the horizon; this had been her own lifetime habit. A simple thing like fire was of the utmost importance and a pioneer family always kept the fireplace lighted. If it went out, someone might have to walk miles to a neighbor for a pan of hot coals to get it started again.

With the candle lighted, Sabrina took off her dress and worked the mud from the hem. The three long petticoats were also soiled and she shed them, standing in her brief shift. She was a very slender woman; by the plump standards of her day some men would have said she was skinny. But her legs were tapered and hard, her back smooth-muscled. There was no droop to her stomach; it was flatly muscled and her breasts were firm, unsupported by the shift.

The ink shadows in the room were now a flickering gray as she moved about. Her hair was tangled and she straightened it out the best she could and rebraided it. Dressing quickly, she took the candle with her when she went down the short companionway and in the main room, placed it on the mantle.

Povy and her father were in the other wing. The meal was simple: venison chunk, dandelion greens and sweet potatoes. Priam Thomas was working on his second helping when Sabrina sat down. Povy filled her wooden plate, then leaned back in his chair, a clay pipe sending streamers of smoke toward the beamed ceiling.

Priam Thomas was doing all the talking. "I'll tell you this, Povy, I had a mind to thrash that fella Travis for bein' so bossy. Mind you, I came within a whisker of it." He flourished his knife at Jake Povy for emphasis.

A glimmer of amusement appeared in Jake Povy's eyes. "Was I you I'd go to the other neck of the woods before I hollered that. Ben's a peaceful man but he riles. When he does, he takes hair."

Thomas sulked for a moment, then went on scooping food with his knife. Sabrina ate her meal in silence, then went outside to the wagon. Several Shawnees stood dark and blanket-shrouded on the porch. She gave them a slightly apprehensive glance, then dragged Cadmus Kane's trunk to the tailgate.

The hand on her shoulder was an immeasurable shock. She gasped and whirled, staring into an impassive bronze face and dark, shoebutton eyes. "Wha — what do you want?" Sabrina managed to say.

The Shawnee reached past her, grasped the handle of the trunk and lifted it from the wagon as though it weighed nothing. Povy came out to the porch then. He said, "Consarn you, Shawnee Blanc, you quit pesterin' Miz Kane now!" To Sabrina he added, "No need to get a-feared. He's a friendly cuss, an' been with white folks most of his life."

Shawnee Blanc still held the trunk as thought awaiting her decision. Her smile, although brief, was encouragement enough. When she went inside to her room, he followed, bearing the trunk on his heavy shoulder.

She got the candle from the mantle and set it on the floor. Shawnee Blanc stood by the open door, watching with a completely blank expression. For an instant she thought of dismissing him, but then put the notion aside; he obviously meant no harm and somehow she felt not the slightest bit nervous. She had imagined that Indians would frighten her.

Opening the trunk, she slowly removed the things that Cadmus Kane had brought her: the carved clock; gay bolts of cloth, too gay to be worn in Pennsylvania; a pair of dancing slippers he had brought home from Philadelphia. And the conch shell, such a useless thing, yet precious because of its very uselessness. Able Kane had been quite angry when Cadmus had brought it home, but then, Able never dreamed. He could find little pleasure in holding the conch to the ear and listening to the sea roar, a sea he had never seen, probably never would see.

Sabrina put it to her ear and listened to the rolling breakers smash against a rocky shore line and by closing her eyes could see the white foam and the masses of green water. Shawnee Blanc touched her

42

hand and she opened her eyes quickly. He wanted the conch shell and for an instant Sabrina thought of resisting, but instead she handed it to him.

The Indian turned it over in his hands, peered into the opening and made probing tests with his fingers. Then he put it to his ear and on his face appeared a most dismayed expression. He suddenly handed the conch shell back to Sabrina and wheeled, running out of the settlement. In a moment he was back with five more Shawnees. They babbled to themselves in low voices and Jake Povy heard the disturbance, his heavy boots thumping as he approached to see what was going on.

"Git outa the way there! Shawnee Blanc, what the devil you doin'? Pesterin' Miz Kane again?"

Shawnee Blanc was passing the conch shell to his friends and each had his listen. Each thrust his fingers inside, trying to find the animal making this noise like the sea. Povy took it away from them and said, "You got to excuse Injuns, Miz Kane. They're heathens an' think this is magic."

"It's just a sea shell," Sabrina said. "My, what a lot of fuss —"

Povy handed the conch shell back and Sabrina put it away in the trunk. Then Povy shooed them out of the trading post, but Shawnee Blanc came back as Sabrina was about to close her door.

"Big medicine," Shawnee Blanc said and squatted against the wall. He pulled his blanket around him and plainly indicated his intention to remain there all night.

"Go away," Sabrina said. "Shawnee Blanc, go home!"

"Big medicine," he said.

She closed the door. There was no bar on the inside, and she wondered if she shouldn't slide the trunk against the door, then decided that the whole idea was silly.

She shed her clothes and then used one of her petticoats for a nightgown. A breath against the candle flame brought darkness into the room and she settled on the straw pallet. She lay back, her eyes closed, the night pressing against her like thick, black velvet. She heard several men come into the main room and a moment later there was loud laughter.

From across the village an Indian whooped once, then fell silent under the scolding tongue of a woman. For a time she lay in the darkness, listening to the night noises, the stirrings of Shawneetown. Then a new sound came through the walls and her attention sharpened. From somewhere in the night, Benjamin Travis struck a few chords on his banjo and began to sing:

> This lovely lass around we pass,
>   And crown her queen of the Ma — aay;
> No fairer form could wreaths adorn,
>   This merry meeting da — aay.

Travis sang on and Sabrina was filled with a sudden and overwhelming envy for this man because he could laugh and be free from care. She supposed he would always be that way, somewhat irresponsible, never satisfied; there was no hint of security in Benjamin Travis' manner. She supposed Able Kane would say that there had been none in Cadmus either, that the two men were alike, yet Sabrina sensed a vast difference. Cadmus Kane had been without hardness, a man easily molded by others. Benjamin Travis was the opposite, a strong-willed man, but not a good provider. Cadmus had at least been a good provider, if little else.

The song ended and there was a moment of appreciative whooping. Then, as Sabrina listened, he whanged out a few more introductory chords and began another, a ballad of lost love:

"The wintry clouds were wild above;
    My scalding tears, — they burn.
Where is the dwelling of my love?
    O, when will he return?
I've searched each cave for miles around,
    And e'en the wild beast's den;
But trace nor track of him I've found,"
    Cried Nancy of the Glen.

"Perhaps the wolves that heart have torn
    That loved me aye so true,
Or else some artful maid has borne
    Away that love, my due.
The pigeon seeks her absent mate,
    So doth the mountain hen:
I'll fly, I'll know my Charlie's fate,"
    Quoth Nancy of the Glen.

Her scanty wardrobe, all she had,
　　Was gathered, wild and fast;
Through storm and beating sleet she fled,
　　Nor feared the driving blast.
Her track the blood left pure and warm
　　On rock and thorny stem,
And scenting wolves howled with the storm
　　For Nancy of the Glen.

To gain the pass she urged her flight
　　Before the setting day;
But gathering storm and thickening night
　　O'ertook her on her way.
Against the tree, beside the gulf,
　　Far from the haunts of men,
In bitter anguish threw herself —
　　Poor Nancy of the Glen.

'Tis morn. Hark! Not a breath is heard;
　　Nor wolf, nor hawk, I see:
The storm howls not; no spray is stirred;
　　Yet Nancy's by the tree.
But O, her beauteous form and eye
　　Were cold; and angels then,
On cherub wings, came from the sky
　　For Nancy of the Glen.

The Indians whooped again and one of them banged on a shield made of dried hide. Sabrina heard Benjamin Travis laugh, a clear-toned sound breaking over the guttural voices of the Shawnees. She wondered what kind of a man he really was to sing ballads to savages. Could he be like a comet she had once seen, fast moving, but without a destination save oblivion?

He played another song, more softly this time and before he reached the end of it she was asleep. Later in the night she woke briefly when someone slammed a door, then when all was quiet, drifted off again.

Jake Povy's knock roused her in the morning. "Sun up," Povy called and went away. She smoothed her hair and clothes, then dressed and went outside and around the trading post. Shawnee Blanc waited on the front porch and he went with her, three paces behind like a watchdog.

A well and wash trough stood in back of the store and she scrubbed her face before going inside for breakfast. Her father was just finishing his meal. He looked at Povy and asked, "How much for the fixin's?"

"A dollar," Povy said. "Or trade for coffee. I'm short."

"Pay him the dollar," Priam Thomas said and sauntered outside.

Povy was a little offended to find a woman holding the purse strings and he hastily took the dollar. He acted as though he were afraid word of this would get around; a woman running a man's business was downright dangerous.

Nevertheless he felt compelled to express his sentiments. "Damned if I'd let a woman stand Sam for me," he said flatly, then clumped outside. Sabrina ate a bowl of pap and some sowbelly before leaving the table. When she returned to the room she found the trunk gone. She went directly to the porch in time to see Shawnee Blanc loading it into the wagon.

Her father stood to one side, content to let someone else work. Povy was admiring Benjamin Travis' two no-horn cows tied to the rear of the wagon.

"I thought I told him —" Sabrina began, but Povy interrupted.

"He give 'em to you, Ma'am. Ben's like that."

"I don't give a hoot what he's like!" Sabrina said quickly. "Mr. Povy, I don't want to be beholding to anyone. Call Mr. Travis and have him untie those critters."

"'Fraid I can't," Povy said. "Ben left around midnight. Took the spare horse and some of his trappin's. He left some saws an' tools in your wagon. I guess he figured your haulin' 'em was payment enough for the cows."

"Haulin' them?" Sabrina frowned. "Mr. Povy, I'll likely never see Benjamin Travis again."

"Don't expect that's so," Povy said. "Ben wanders about a good bit. He'll be callin' for his goods one of these days."

"What a slipshod way to conduct business," Sabrina said. "The idea! How does he know where we'll be? I haven't decided for myself yet."

Jake Povy chuckled. "Miz Kane, you're just gettin' yourself in a plaguey hobble over nothin'. We keep track of folks that's movin' into the country. Wherever you settle, the word'll get back. An' that Ben moves about, a real restless man. He'll sure turn up, especially around Illinois Town. Him and a couple of fellers there has a

48

little disagreement to settle." Povy smiled. "An' that Ben's all hell for settlin' his disagreements."

"I suppose there's nothing I can do about this," Sabrina said.

"We ought to be thankful for the cows," Priam Thomas said. "He's got a swod of good tools there. Be right helpful when we start to build. That fool Cadmus'd rather have taken knick-knacks instead of tools."

"We'll not use Mr. Travis' tools," Sabrina said firmly. "Papa, I'll not be beholdin' to a shiftless man." She lifted her skirts a little and climbed into the wagon. "Thank you, Mr. Povy. I do say you've been most kind." She looked back and saw Shawnee Blanc, his meager belongings in a bundle over his shoulder. Sabrina became alarmed. "Where's he going?"

"With you," Povy said.

"But I don't —"

"Now Miz Kane," Povy cautioned, "there ain't a thing you can do about it. He'll be a heap of help to you, bringin' in game, makin' camp. An' he won't be no fuss either."

"We can use a man," Thomas said, thinking about all the firewood Shawnee Blanc could carry.

"Sure been a pleasure to meet up with you folks," Povy said. "When you see Ben, give him my howdy."

"I'll give him a piece of my mind," Sabrina said. "Get in, Papa."

"Suppose I better," Priam Thomas said and climbed onto the seat.

Sabrina slapped the team with the reins and drove out of Shawneetown, following the trail westward. All that day they traveled at a walk, through lush grass land and rich forest glades. Shawnee Blanc was like a dog, sometimes ranging ahead of the wagon, at other times to the sides, poking into every bush and hollow. By mid afternoon Sabrina lost track of the creeks they had crossed. That evening she selected a campsite on the north bank of Saline Creek.

Shawnee Blanc fetched the firewood and she fixed the supper. Sometime during the afternoon the Shawnee had caught three tree squirrels. Sabrina made a stew, then after the meal cleaned the pot and climbed into the wagon to spread her blankets.

Priam Thomas stomped around a bit, clearly indicating that it was his intention to sleep in the wagon. Finally he said, "Expect you want me to bed down on the ground."

"It's dry enough," she told him and fell asleep.

Birds woke her as the first faint flush of day brightened the east. Shawnee Blanc came out of the brush with two rabbits, carrying them by the long ears. Sabrina started a fire and made a meal. Her father was in a grumpy mood and spoke sparingly, mostly mono-syllables. They were in the wagon and moving by the time the sun rose over the treetops.

That night they stopped near a small cabin owned by a Dutchman and his very large family. The Dutchman spoke little English, and since Sabrina was ignorant of Dutch, the conversation was restricted to hand waving, which established the direction from which they had come and the direction in which they were headed. Sabrina ended up paying the Dutchman twenty-five cents for the privilege of sleeping in the three-sided log lean-to.

The next morning they departed early, the half dozen children running alongside the wagon for a mile or two. That noon they watered the team in a wide creek, then crossed at the ford. They spent the night in the open, on a sea of hip-high grass. Because Priam Thomas had not yet learned to carry wood in the wagon, the meal was cold and quite unsatisfactory. He complained about this until he fell asleep and even then muttered comments in a droning voice.

Toward noon the next day they once more reached timber. Priam Thomas wanted the wagon stopped long enough for him to chop some wood in the event they again slept on the treeless prairie. Before dark they reached the settlement of Liberty and after supper Sabrina Kane walked down to the bank of the Mississippi and sat alone, watching the dark water. Not alone, actually, for Shawnee Blanc was like a shadow three paces behind, but by this time she had become so accustomed to his presence she could almost forget he was there. During the day her thoughts of Cadmus Kane could be controlled, but the shroud of darkness allowed her the isolation she needed to grieve. To some men he might not have been much, but to Sabrina he was her buckler and gorget, her protection against the many things she had learned to fear in other men. A woman needed love, and Cadmus Kane had loved her.

Now there was no more. After a while she got up and returned to the village.

Liberty was a growing town. Already there were four streets and a hundred and fifty permanent residents. Along the river a quay had been built to serve the river traffic; several boats were tied up there, taking on or unloading cargo. In Liberty Sabrina saw men who were akin to Benjamin Travis, buckskin clad men with long rifles and dangerous lights in their eyes. Men from across the Mississippi, from Missouri country, a wild and uninhabited region of fierce Indians and riches beyond imagination.

These men came across the river with bundles of furs and tall stories and an appetite for pretty girls and strong liquor. Liberty had few pretty women, at least unattached, so the town tried to atone for this deficiency with whiskey, which was served at a nickel a mug. After the third mug, only the strongest man was a match for shrewd Yankee traders who bought the furs for a quarter of their value.

Priam Thomas, fortified by several tots of Bald Face, wanted to stay on here. He spoke with half-drunken abandon of the fertile land, the limitless opportunities waiting for the right man to come along. Sabrina Kane agreed, and with Shawnee Blanc's help, put him to bed in the wagon.

The next morning they drove out of Liberty. Priam Thomas nursed a severe headache without benefit of Sabrina's sympathy. Even Shawnee Blanc, who had tasted many times of the white man's firewater, grinned and tapped his head, amused by Thomas' discomfort.

52

A long day's travel carried them to Kaskaskia, in a few years to become the first capitol of Illinois. But in 1811 the town was a mere cluster of rude cabins, with a trading post and a quay for river boats. By now, Sabrina Kane was beginning to understand something of the country. Every town had a trading post, but more correctly, every trading post soon found a town growing around it. The river held the key to Illinois, for on this broad waterway, boats arrived from New Orleans and Europe. At the Illinois trading posts, goods manufactured in England and France could be purchased, either by dollars, credits or furs. And other rivers linked Illinois with the world: The Tennessee where a man could pole a raft from Nashville or Chattanooga or the Ohio; it was not uncommon to find people in Illinois who had made the water journey from Pittsburgh or Charleston.

Trade was the answer to everything. A man could have the best piece of land, but if he couldn't move his produce and make a profit, then he became a squirrel hoarding nuts.

At Kaskaskia, Sabrina Kane stopped.

Near the west edge of town she found a small, unoccupied cabin and a few inquiries assured her that the former owner had moved upriver to Prairie du Rocher. Satisfied that she could do no better for nothing, Sabrina informed her father that this was their home and began to unload the wagon.

The first two weeks were difficult. The old chinking had to be pulled out and new mixed to replace it. The fireplace drew badly and the door needed fixing. Priam Thomas, much to his disgust, was put to work building a lean-to out back. When this was finished, Sabrina carried his belongings out to it and told him this was his new home.

There was little conversation between them that evening.

Movers came through Kaskaskia every week, some in small groups, and once, a large train of nineteen wagons. The movers stayed a few days, looked the country over, and invariably moved on to the north, Prairie du Rocher, Cahokia or Prairie du Pont. Sabrina Kane watched these people, studied them, listened to their talk. During the third week she decided to move again. She spoke to her father of this.

Priam Thomas banged his hand palm down on the table. "I ain't goin'!"

"All right," Sabrina said evenly. "I'll leave you two of the horses to plow with and half the seed. That's fair enough."

"Wh — why're you doin' this to me, Sabrina? What do you want to go on for; there's no reason, child. You got this place and some land around it. What do you want from life?"

"A better one than I had. A better one than mother had. This isn't really my place; I just moved in. The other movers are going north along the river. That's where I've decided to go."

"It's a man's place to decide," Thomas said. "Your ma was always runnin' over me, now you."

"Stay if you want," Sabrina said. "I don't care."

"You know I'm no good without you." Priam Thomas spread his hands appealingly. "You're a drivin' woman, Sabrina. You're hard on a man. Hard on me an' Cadmus too." She started to protest. "Yes, you was! Always makin' him do the things he never really wanted to do or had the gumption for. You been that way to me, too. This last ten years I ain't had a minute to myself. Since you been fourteen an' took over the house from your ma, it's been 'do this, do that,' and no peace if I didn't."

"What have I ever asked you to do besides work, which every man should do without being told?"

"Work I don't mind," Priam Thomas said. "A man just hates to be the hand for someone else's ambition, that's all."

She was angry. "You want to be like Benjamin Travis? With only the clothes on your back?" She took a deep breath. "Papa, I'm not going to argue about it. I've had my say. We'll leave tomorrow."

"All right, Sabrina, all right! You may be right about Ben Travis, but by Jehoshaphat, he's got his freedom! Been so long since I've been fishin' I plumb forgot how."

"You want to go fishing, then go!" Sabrina snapped.

"Ain't the same, goin' by command. You don't understand — a man's got to feel that he's a man. That he can do what he pleases when he pleases. You take that away from a man, Sabrina. You took it away from Cadmus, and I guess that's why you didn't marry Able; he wouldn't have put up with your nonsense a minute." He got up wearily and went to the doorway. He stood there, looking at the village. Then he turned back to her. "You've made plain my shortcomings, but you've got your share."

"I never pretended I didn't."

"Guess you didn't," Thomas agreed, "but your chin gets stubborn and your eyes get determined as if you was darin' a body to remind you of 'em. You learned to hate men, Sabrina, danged if you ain't. A man like Cadmus was weak enough for you to twist around to doin' what you wanted, but not strong enough to get your wants."

"That's a filthy thing to say!" Sabrina shouted. "I loved him! And he knew it!"

Thomas shook his head slowly. "I guess you really think you did, but it wasn't real, Sabrina."

"I've heard enough!" She began to clear the table.

"No you ain't!" Thomas took her arm, pulling her around. "I got my wind up and you're goin' to hear me out just this once. No need to look at me that way. I ain't much and I know it; you've showed me that often enough. Maybe I'd have been more if I hadn't been told so many times what I wasn't!"

"You can't plow a furrow when you're on your knees askin' for help," Sabrina said scornfully. "All those fancy notions about Able Kane; you wanted me to marry him because he had a big farm and would have let you loaf around until you died. It wasn't me you was thinking of, Papa. Don't stand there and tell me it was." She jerked her arm free of his grip. "Ma went through twenty years of wondering where the next shilling was coming from while you laughed because you didn't care. Well, no man will ever make an old hag out of me! If I ever marry again, it'll be to a settled man, a providin' man, but he'll be one that'll let me have my say. It's my life I'm sharing."

"A man's got to run his own business and a woman's got to go along, for better or for worse." Thomas shook his head. "Girl, I ain't sayin' it's wrong to be so all-fired independent, but a man just don't understand a woman like that. Cadmus didn't."

"He did! Papa, he did!"

"Nope," Thomas said. "He didn't. He loved you and he put up with your nonsense, but he didn't understand it. Able didn't either, but he would have put a stop to it, had you married him. You want a settled man, you say. A providin' man. You want a man to taw the line when you say jump. No man'll do that."

"That isn't what I want," Sabrina said. She sat down and rubbed her forehead. "Papa, I want a man who'll — look at me as a — a partner, not just someone to cook the meals and keep the bed warm. I'm alive, Papa, a person, not a — a cow."

"Funny," Thomas said, "but you're goin' at this all wrong, Sabrina. You'll find a man, but he'll be some man. Likely tamin' you to the cradle'll be a heap of work, but he'll do it without raisin' a sweat." She opened her mouth to protest, but he silenced her with a raised hand. "Your trouble's that no man's ever made you feel like a woman. When that happens you'll —" He stopped to swing his head toward the open door. "What's that I hear? Did you hear that?"

He went to the doorway without waiting for her answer. Sabrina came up and stood beside him. Shawnee Blanc, who never came into the cabin, was smiling, looking off into the timber. A hundred yards of flat ground ran to the timber's edge and from a break in the trees Benjamin Travis appeared, the twangy thump of his banjo coming bell-toned across the distance. He was leading his horse, laden with furs and assorted plunder. A small boy sat on his shoulders. His long rifle was thrust crossways between the boy and his own back, leaving both hands free to play the banjo as he walked. The boy was laughing and clung tightly to the fur of Travis' coonskin cap.

Travis made his way to the edge of the village. Families came to the doorways as he approached and children followed him in small droves. He smiled and spoke to them in a way all children understand, with a song. He came on toward Sabrina Kane's cabin unknowingly and when he saw her dearborn wagon and the two brindle cows, he gave one loud concluding whang on his banjo and stopped. He disbanded the children with soft, meaningless threats and a wave of his hand.

Sabrina snorted through her nose and turned from the door. "He can charm a bird out of a bush but never does a lick of work."

Priam Thomas frowned at her but waited until Travis approached the stoop. Thomas said, "Well there, come in and set a spell."

"Thank you kindly," Travis said. "I've come a far piece." He bent down so the boy wouldn't crack his head against the door frame. He placed his banjo against the wall, unslung his rifle carefully and leaned it next to the banjo. Sabrina was at the fireplace, stirring a kettle of broth hanging from the crane. She had her back to him and from the set of her shoulders showed little inclination to turn around. Benjamin Travis observed her through narrowed lids, a mild amusement in his eyes. He had a man's frank appreciation for a shapely woman.

"Ain't you got a howdy for me, Ma'am?"

"Hello," Sabrina said. She turned, still holding the wooden spoon. "I've a few words to say to you, Mr. Travis."

He saw the temper in her eyes and his smile widened to disarming proportions. "It'd be my pure pleasure to chat, but I've come a scandalous piece with this little tyke an' he's plumb tuckered out." Travis stretched his arms upward for the small boy and lifted him down from his shoulders. The boy laughed and clung to the coonskin cap. "Ain't he a cute little jigger?" He held the boy toward Sabrina. "Why don't you hold him for a spell?"

Shawnee Blanc looked around the door. Travis said, "There's some tobacco in my possibles. Go get it an' stop sneakin' around like you was fixin' to lift hair."

"You good friend," Shawnee Blanc said and went after the tobacco.

"Mr. Travis," Sabrina said, "about the cows and —" She looked at the boy. His hands and face were dirty and for clothes he wore a deerskin tied by a cord around his middle. "Mr. Travis, have you fed this child?"

"Fed him?" Benjamin Travis strangled a smile to look thoughtful. He caught Thomas' glance when Sabrina wasn't looking and winked. "By doggies, I forgot about feedin' him, Ma'am! He cried once an' I gave him a bite of my tobacco. He seemed to like it."

"Oh, you're terrible!" Sabrina said in disgust. She snatched the boy from his arms and set him on the table. He was a moon-faced child, nearly three. His hair was dark and he watched her with round, fascinated eyes as she set a bowl of pap in front of him. He took the proffered spoon, loaded it, then flung the mush on the floor. Sabrina sighed and began to feed him.

Benjamin Travis rocked back and forth on his heels, highly pleased. "Give a woman a youngun an' she'll be happy," he said. Sabrina turned her head and gave him a disgusted frown. Travis grinned at her. "He sure takes to you, Ma'am. I was hopin' he would, 'cause I meant to give him to you."

Sabrina knew a sudden alarm. This man was beyond prediction; he was insane. "Mr. Travis, you can't leave him here!" She glanced at her father, but there was little hope of help there. "This — this is beyond reason! We have laws!"

"He ain't big enough to forage for himself," Travis said seriously. Had she bothered to look into his eyes she would have seen the telltale shine of humor, but anger blinded her. "Injuns give plews an' horses; ask Shawnee Blanc if they don't. But I only got one horse left and I need him. The plews I trade off, so I'll give you the boy."

Sabrina Kane was furious. Only a man could have so complete a disregard for others; this was her thought as she stood before him, fists on her hips, her face inches from his. "Mr. Travis, we don't give human beings away! Where did you get this boy? Stole him probably. Now you take him back, do you hear? Take him and your no-horn cows and your truck from my wagon. Then git!"

"Now, Sabrina, Ben's only havin' his little jo —"
Thomas closed his mouth with a snap for Sabrina gave
him a venomous glance.

"The cows was a gift, too," Benjamin Travis said. "It
ain't proper for a man to take back what he gives."

"I'll not be beholdin' to the likes of you!" Sabrina
snapped. She watched Travis' smile grow bolder and
knew then that he was baiting her for his own amusement.
She hated him for his smug male superiority.

Travis said, "Seems that you're already beholdin'.
That's why I figured you'd take the boy, to sort of even
up. After losin' your man an' all, the boy'd take your
mind off your problems. Give you somethin' to do."

By closing her eyes for a moment, Sabrina was able
to kick her temper under control. She spoke quietly.
"Mr. Travis, whose boy is this?"

"Well, I don't rightly know," he admitted. "His name's
Bushrod, but he couldn't tell me what his last name
was."

"But he belonged to someone and you took him. Is
that right?"

Travis looked at Priam Thomas as if to ask whether
he should let this go any farther, then something he saw
crystalized the decision. "I reckon that's a fact," he said.

"Mr. Travis, I haven't decided whether you're
touched in the head, or just a simple, good-natured
fool." She stamped her foot in exasperation. What
angered her most was his total lack of response to her
demands. But most men were like that; they ignored a
woman. "You have to take this boy back to his parents!"

"Can't," Travis said simply.

"Can't or won't?"

"Can't see how it'll make much difference," he said. "You've already made up your mind about it."

She turned away from Benjamin Travis, her arms crossed over her bosom. "Mr. Travis, I have troubles of my own. I don't want the boy. Do you understand? Just take him away."

The change in his manner was a shock even to her. The gaiety left Benjamin Travis' eyes and he suddenly became a stranger. There was a brittleness to the tight-drawn skin over his cheekbones and in his voice the warmth of autumn faded to the chill of winter. "Guess I made a mistake about you," he said. "I thought you was a kindly person. Brave, too, the way you held yourself after your man died. But I was wrong. If you're so all-fired selfish you can't find a corner for him to sleep in, or an extra bowl to feed him out of, then I guess he's better off someplace else." He put the boy back on his shoulders, replaced his coonskin cap, picked up his rifle and banjo, and walked out.

Priam Thomas said, "I'm not proud of you, Sabrina," and followed Benjamin Travis.

Sabrina opened her mouth to call to him, to bring him back, for she was sorry now that she had not penetrated Travis' easy manner to the serious man beneath. But she knew the time had passed for calling him. He was not the kind of a man who came back on a whistle.

Travis stopped when Thomas halloed and waited for him. Thomas said, "Pay her no mind. She's upset. She'll change her mind."

"No need for that," Travis said, " 'cause I only ask a body somethin' once."

Thomas could no longer contain his curiosity. "Where are the boy's folks?"

"Dead," Travis said simply. "You live here awhile, you'll know about them things. You know an' you don't ask a lot of damn fool questions about the obvious."

They walked through the settlement to the trading post. A group of men lounged on the porch and they yelled their greetings at Benjamin Travis.

"Ben, what you got there, Hoss?"

"His pelt's poorly, Ben."

"What'd you catch him with, sugarhards?"

Travis grinned at them. "I'm buyin'," he said and they all went inside. The bar was a long, heavy plank set on two short cuts of walnut tree. Travis set the boy down and placed the banjo close by. The boy amused himself by picking the strings. Caleb Stiles, who ran the trading post, came out of the back room as the men lined up. "Rum," Travis said, indicating them all with a sweep of his hand. He laid a Spanish dollar on the rough wood.

Stiles drew from a barrel and when the mugs were filled, set them on the bar. He looked carefully at the boy, then at Benjamin Travis. "Ain't he from around Pond Slough?"

"Yep," Travis said. The talk fell off and Caleb Stiles studied the boy's hair color and his eyes, pausing long on the formation of his face.

"Seems that I've seen his tribe before. Where'd you find him, Ben?"

"Hidin' in the smokehouse," Travis said. He lifted his mug and saluted the gathering. "Here's to the country Jakes."

The others hoisted their tot of rum and the talk built up again.

Caleb Stiles had a one-track mind. "Ben, I got kin down there. Was it big?"

"Not big. A small party of Crees. They hit two places, then moved across the river." He smiled at Caleb Stiles. "You sell good rum."

"Sure," Stiles said. "The best, Ben."

"Fetched you some Baltimore papers," Travis said. "That danged fool Fulton's runnin' a steamboat on the Hudson river."

"They ought to pass a law," Stiles said flatly. "A thing like that'll blow up an' kill somebody." The news was worth a little more rum on the house. Stiles put a dram in each mug.

"Then there's this French feller," Travis said. "Can't remember his name, but he's figured out a way to preserve fruit an' stuff in glass jars."

"Lord help us when the women find this out," one of the men said. "You'll make a fortune off'n them jars, Stiles."

"If I could get 'em here without bustin' every damn one of 'em," Stiles said.

Priam Thomas had been listening to this talk and tried to enter into it, but he kept thinking of Travis' brief remarks about Pond Slough. He considered asking Travis for more detail, but when he looked at the tall man's face he understood that here was a man one did not question or ask for explanations. Benjamin Travis believed that a man understood what he wanted to understand and all the explanations in the world would not change his mind. Priam Thomas turned his attention to the others, sure that he had discovered an important truth about Ben Travis.

To forestall further conversation, Benjamin Travis walked to the open doorway and stood there, looking out toward the river. Two keelboats were loading up with furs for the trip down river. Another boat was unloading, and while he lingered there, still another worked upstream and tied up to the quay. Upriver traffic was always worth watching. From the south came all the manufactured goods and the news from a world that sometimes seemed far away.

The river was over a hundred yards from the trading post, yet Benjamin Travis' keen eyes identified the three new arrivals. He turned his glance to Priam Thomas, but Thomas was telling a story and showed small interest in what went on outside.

Moving away from the door, Ben Travis went to the bar, picked up his rifle and returned to the door. Only this time he leaned his shoulders against the wall, out of sight of anyone coming up the road. He held his rifle negligently as he waited.

He heard Fountainbleau's voice before the *voyageur* reached the porch. Thomas, still talking, failed to notice; then Fountainbleau and his two companions came into the building. Shadows filled the doorway and Travis drew a deep breath. The Frenchman stopped just inside while his eyes adjusted to the dim light. He carried a long-barreled fusil and shouted, "*Eh bien!* It has been a long time, *mes gens!*"

Priam Thomas turned because he was irked by this interruption. With each man recognition was simultaneous. "*Mere de Dieu!*" Fountainbleau exploded and cocked his fusil before throwing it to his shoulder.

Benjamin Travis swung his leg, catching the Frenchman under the arm. The heavy-caliber fusil went off with a roar, then fell as Fountainbleau staggered to retain his balance. A haze of powder smoke hung in the room and the two *voyageurs* with Fountainbleau reached for weapons.

"I wouldn't, *mes amis,*" Travis warned softly. He pointed his flintlock at them and neither chose to challenge his shooting ability.

Fountainbleau had recovered from his surprise. He bent to retrieve his fallen musket, but Travis stepped forward without taking his attention from the others and kicked it into the corner. "You won't need that, Frenchy."

"Name of cow! What you would have a man do?" He pointed to Priam Thomas. "You — how you say, disarm a man before his enemies?"

Travis' soft laugh worried Fountainbleau. "Frenchy, when I heard you put 'em ashore an' kept their dollars, I said, 'That Frenchy is goin' to show up for a whoop-up.' An' here you are, Frenchy, all set to spend them dollars."

"There's no need for —" Priam Thomas began, but Benjamin Travis interrupted him.

"Frenchy, Mr. Thomas ain't riled about the money, but the way you manhandled Miz Kane."

"Sacre Bl —"

The men in the room muttered angrily, cutting Fountainbleau off. Stiles said, "You mean that this low sausage laid a hand on Miz Kane?" He glared at Fountain-bleau. "By God, I got a rope here that'll fit his neck!"

"No need for that," Travis said. "Mr. Thomas'll handle this in his own good way."

This talk about handling things was beginning to make Priam Thomas nervous. He said, "See here now, Ben —"

Travis cut him off. "Mr. Thomas, you just be quiet. This is an affair of honor an' it ought to be settled with a duel. In that case, the principles ain't supposed to speak with each other."

"A duel?" Fountainbleau licked his lips. "M'sieu Travis —"

"Shut up!" Stiles said. "Or you won't live until Thomas can kill you."

"Now don't wear yourself out cussin' this sausage," Travis said. He reached to the back of his belt and drew his knife. Flipping it in his hand, he threw a neat turn and a half. It sank true near Priam Thomas, quivering as though alive. "You got a blade, Frenchy, so we'll settle this with a reg'lar sifter, cut-the-buckle and chicken-flutter set to. Stiles, you got some yard goods they could hold twixt their teeth?"

"I surely have, Ben. The rest of you gents keep an eye on Frenchy's friends so's we don't have no outside interference."

They seemed eager to do this and Fountainbleau's two *voyageurs* were held in one corner. Fountainbleau looked at the open doorway and gauged his chances, but Travis' ready rifle discouraged him. Sweat began to make his face slick and he licked his lips. Priam Thomas, still by the bar, looked at Travis, but the tall man only winked.

Caleb Stiles came up with a piece of flannel nearly three feet long. He said, "You want I should lock the door, Ben?"

"This won't take long," Travis said. He gave Fountainbleau a push that sent him into the center of the room. The Frenchman stopped and stood stiff-legged, watching Priam Thomas with unwavering attention.

At Travis' insistence, Thomas reluctantly shed his coat. Fountainbleau was divested of his capot and Travis made him draw his knife. "M'sieus," Fountainbleau said, "I will return the dollars! Every sou!"

"It ain't the money, Frenchy," Travis said. "It's your layin' hands on Miz Kane that's goin' to get you killed."

"Now, Ben —" Thomas began.

"M'SIEUS! I WILL MAKE THE APOLOGY MANY TIMES!"

"*Fermez la bouche!*" Travis said. "*Vous parlez trop.*"

"*Mon Dieu!* It is wicked to duel!"

"You should have thought of that," Stiles said. "Pick up your knife, Thomas. Open his yellow gizzard."

Sabrina was right, Thomas decided. They're all crazy! Nevertheless he picked up the knife and held it. "If he wants to pay me —" Thomas began, but Travis interrupted him.

"Nosiree, this is an affair of honor!" He motioned to Caleb Stiles. "Put the cloth in their mouths."

Fountainbleau wouldn't take his until Stiles struck him. Thomas appeared to be hypnotized. All seemed satisfactory to Benjamin Travis and he stepped back. Both men breathed through their teeth, the whistling loud in the room.

"Go to 'er," someone shouted and Fountainbleau made a frightened stab for Thomas' breast. How Thomas ducked that one Travis never knew, but the knife merely ripped through the shirt and inflicted a shallow wound on Thomas' chest. He yelped with pain and swung his fist at Fountainbleau's face, forgetting that he had a knife in his hand. The blade went through Fountainbleau's cheek, broke two teeth, then split him through the mouth as Thomas wrenched the blade free. The Frenchman's cry was more of fright than pain, although the wound was ghastly.

He released the cloth from his teeth and drove against Thomas, driving his knife blade cleanly through the muscle of Thomas' upper arm. Like a wild man, Priam Thomas bore into Fountainbleau. Thomas' eyes were glazed and he brought his knife fist down, trying to hit the Frenchman on top of the head. But Fountainbleau jerked to one side and took the blow over the ear, and it was cleanly severed. Clapping one hand over the blood spout, Fountainbleau fell back, his knife clattering to the floor.

69

Then he looked down and saw his ear on the dirt floor and collapsed in a loose heap. Travis who observed everything with quick, shifting glances saw Priam Thomas' knees start to bend and rushed forward, grasping him, supporting him as he shouted, "Did you ever see the beat of it? Why Thomas is a wildcat! He'd have carved that poor French louse into sausages if Frenchy hadn't lost his stomach!"

This was enough to excite the onlookers' imaginations and within a minute everyone present believed that Priam Thomas, the finest knife fighter east of the Mississippi River, had beaten Jacques Fountainbleau without half trying.

"Let's get some more rum into him," Travis said and Caleb Stiles hurried behind the bar. "Don't you know a he-cat like Thomas here wants his rum after a fracas?"

Stiles seemed ashamed that such an important detail had slipped his mind. Travis held the cup to Thomas' lips while he drank, then threw it into the fireplace with a crash. All the men cheered loudly and Stiles furnished another round.

Thomas' wound was bleeding freely but he was not seriously injured. Travis made a show of dressing the arm wound and Thomas, fortified by the second tot of rum, insisted on ignoring the slash across his chest. Thomas was a man anesthetized by the miracle of still being alive.

In the corner, Fountainbleau's men still waited and at Travis' slight signal they came forward. They stood nervously while he emptied Fountainbleau's poke, counted out eighty Spanish dollars, then put the rest back.

"Get him out of here," Travis said. "Take his ear with you. If'n you sew it on right away, I hear tell it'll grow back on."

"*Oui, M'sieu,*" one of them said.

As they prepared to lift Fountainbleau, Travis halted them once more. "In the event you two sausages mean to back-shoot me, remember this." His pointing arm singled out a small knot in the pine door. When the Frenchmen turned their heads to look, Travis shouldered his rifle in one smooth motion and shot the knot out.

They said nothing, but they were impressed. Travis reloaded his rifle carefully, paying a strict attention to Priam Thomas. Thomas finished his tot of rum, but refused the next round being pressed on him. "Seems I ought to be gettin' home," he said. The fury of past moments was beginning to work on his nerves.

"I'd be obliged to go with you," Travis said and hustled him from the trading post before objections could be voiced. Behind them was a burst of ribald singing and the memory of a fine fight. Night had fallen and the settlement was quiet. They walked slowly and carefully through the soft dark.

"I don't see why you done this to me," Thomas said. "Shovin' me into a cuttin' fight. I thought you was my friend." He began to tremble and Travis stopped until this wore off.

Travis was a stone-silent man. As they approached Sabrina's cabin, he saw her silhouetted in the doorway, the hearth fire shooting a flickering light behind her. Travis said, "Light a candle, Ma'am."

There was a premonition in his voice, enough to turn her. By the time they stepped inside she had two candles set in dishes on the table. When she saw the blood on Thomas' shirt her mouth formed into a shocked, round O. Then she hurriedly led him to her bed and pushed him back.

"What in the world happened?" She spoke to Travis while trying to remove Priam Thomas' coat.

"Knife fight," Benjamin Travis said easily.

"With who? Over what?" She shot him an unbelieving look. "Papa never fights. He hasn't raised his hand in anger for so long he's forgot how!"

"He remembered tonight," Travis said. "He cut Fountainbleau's ear plumb off."

"He what? You're lying. Papa's a meek man!" Her hands fluttered as she attempted to inspect her father's wound, but quite unexpectedly he pushed her hands aside and sat up.

"Meek, am I?" Priam Thomas was shouting. "I put a cloth in my mouth and fought him proper, ain't that so, Ben?"

"It most surely is," Travis said and there was a great wisdom in his eyes. "A man's more than he usually thinks he is, Thomas. Like as not that sort of slipped your mind through the years."

"I won't forget it now," Thomas promised.

Sabrina Kane understood none of this. She stood up quickly, whipped around and struck Benjamin Travis in the face with her open hand. "You let him do this! He could have got killed, but you wouldn't have cared!"

"I expect he could have," Travis admitted. The friendliness he had formerly shown her was now gone. "As a fact now, I started the whole thing."

This bald admission made her so angry that she trembled. "Mr. Travis, I have a rifle. If you ever come near me again, I'll shoot you; do you understand that?"

"For a fact, I do," Travis said. He turned to the door, pausing there. "Ma'am, for bein' a married woman, you sure know next to nothin' about a man."

"I'm getting acquainted with you!" she snapped. "Now get out!"

Benjamin Travis looked at her for a brief instant and was gone. Sabrina turned to her father, meaning to help him, but he was standing. She rushed to his side, but he fended her reaching hands away.

"Just let me be," he said with a new dignity.

"Papa, you've been hurt! I want to help you."

"I'll live," he said. "And I'll take care of myself. You made it plain that's the way you want it."

She wrung her hands. "Not when you're hurt." She bit her lip. "Oh, how I hate him! I've had nothing but trouble since I met him."

"You're a fool," Priam Thomas said. "A blind fool."

"I'm not going to stay here any longer. Not as long as he's here," Sabrina said. Without another word she began to gather her things, carrying them to the wagon.

"You're running," Priam Thomas said when she came back for another load. "You're runnin' from Ben Travis."

"Yes, I'm running. Does that give you satisfaction?"

"No," he said and watched her move her trunk, then the bedding. "It won't give Ben none either."

In an hour she was packed. She had taken Benjamin Travis' things out of the wagon and stacked them by the cabin wall. She told her father, "I'm leaving. You'd better come, too."

"I'll go," Priam Thomas said flatly. "But because I want to go. You did a bad thing, orderin' him off. A stupid thing."

"I don't understand you sometimes." She looked at him oddly. "He got you into a fight; you could have been killed. And taking that boy — he has no respect for other people's rights. Absolutely none!"

"What do you know about it?" Thomas asked. "You don't know because you can't see. You're so blind, Sabrina. You look at Ben Travis and you don't see him at all. I'll tell you where he got the boy. At Pond Slough, some place south of here. That's where he got him, after the boy's folks had been killed by Crees!"

For a moment Sabrina stood in shocked silence. "Why didn't he tell me that? Why didn't he?"

"Because he ain't the kind that explains everything. He expects you to have sense enough to figure somethin' out for yourself. You got to see the man, understand him. You got to open your eyes, Sabrina. You got to think about other people besides yourself." Thomas lowered his voice. He spoke almost reverently. "Tonight somethin' came back to me that I ain't had for a long time, my guts. But Travis did it for me, put me into somethin' I couldn't back out of. Oh, I was scared, Sabrina. Really scared, but I found out Fountainbleau was as scared of me as I was of him."

"Am I supposed to thank him for that?"

"I guess you wouldn't," Thomas said. "But don't talk again' him to me. I don't want to hear it."

He moved past her and went outside to mount the wagon, gasping when the lift pulled at his slashed chest muscle. He sat on the seat, breathing heavily. Finally he looked down at Sabrina and said, "You comin'?"

"Do — do you suppose he'd listen to me if I went to him?"

Priam Thomas shook his head. "He ain't the kind of a man that wants a person humble. Was he to pass this off, I doubt he'd ever make mention of it."

Sabrina stood by the wheel, undecided. She had made her brag about leaving, but now she realized how wrong she had been. Yet she could not retreat; she never had and long ago had vowed never to go back on anything she said. This was her way, she supposed, of competing with men, to make her word as good as theirs, force them to accept her at her word.

She mounted the wagon.

When she drove out the two brindle cows were still tied behind the wagon, but she told herself that the only reason she couldn't leave them behind with the rest of Travis' traps was that the cows needed tending. When she settled in her final home, she would find a way to return the cows.

Shawnee Blanc walked behind the wagon, a disgusted expression on his face. Finally he came up to Thomas' side of the wagon with a long willow switch.

He offered it to Thomas with this advice: "Woman talk all time. You beat. Stop talking."

Thomas laughed and Sabrina shot him a withering look. "You keep your heathen opinions to yourself!" Shawnee Blanc looked crestfallen and returned to his place behind the wagon.

Her father's heated speech still bothered her, for he had changed and she was not too sure that she liked it. Her mother had devoted years to patient disapproval in order to steady Priam Thomas to his tasks but even then he did his work reluctantly. A man's independence was a woman's curse; Sabrina had learned this the hard way. Now her father was showing the old signs and she could thank Benjamin Travis for this. Yet she viewed the matter with a frighteningly new perspective. Quickly, unerringly, Benjamin Travis had divined Priam Thomas' character and done something about it. All men, it seemed, resented seeing another under a woman's thumb. It was, she supposed, an affront to their imagined manly superiority. Little matter when there were mouths to feed and a man went hunting when he should have been cradling wheat. The wheat could always wait for a man's pleasure.

Everything waited for a man's pleasure, and this riled her anew.

She had to drive past the trading post and through the open door came the sounds of Benjamin Travis, singing to the accompaniment of his banjo. Somehow the sound of this gaiety was insulting to her; obviously the man was without sensitivity. He had not paid the slightest attention to her anger or her feelings.

On sudden impulse she stopped the team, set the brake and climbed down. Shawnee Blanc grinned, wrinkling his copper-face. "You buy *scootiwaboo?*"

He patted his bare stomach as she pushed past him, walking without hesitation in to the trading post bar. Priam Thomas was shocked. "Sabrina! Dang-bustit, a woman don't go among drinkin' men!"

She ignored him and went in. A strained hush fell over the group. Even Benjamin Travis looked at her oddly and laid his banjo aside.

He had been drinking; he was unsteady on his feet. The boy sat on the bar by his elbow, sucking on his fingers. He seemed quite content to remain there. Sabrina walked up to him, placed him on her hip and said, "I've changed my mind, Mr. Travis."

She didn't wait for him to object but went outside, handed the boy into the seat, got into the wagon and drove from the settlement. For once Priam Thomas remained silent and she was grateful, for her own impulses were not as clear as she would have liked them. For twenty minutes she held the horses to a walk, then suddenly turned them around in the trail and went back. Passing the trading post, she drove directly to the cabin and got down.

One by one she loaded Benjamin Travis' things into the wagon.

CHAPTER
FOUR

For five days Sabrina Kane and her father drove in a northerly direction, through hilly grass lands and across flat stretches of prairie. On the sixth day she paused on the breast of a hill to rest the team. Below and beyond where the Mississippi made a yawning bend lay Illinois Town, sprawled on a broad, grassy flat, surrounded on three sides by low rolling hills and rich timber. On the west side of the river lay St. Louis, gateway to the vast Missouri Territory and all the unexplored riches beyond to the Pacific Ocean.

"Quite a sight," Priam Thomas said.

Sabrina brushed a strand of hair away from her eyes, then lifted the boy, Bushrod, to her lap so he could see. On the Mississippi, a crew of *voyageurs* strained on the cordelle, their singing coming faintly across the distance.

Beneath the sharp brightness of the early morning sun, Illinois Town was a rough diamond displayed on nature's green breast. The houses were hewn timber set upright in the ground and chinked with stone and mortar. None were more than one story high. All had porches on at least two sides; some on three or four. The roofs were quaintly pitched, starting steep at the gable and ending flat at the porch eave. All the houses, except those of the Americans, were patterned after the French houses in Toulouse. Surrounding each was a garden formed by fruit trees in full bloom.

From the moment she saw Illinois Town, Sabrina Kane knew she wanted to live there. The Indian, Shawnee Blanc, had his long look, then grunted; he did that when he approved of something.

Urging her team on at a walk, she drove past the farms where fourth generation French, descendants of La Salle and Ibberville, worked. Their farming methods had remained unchanged through the years. Horses pulled small wooden carts that held little more than a large wheelbarrow. Oxen were yoked by the horns instead of the neck and driven with whip instead of 'gee' and 'haw'.

She passed Americans and from their cabins and manner of farming placed them as being from Kentucky, Virginia or Pennsylvania. Past the forest perimeter lay the Indian nations: the Kickapoos, Sac and Fox, Shawnee, Winnebagoes, Menominies, Pottawatomie, and farther north, the fierce Sioux.

As she approached the center of the settlement she saw the Catholic Church, decaying along with the other buildings of the French fur company, who had won this town from the British in 1778, only to lose it to the Americans a few years later. A cluster of newer buildings marked the enterprise of Jethro and Clem Sweet, and toward these Sabrina drove her wagon, stopping by the sheltered porch. Only then did she recognize the man sitting there.

Jacques Fountainbleau's head supported a thick bandage. He gaped at Sabrina and her father, then sprang from his stool and bolted through the door, calling to someone inside the building. A moment later he peered around the door frame, but when he saw Thomas holding his flintlock, he ducked back inside and stayed there.

By the time Sabrina had dismounted and put the boy in the back of the wagon, another man had come through the door and off the porch. He was a big man, even taller than Benjamin Travis. He wore tight, velvet breeches with a short coat and a felt hat with a wide ribbon wound around it for a band. Into this was thrust his long-stemmed pipe. His hair was braided into a queue, the ends tied with a colored silk ribbon. His shoes were of fine leather and instead of lacing, were held together by three silver buckles. He was a man in his early thirties, with a broad, handsome face, completely clean shaven. With a flourish he uncovered his head and said, "Jethro Sweet, the most man in these here parts. You want anything, then come to me. Don't waste your time with anyone else; I'd have to do it anyway. At your pleasure, Ma'am."

From the manner in which Sweet studied her, Sabrina was certain that Fountainbleau had told him about her and Priam Thomas. Nevertheless, she introduced her father and herself.

"I intend to farm," she said, as if that explained everything.

Evidently it did to Jethro Sweet. "You've come to the right place," he said. "Illinois Town is mostly mine for as far as you can see." He waved his hand to the north, toward the timber's edge. "Step yourself off what you want, but don't be a hog about it. I'm givin' it to you 'cause you're a woman and a doggoned, all-fired handsome one, too." He looked at Shawnee Blanc. "That your Injun?"

"He travels with us," Sabrina said.

"I don't want him hangin' around the tradin' post," Sweet said. "Anythin' I can't abide an' that's a lazy man, 'specially an Injun." He glared at Shawnee Blanc. "You understan', Injun?"

"He won't bother you," Thomas said suddenly. "You say this land's yours. How do you mean, yours?"

"'Cause I say it's mine," Sweet said flatly. "Don't that suit you?"

"I've worked other men's land before," Thomas said. "It's poor doin's. I want to have title to the land I farm."

"I said the land was mine," Sweet repeated. "Folks around here all work for me. They bring their yield to my store. I give 'em fair trade. You folks either take it or leave it. You go north of here the Injuns'll kill you inside of a year."

"We'll take it," Thomas said. "But I'll likely talk to you about this later."

"No talkin' to be done," Sweet said. "I tell a man; that's all there is to it." He again pointed to the timber north of town. "Take a goodly passel. Another fella wants it, but he ain't comin' back to claim it. It's yours as long as you trade with me."

"And what if we want to take our goods down river?" Sabrina asked.

Sweet frowned, then switched his eyes to Priam Thomas. "You all the man she's got?"

"What I lack in size," Thomas said, "I make up with a big stick."

Sweet laughed. "Then I won't lose sleep about you takin' your goods down river." His glance touched Sabrina. "You'll get a man quick enough. There's single men around here lookin' for a woman with your figure."

Blood vaulted into Sabrina's face, but she kept her voice under control. "I'm not looking for a man, Mr. Sweet."

"There won't be much you can do about it. Was I to say it, they'll be around your lodge thick as flies after a honey house."

Another man came through the doorway to the porch edge. He looked at Priam Thomas and said, "Is he the one who cut Jacques up? He ain't much, is he?"

"My brother, Clem," Jethro said. "Put on your manners now, Clem."

Clem Sweet was a copy of his older brother, but his tastes ran to buckskins and chewing tobacco instead of a pipe. He was a dark-haired man, built like an oak smokehouse and big enough to hunt bears with a switch. His shoulders were the widest Sabrina Kane had ever seen.

He shook hands gravely with Sabrina and her father. "Which passel did you give 'em, Jethro?" He kept his glance on Sabrina when he spoke. She felt his eyes on her rounded hips and her full breasts, as he smiled, cleared his throat and kept on looking.

"The one Ben Travis wanted," Jethro said. "Clem, dang your hide — you hear me?"

"Sure," Clem said. His expression indicated that he didn't give a hang about Ben Travis. Sabrina tried to stare him down but Clem's boldness proved too much for her. She pulled her eyes away from Clem Sweet's. Even Cadmus Kane had never looked at her that way.

"Travis won't be back," Jethro said. He spoke with the confidence of one who has had his own way for so long that he was certain no one would cross him. He looked at his brother. "Get your mind on business! I told you that a hun'red times."

Bushrod, who had been dozing in the wagon, awoke with a wail. Both the Sweets looked surprised. Clem said, "You got younguns, Ma'am?"

"A small boy," Sabrina said. Then quite unexplainably she tried to rationalize his presence. "He isn't mine. His parents are dead. Benjamin Travis gave him to me." Jethro shot Clem a look of surprise, then his eyes narrowed, screening his thoughts. Sabrina went to the wagon and lifted Bushrod down, shifting him so that he straddled her hip.

"I was thinkin' it was mighty strange you should have younguns, you bein' so shapely still," Clem said. "Ain't that what you thought, Jethro?"

Jethro Sweet waved his hand impatiently. "Where'd Travis give you this kid?"

"Kaskaskia," Sabrina said. She regarded Jethro Sweet carefully. "You look concerned, Mr. Sweet."

"I ain't worried," Jethro said flatly. "Travis has been gone five months. I ain't seen hide nor hair of him."

"But you might," Sabrina said and put Bushrod back in the wagon. She climbed onto the seat and Priam Thomas joined her. She lifted the reins, as she paused to add, "I have some tools in my wagon that belong to Benjamin Travis."

When Jethro swore beneath his breath, Sabrina drove away. Jethro watched the wagon for a time, then turned and put the boots to a dog lying near the door. The dog took off yelping. Jethro went into the back where he kept his sleeping rooms. Clem followed him. Fountainbleau, leaning against the bar with a jug, watched them pass through.

"Go over an' help the pretty widow," Jethro said.

"Thought I'd go to the river," Clem said. "The cats is bitin' somethin' fierce." He laughed. "I'd as soon go over after dark, Jethro. What the hell can a man do in the daytime?"

"She was lyin' to me," Jethro said. "She's Ben Travis' woman."

"Ah now —"

"I say she is!" Jethro struck his palm with his fist. "You heard her say she had Ben's traps. And he give her the kid. He's sent her on ahead, afraid to face me himself. Now you get over there and make yourself useful; you hear?"

"Sure, I'll go."

"Then get out of here. I want to think."

"If she don't want me around, can I go fishin'?"

"You go near that river without me sayin' so an' I'll break your back. Travis is comin', an' when he gets here, I want you to take him."

"Maybe I can't lick him by myself," Clem said.

Jethro cursed him. "Can't you lick anyone in Illinois Town?"

"Yes, but —"

"Then you put a head on Travis when he gets here, you understand?"

"All right," Clem said, turning to the door.

"Now do some work over there! Don't stand an' gawk!" Jethro listened to his brother's ponderous steps leaving the building.

Sabrina selected a site near spreading oaks, bordering a twenty acre pasture. She could see why Benjamin Travis wanted this spot for it was rich in timber, yet there was a smooth-crowned hill on which to build a cabin. Near the edge of the woods wild raspberries grew in choked profusion, and years before someone had planted plum and peach trees; they were in full bloom now with the promise of a limb-breaking crop. She parked the wagon near the creek that wound around the base of the hill and began to unload. Priam Thomas insisted on doing his share but Shawnee Blanc pushed him aside and did all the work himself.

Thomas seemed troubled and finally came out with it. "Sabrina, seems to me that there was no need to tell the Sweets you had Ben's things. Plain as the nose on your face, they have a quarrel with him. It didn't do Ben any good to have you warn 'em."

Priam Thomas was right; Sabrina admitted it to herself and was sorry she had spoken so hastily. She supposed that Benjamin Travis' galling self assurance had prodded her into speaking, but now that she had upset everything, it seemed a childish way of striking back. And now Priam Thomas was placing her in a position where she had to defend herself. Men were always doing that to a woman, especially men like Benjamin Travis who acted like they knew everything.

"It won't kill him to get some of the sass taken out," Sabrina said. "He acts like a tomcat on a back fence anyway."

"You think the Sweets don't?" Thomas snorted. "Their land! Hell, this is free land!"

"Free or not," Sabrina said. "Jethro Sweet is a successful man, which is more than you can say for Ben Travis."

"Maybe so," Thomas said, "but somehow self-made men are always inclined to be a little too proud of the job."

This type of generalized argument irked Sabrina. She flared, "I suppose Benjamin Travis isn't? He just shoves people around and does what he thinks is good for them. Does he ask? Did he ask me if I wanted Bushrod? No, he forced me to take him. Don't deny it."

Priam Thomas grinned. "Seemed to me, Sabrina, that you wanted the boy pretty bad. Bad enough to walk into a drinkin' place after him."

"Oh," Sabrina snapped, "you're disgusting to talk to!"

86

"Well," Thomas said, "I think it was none of your business, tellin' the Sweets that Ben was comin' back." He looked past her shoulder and in a softer voice said, "Comp'ny."

Clem Sweet arrived grinning, his eyes bold. "Howdy, Ma'am. I come to help."

"I told you we'd manage," Sabrina said. He stood near her and she could smell the sweetness of his chewing tobacco. She went to move past him but he put out his arm easily and braced it against the wagon box like an oak bar.

Shawnee Blanc straightened after placing a heavy trunk on the ground. His eyes were cold coffee beans as he watched Clem Sweet. In Shawnee Blanc's belt a heavy trade hatchet was thrust and he grasped the head, standing that way.

Clem transferred his chewing tobacco to the other cheek. "What's that Injun think he's doin'?" He waved his free arm. "Get away from me, Injun!"

"You get away," Sabrina said evenly. "I have an idea he can throw that hatchet straighter than you can shoot."

"Hell," Clem said, "I meant no harm." Then he dropped his arm. He picked up Thomas' axe and without another word walked to the timber's edge and began selecting trees.

Priam Thomas said, "Funny Shawnee Blanc got his back up that way?"

"Him bad," Shawnee Blanc said.

Throughout the rest of the day Clem Sweet's axe rang steadily and when dusk fell he went home, not

87

stopping at Sabrina's camp. She had been anticipating his return, dreading it for in Clem Sweet she read trouble. Yet when he went on to the trading post without stopping, a deeper worry began to ferment.

Priam Thomas said, "That was nice of him, wasn't it? All that work without a lick of thanks."

Remembering Clem's eyes when he looked at her, Sabrina said, "When a man does something for nothing, watch out, because he's got an eye out for his pay."

"Now Ben Travis never struck me as that kind," Thomas said.

"They're all that kind," Sabrina said flatly and began a pot of Hoppin' John, which was meat scraps, peas and shaved peppers, all cooked into a stew.

Shawnee Blanc accepted anything Sabrina cooked, but he would never eat at the fire. If she put his food in a bowl he would dump it onto a piece of bark and sit along the shadowy fringes of the fire, eating it with his fingers. He spoke little, but his eyes saw everything. It seemed that he had an almost divine perception, for a scant instant before Sabrina decided they needed more wood, Shawnee Blanc would rise and fetch some. He perceived her every wish a moment before she wished it.

The arrival of a new family in Illinois Town had not gone unnoticed, but on the frontier a man worked while the sun was up and did his visiting when it went down. After supper the neighbors began to gather. The first to arrive was Ninian Lockwood, the nearest neighbor who lived a half mile to the west. Lockwood was a tall, slow-spoken Kentuckian. He wore his beard tucked into his shirt collar and his hair queued up in the back. He brought along his wife and seven children who ranged from a babe in arms to a boy of thirteen.

Priam Thomas introduced himself and Sabrina. The children gathered around Bushrod, who stared for a moment, then joined them in play. Mrs. Lockwood was a heavy woman, forty some, and hard work and too many children had sapped her vitality. She sat down wearily as though she rarely had time for the luxury of rest.

Lockwood looked around him and said, "Picked a nice place. This land will grow anything as long as it's corn, wheat and punkins." He got out his pipe, crushed tobacco into it, then bent over the fire for a light. He straightened, puffed contentedly, and said, "As I recall, Ben Travis put his bids on this piece. Said he'd be back to claim it."

"So we've been told," Priam Thomas said. "Sweet picked this for us."

Lockwood grunted and on his face was a momentary displeasure, as though a distasteful thought had occurred to him. "Jethro Sweet picked all the places," he said finally. "You met up with Ben Travis?"

"Yes," Sabrina said. "We know him."

"I was talkin' to your pa," Lockwood said in the same tone he used when his children interrupted. "Nice fella, Travis. He's in for a row with the Sweets. With Clem; Jethro has him do all his fussin' for him. Travis knows it, an' don't give a whoop'n holler neither." He stopped talking and turned as another family reached

89

the camp, Shadrach Bond and his brood. Bond was heavy and middle-aged. When he greeted them there was a touch of Tennessee in his drawl. His wife was a spare woman, almost frail. They had five children, the youngest nearly eight. Ninian Lockwood said, "We was talkin' about the Sweets, Shadrach."

"There's pleasanter subjects," Bond said. "Can you spare me a bit of that tobacco, Ninian?" He took a pinch, crowded it into the bowl of his pipe and took his light from Lockwood's pipe, holding the bowls together. He spoke to Thomas. "Seen Clem workin' here today."

"Yes," Sabrina said. "He offered his help."

Bond glanced at her, then spoke again to Thomas. "You mean to grow crops?"

Thomas nodded.

Lockwood said, "You'll have to sell to the Sweets."

"We'll sell where we please," Sabrina said.

"I was talkin' to your pa," Lockwood said again.

"Since I'll be doing half the work I got half the say," Sabrina said. "If you don't like that, go home."

Since Lockwood had never had a woman talk that way to him before, he was a little surprised. "Hell," he said, then closed his mouth.

"Pretty late in the season to be plantin' anythin'," Bond said. "I suppose you could break your backs an' get enough to tide you over the winter."

"There must be some way to get along," Sabrina said. "Who gets all the profits?"

"The Sweets," Lockwood said. "He'll stop you from goin' down river."

"He might stop one boat," Sabrina said, "but could he stop a half dozen?"

"Maybe not," Bond put in. "It's never been tried. Anyhow, I wouldn't want to come back with Clem waitin' on the landin'."

Bond and Lockwood exchanged glances as though they had discussed this many times before and reached no satisfactory conclusion. "Thomas, you ain't big enough to cross Clem and Jethro," Lockwood said. "And they're big enough to cross anybody."

"Exceptin' Ben Travis," Bond said quickly.

"Well," Lockwood argued, "we ain't sure Ben can do it either. Ben made his talk, but he ain't here to back it." He puffed to keep his pipe going. "Ben told the Sweets last fall he was goin' to put himself in a sawmill right where you're standin'. Then he pulled foot. That was five months ago. There was some soldiers here then, from Fort Dearborn. Talkin' about buildin' a shot tower so's they'd have cannon balls handy to fight the Injuns. The Sweets said no. Ben Travis said he'd be right glad to build a shot tower in the spring. Any day now I've been expectin' them soldiers to come back an' find Travis has skipped." He sighed. "Never could figure Ben out. Didn't seem too steady a man to me, always goin' off someplace instead of settlin' down. Still, I liked the way he spoke out again' the Sweets. Sorta like he meant it. Too bad. Some folks pinned their hopes on Ben."

"They pinned their hopes on an empty-headed fool," Sabrina said quickly. "All he can do is sing and play the banjo and make trouble for people."

Bond looked offended. "Girl, there's more to the man than that."

"I've never seen it!"

Bond shrugged. "Then you don't know him very well."

"I know that he's irresponsible," Sabrina insisted. "And he's arrogant. He's no different from the Sweets, only more shiftless."

"That's enough!" Priam Thomas snapped. Sabrina shot him a surprised glance but Thomas ignored it. "Ben Travis'll be back. I say so because we've got his things in our wagon. He wouldn't have give 'em to us unless he meant to come back."

This created a stir. Sabrina listened to it, tried to understand how Benjamin Travis could merit such confidence. And she was annoyed with her father for forcing her to add to the Travis legend. The man needed taking down, not building up. Why, the very manner in which he conducted his business affairs shocked her. He had never asked her destination or told her his. He had just placed his things in the wagon and trailed along behind, free of the bother. She supposed that if she had settled in Prairie du Rocher or Kaskaskia, he would simply have thanked her, taken his things, and found another gullible fool to do his bidding.

Shadrach Bond brought her mind back to the moment when he asked in all seriousness, "Is Ben Travis your man?"

For a moment Sabrina was too stunned to speak, then so angry she could not trust her voice. Lockwood, more observant than Bond, said, "No need to raise the hatchet. You could do worse."

"I doubt that," Sabrina said.

Others came into their camp and one by one gathered around the fire. The talk went to many things such as the prospect of a good year, but soured when they thought of the profits, all going to the Sweet brothers.

The children had been playing at the edge of the camp, their sharp shrieks of pleasure clear in the night stillness. Suddenly they stopped chasing each other and when the yelling died off, the silence was a pressure that made everyone turn their heads. From the edge of the fire Jethro Sweet stepped toward them, smiling. "Fine evenin'," he said and looked at each man in turn. He had a way of applying pressure with his eyes. This, coupled with his bold, assured manner, made men step back involuntarily to make way for him. He looked now at Sabrina Kane. "It's a custom of the country to offer a man somethin' when he comes to call."

"There's coffee in the pot," she said. "Help yourself."

Sweet's glance touched Priam Thomas. "Was she mine I'd teach her to keep a civil tongue in her head."

"She ain't yours," Thomas said.

Sweet moved to the fire and filled a cup, then stood with his back to the group. The children had formed a silent ring near the wagon, watching Jethro Sweet as if he were the embodiment of the Bogy-man. He spoke to Thomas without turning to him. "A woman's place is with women. Tell your daughter to go gab with the others. What I have to say is for men, not petticoats."

"I do as I please," Sabrina said. "And now it pleases me to stand by my fire."

Sweet's head came around slowly. The firelight reflecting in his eyes gave him a foreboding appearance. "When I came here the French chippies ran in the streets. I had every tough in St. Louis over here after 'em. The chippies are gone. A woman's a lady here or she moves on. Remember that."

"Now wait a min —" Thomas began.

"When I talk to you, I'll call you by name," Jethro said slowly. He smiled at Sabrina Kane. "I've a great respect for ladies, Ma'am. When they're ladies."

"Meaning?" Sabrina's eyes were bright with anger.

"Meanin' that you ought to find a man an' start raisin' younguns, an' then you'll be too busy to poke your nose in man's business." He turned away from her, having had his say. "You fellas been talkin' behind a man's back again. And that's unfriendly. You don't want to be unfriendly, do you?"

Both Lockwood and Bond fidgeted and looked at the ground. Priam Thomas, surprisingly, locked eyes with Jethro Sweet and didn't give an inch.

Sabrina said, "If you're through threatenin' folks, get out of our camp."

"I've said my say to you," Sweet said. "You want to talk to me, then get a man to say your say." He singled Pierre Menard out of the gathering and began to crowd him with words. "You fellas don't want to make a mistake now. Lige Hanks got Clem riled, an' you all know how peaceful Clem is. I told Lige not to flourish

94

his axe aroun' that way, but Lige was a stubborn cuss. He had to go and get himself killed."

"What kind of a man are you?" Priam Thomas asked.

"Why, a kindly man toward those who're kind to me," Sweet said. "Then again, a rough man when folks speak out against me." He finished his coffee, tossed the grounds in the fire and put the cup aside. "When I come here I had to shoo the Injuns off to make room for my tradin' post; the French had the Injuns livin' with 'em. I built all this, an' I run things. You find anythin' wrong with that?"

"Don't sound free to me," Thomas said flatly. "Is that why you're so all-fired again' Ben Travis, 'cause he won't knuckle under?"

Jethro Sweet laughed softly and turned to Sabrina. "You know, I had the idea that Ben Travis was your man." Sabrina opened her mouth to deny this, but Sweet cut in. "It wasn't had to figure. I expect Travis'll come soft-footin' it along an' just push me aside, or try."

"Benjamin Travis is not my man!" Sabrina said. "I know him, yes. And if I seem involved with him it's only because he can tangle a person up so that it looks bad."

"You're a liar, Ma'am," Jethro said evenly. He looked around at the men. "Any of you gents want to take exception to that? I didn't think you did." He turned his head again to Sabrina, his eyes flat and expressionless. "I'm not the fool you thought me. He'd have never sent his woman ahead if he wasn't comin' back."

"That's not true!" Sabrina looked at her father. "Papa, convince him!"

"How? A wink's as good as a nod to a dead mule."

"Mr. Sweet," Sabrina said, "we met Benjamin Travis right after my husband died, near Shawneetown. He went there with us. I didn't see him again until we got to Kaskaskia. That's the truth!"

"What about the boy?" Sweet asked. "Where'd you get him?"

"At Kaskaskia. Benjamin Travis asked me to keep him. The boy's parents are dead. Someone had to raise him!"

"You knew his parents?"

Sabrina rubbed her hand across her forehead. "No."

"You must think I'm touched in the head," Jethro Sweet said. "You expect me to believe a woman'd take a stray youngun from a man she knew only slightly?"

"It's the truth!"

"Why? You must have had a reason."

"Oh, I don't know," Sabrina said. "That's Ben Travis anyway; he makes you do things that seem crazy when you think about 'em."

"But I ain't crazy enough to believe 'em," Jethro Sweet declared. "Ben said he was comin' back with tools, but he knew I'd never let him in the settlement with 'em. So he sends 'em on in with his woman. Well, I'll tell you somethin'. He'll never cut a stick of timber in these parts. Clem'll break him in half if he does. And when them rambunctions are over, I'll have him move you and your pa out!"

"I ain't big," Priam Thomas said calmly, "but I can pull a trigger. You want to get shot serious, then raise your hand to my daughter."

"I never bother with women," Jethro Sweet said. "And I never threaten a man unless I mean it."

"Well," Thomas said, "I meant it."

Near the river a man halloed. Jethro Sweet pivoted his head sharply as though he recognized the voice and didn't like the sound of it.

"Who's that?" Thomas wanted to know.

"Shut your mouth so I can hear," Sweet said. He had come into the camp unarmed to show his fearlessness and now the regret was plain on his face.

The man halloed again. Then Sabrina Kane heard another sound, a man singing, and quite unaccountably her breathing quickened. Silently she chided herself for this unwonted behavior. She told herself that her only joy in seeing Benjamin Travis again was that this terrible matter about her being his woman would be cleared up forever.

The children had heard that voice before for they wheeled and ran off into the night, yelling loudly, gleefully.

Ninian Lockwood looked at Bond and said, "Glory be! Speak of the devil —"

Thomas said, "Looks like you can make your threats to his face, Sweet, seein's how you hate so for a man to talk behind the back."

Benjamin Travis was nearer now and they could hear his song:

How glorious the scene, and how joyful the day,
In the old woods of green, in the young month of
May!
So in hearts that are spotless, on earth they may
stay,
And old blossoms hold them, 'tis May — always
May.

Jethro Sweet looked at Sabrina, a light of triumph in his eyes. "What'd I say? I knew he'd come taggin' along." He laughed. "Sneakin' in at night like some damned weasel after a chicken!"

"That's not so!" Sabrina said hotly. "Mr. Sweet —" She saw that words would mean nothing now and turned her back to him. Half beneath her breath, she said, "Damn you, Ben Travis! Oh, damn you anyway!"

The gathering around Sabrina's fire remained motionless until Benjamin Travis stepped into the light. The children followed him in a group, only he had two more than had gone out to meet him. He carried one on each arm, a naked little Indian girl of four, and a white boy about seven. Neither had seen soap and water for a month, judging from the dirt on them.

Travis' eyes moved like the swift slash of a knife, taking in everyone, including the bulk of Jethro Sweet. But it was on Sabrina Kane that his glance stopped and Jethro placed damning importance on this. Travis grinned and set the children down.

"Bet you thought I'd never get here," he said.

"Ha!" Jethro's whoop was one of success.

Sabrina stamped her foot angrily. "Why did you have to say that?"

"Just what did I say?" Travis asked with great innocence. He looked at each of them, then bent to urge the children forward. "Sure are cute buggers, ain't they?"

For the first time Sabrina really looked at them. "Oh my goodness!" she said and snatched up a blanket to cover the girl's nakedness.

"Where'd you get that Injun kid?" Jethro Sweet asked.

Slowly, indolently, Travis looked at him. "Some business of yours?"

"You know I run the Injuns out. Now you bring one in."

After considering this for a moment, Benjamin Travis said, "I got 'em across the river. They've been livin' with old folks." To Sabrina he said, "Guess they're hungry. They ain't had a bite since mornin'."

Jethro Sweet pushed Shadrach Bond to one side so that he faced Travis. "You givin' 'em to her?"

"I don't want 'em!" Sabrina shouted. "He's got no right to bring them kids here!" She looked pleadingly at Jethro Sweet, but the man had already made up his mind. "Ben Travis, what makes you think you can —"

"I figured Bushrod would get lonesome," Travis said. "Two more won't eat much, an' they're naturally quiet. Injun kids is that way an' the boy's been a prisoner for a year; he picked up a lot of their ways."

"Now who's the liar?" Sweet asked this of Sabrina, who could not give a ready answer.

A fleeting annoyance crossed Benjamin Travis' face, but this was the only break in his good humor. He looked at Sweet and said, "I'm tryin' to tell the lady somethin' but you keep stickin' your bill in. Don't do it again." He spoke in an easy conversational tone and he kept smiling while he talked, but only a very stupid man would have failed to understand the warning. His rifle was on his shoulder with his banjo and he set the rifle butt first on the ground, cupping his hands over the muzzle. "As I was sayin', the girl's ma took sick a year past. Her pa was killed fightin' the Sioux up north. With winter comin' on an' the old folks stove up some —"

"Winter's seven months away!" Sabrina said. "Mr. Travis, will you tell Mr. Sweet that you're not my — my man?" She nearly choked getting it out.

Travis chuckled. He looked at Jethro Sweet's scowling face and said with maddening sincerity. "You know I can't rightly do that, Sabrina. After all we been through together."

"Been through togeth — Oh, you're hateful! Take these filthy urchins and get out of my camp!"

"I'll tell you, too," Jethro Sweet said. "I told you before but it seems you didn't take me serious like."

"As a matter of fact I didn't hear you at all," Travis admitted. "Seems that you're always blowin' off about somethin' and there was an oriole singin' in the lilac bush. Mighty pretty, orioles singin'. A heap better than listenin' to your bellerin'."

Jethro Sweet stood still and stared at Travis, unable to believe what he had heard. He could not recall a time when a man had talked to him in this manner, and from his expression, everyone could see that he was toying with the idea of doing something about it. Sabrina looked from Travis to Sweet. Travis seemed not at all worried and it was only when Jethro Sweet spoke that she realized she had been holding her breath.

"Maybe you'll hear me now; there ain't any birds singin' to bother your ears. Stay the night — I'll begrudge no man that — but leave in the mornin' and take this tribe with you."

"Why should I do that now?" Travis asked. "Didn't I go back east for saws an' truck like that? Why, I've been pullin' foot for three months, just gettin' back." He shook his head. "In the mornin' I intend to walk off my cabin."

"An' Clem'll be here to see that you don't," Jethro said.

Travis grew serious. "Don't send Clem aroun' here. You want your trouble, then make it yourself."

"Clem does what he's told," Jethro said. "I got to protect what's mine; you can see that. You take what you want now there'd be nothin' to stop you from takin' more later."

"That's right," Travis said, "there'd be nothin' to stop me, 'ceptin' I'm not an overgrown hog like you."

Blood stained Jethro's face and his breathing deepened. "Clem'll move you out in the mornin'."

"Suppose we just wait until mornin' an' see," Travis said. "But don't send Clem. You come move me."

"Clem gets up early," Sweet said and pushed his way out of the camp. The Lockwoods gathered their brood and went home. Shadrach Bond wanted to stay a little longer, but his wife pulled at his arm and they left. The others followed.

Priam Thomas turned to add more wood to the fire. Sabrina faced Benjamin Travis, her cheeks stiff with anger. "Mr. Travis, perhaps you can explain your behavior!"

"I'll sure try," he promised. "Like I said, the kids was wit —"

"We'll talk about them later," Sabrina said. "I want to know what you meant by telling Jethro Sweet that I was your woman. I wouldn't have you on a bet! Is that understood?"

"Yes, ma'am." Benjamin Travis failed to look contrite. "But I can't recollect tellin' Jethro anythin' of the sort. I just said —"

"I know what you said!" Sabrina shouted.

"No need to yell. I ain't deaf."

"Deaf, dumb, blind; you're all of those things!" She bit her lips to keep from crying. "Mr. Travis, you're the worst thing that's ever happened to me. At my husband's grave you lied about the Shawnees so I'd do what you wanted me to do. In Kaskaskia you played on my sympathy and when that didn't work, bullied me into taking Bushrod."

Travis' smile teased her. "You sure that's exactly the way it was?"

"It doesn't matter," she said. "Now you've spoiled everything for me here, not to mention bringing me two more children to take care of — and one an Indian at that!"

"Well," Travis said, "Shawnee Blanc's an Injun and —"

"Shawnee Blanc takes care of himself!" She massaged her palms together. "The thing that's unthinkable is Mr. Sweet believing I'm your woman."

The two children huddled near the wagon, the little girl clutching the blanket around her. They looked at Sabrina with bright eyes and she pulled her own away quickly. There was something irresistible about a dirty child; all of her woman impulses directed her to wash them.

"You don't want these younguns?"

"No," she said quickly. "Take them and get out. Never come back."

"You sure don't mean that," Travis said. "Won't you keep 'em here tonight? I could take 'em some place else in the mornin'."

"In the morning you're going to meet Clem Sweet," she reminded. The thought of Sweet's bulk made Travis seem almost pale and slim by comparison, and she felt the rise of a nagging fear. However, he seemed complacent about the whole thing and this prodded her to say, "Don't you ever worry or think ahead?"

"Not much," he said. "Tomorrow's bad enough when it gets here."

"The children can stay the night," Sabrina said. "It's the least I can do. Papa, heat some water so I can wash them."

Priam got the wooden tub from somewhere in the scatter of belongings and set a large iron kettle of water on the fire. Benjamin Travis spent a moment standing on one foot, then the other. Finally he said, "Ma'am, I had this place all picked out. I don't see how we're both goin' to live on it." He scratched his head. "I reckon you hate me proper; I've caused you a heap of trouble, accordin' to your lights. But you think on it a spell and you'll see that I've only got you to actin' like a woman. An' a mighty handsome one you are."

"I don't need your compliments!" Sabrina flared, but a part of her was pleased that he had noticed her. Cadmus had been that way, always telling her small, nonsensical things: how pretty her hair looked or how shapely she was. A woman liked to primp for a man when he noticed. Most men noticed but so few ever spoke that a woman soon began to think of herself as some kind of domesticated draught animal.

She scrubbed a hand over her eyes. "Mr. Travis, is it possible that you ignore logic? I don't even have a roof over my head yet you expect me to care for three children."

"They won't eat much," Travis said, "an' they're used to sleepin' on the ground." He shouldered his rifle. "Guess I'll be goin' an' if it's all right with you, I'll bed down on the hill, seein's how I claimed it first." He stood there, hoping she would look at him and when she didn't, he added, "You're as pretty as a blue-wing teal, an' I'm sure glad you didn't shoot me like you threatened."

He left the firelight before she could turn, striking uphill. Priam Thomas cleared his throat and said, "The water's warm enough now."

Sabrina filled the tub and popped the little girl in first. She smiled at Sabrina and spoke to her, but the guttural sounds were completely alien. The boy chatted with the girl, preferring Siouan to English.

Thomas said, "Strange man, Travis. He's taken a shine to you, Sabrina."

"I haven't taken a shine to him," she said quickly.

"You're a hard one to please," Thomas said. "You want a man who's as steady as a good horse, yet you can't abide that kind. Able Kane was as steady a man as God ever put on this earth, yet you married Cadmus. Didn't make sense to me at the time. I guess it don't make sense to you either."

"Do we have to talk about it?" Her voice was sharp.

"Nope," Priam Thomas said. "We can just forget it. Leastways, I can, but you can't. The world's full of old maids who can't knuckle down to a good man's way."

"Why," Sabrina asked herself softly, "does Ben Travis do these things to me?"

"You mean keep remindin' you that you're a woman?" Priam Thomas paused to think. "I guess it's because he sees you as a woman, Sabrina. Not someone pretendin' she's as good as the next man."

She dried the girl and bathed the boy, then placed them in the wagon with Bushrod. Priam Thomas watched while Sabrina tucked them in. The Indian girl kept repeating one word, softly. Finally she said it louder, "*Day-kan-ray.*"

When the little girl put her arms around Sabrina's neck and hugged her, the boy said, "She's callin' you 'mother'."

Priam Thomas said, "Kids don't hug a man like that. Not with that much feelin'. Ben Travis knew that. That's why he brought 'em to you, Sabrina."

Sabrina felt hot tears behind her eyelids and closed them to trap them there, but they spilled over and ran down her cheeks. With the little girl's arms tight around her neck, she said, "Oh, shut up, Papa! Shut up!"

Then she hugged the child and wept openly.

CHAPTER
FIVE

The pound of a mallet against a stake woke Sabrina Kane and she looked at the sky. To the east there was a grayness near the horizon, the first promise of dawn, and outlined against this was the tall silhouette of Benjamin Travis marking off the dimensions of his cabin.

Shawnee Blanc came from the river, his arms loaded with wood. He dumped it and then struck a fire with flint and steel. Sabrina threw her blankets aside and brushed the wrinkles from her dress. Inside the wagon, the Indian girl stirred. A moment later she climbed down. "*Bdi-he ici-ya waon,*" she said, smiling.

"I don't understand you," Sabrina told her, but she patted her head and the child understood that.

Priam Thomas woke grumbling. He looked to the hill where Travis worked and said, "He could have waited until a decent hour." He moved about, coughing, talking to himself in half tones. "You goin' to let them kids run around naked? It ain't fittin'. Bad enough you traipse around without a bonnet on."

"They're just children," Sabrina said, but she knew her father was right. She made the boy make-shift trousers out of a pair of old pantaloons. He seemed rather proud of them and strutted around the fire, showing off. The little girl's dress was fashioned from an old ruffled blouse, tied around her waist.

Priam Thomas snorted. "What's the use of fancyin' 'em all up? You told Ben Travis you was only goin' to keep 'em for one night." He gave her a slanting look and waited for his answer.

"I — of course," Sabrina said. "Well, they still have to have clothes; you said so yourself." She turned away and began to rattle pots. While she fried the side meat and made the pap, Sabrina kept a watchful eye on Travis up on the hill. The light grew steadily stronger until she could see him clearly and momentarily she expected him to come to her camp, but he didn't. The children ate first. Shawnee Blanc took his food to the edge of the camp and ate with his back to them.

Sabrina piled food on a wooden plate. Thomas eyed it and said, "That's a mighty appetite you got."

"It's for him," Sabrina said, nodding toward the hill. "He don't have sense enough to come down."

Thomas chuckled. "Thought you was mad at him?"

"Well, he has to eat, don't he?" She picked up the plate and walked up the hill.

Ben Travis saw her coming and put his mallet aside. Sweat was slick on his face and his buckskins clung to him damply. He looked at the plate of pap and side meat. "That was mighty thoughtful," he said. "You're a good woman, Sabrina, although you got some funny notions about men."

"What do you kn —" Then she closed her mouth. This man saw too much, made too many guesses too

108

near the truth. Silence and a stiff reserve were a woman's only protection against his kind. Independent men were tricky. They bossed a woman to death and did what they danged please.

"I didn't expect you to have sense enough to come down," Sabrina said. She looked around curiously and from the position of the stakes she could see that he was planning big. She said, "One man don't need all that room."

"I was thinkin' of a family," Travis said easily.

"Your kind thinks only of himself," she said. "You'd give a woman six kids and let the pasture go to *folle avoine*." She turned and gave him a frank look. "We had your kind in Pennsylvania, too."

"Did you now?" He seemed amused at everything she said. "An' what kind of a man was your husband?"

"A good man," Sabrina said flatly and walked over to the position of the front door. She stood there, looking out toward the Mississippi.

Benjamin Travis said, "The fireplace is to your left. A big one. Big enough to heat the whole room."

She turned and walked around the confines of the stakes, her face thoughtful as though she were deciding where the furniture would go.

"Bedroom's there," Travis said. "The one on the other side's for the kids."

"You're takin' a lot for granted," Sabrina said. "A woman's got somethin' to say, you know. Or maybe you want a woman who'll cook and make your clothes and keep her mouth shut."

"A man likes some talk," Travis said. He finished his meal, then set the wooden plate aside. "I sure thank you for the breakfast."

"You're welcome to it," Sabrina said. "It seems to me that you ought to be breaking ground for crops before building a house that big."

"I ain't much for plantin'," Travis said seriously. "I got other plans."

Sabrina snorted. "What'll you do, sit around an' play your wife songs on the banjo?"

"I do other things," he said quietly.

"I've never seen you," she told him. "A woman needs more than a man's pig-headed dreams, Mr. Travis. My husband was a dreamer and not much of a doer. Now he's gone and I'm here trying to make what he dreamed come true."

Travis regarded her thoughtfully for a moment before speaking. "I guess you've told yourself that so much you've got to believin' it. I'd say you was scared of men."

She turned her head and gave him a sharp, angry look. "Are you calling me a liar?"

"You've done that to yourself," Travis said. "They ain't your husband's dreams, Sabrina; they're yours. Big dreams. So danged big they even scare you. That's why you got to tell folks they was your dead husband's or your father's. You're scared to admit they're your own. Women is supposed to work, not dream. That's the way it is an' you're goin' against it."

"That's not true!"

110

He smiled and shook his head. "Then why're you gettin' so all-fired riled at me? You're not goin' to fulfill Cadmus Kane's wants, Sabrina. They're your own yearnin's that you never dared mention 'cause you're a woman."

"I don't have to listen to you!"

"Then look at me an' tell me I'm a liar," Travis invited. "Look at me, Sabrina."

His voice pulled her head and eyes up. She tried to meet his boldly but she failed. "I — I came to bring you some breakfast and I've done that. We have nothing to say to each other."

"Maybe," he said. "But a woman wasn't made to live without a man, Sabrina. One of these nights we're goin' walkin' down by the river an' listen to the frogs sing, an' the crickets talk. We're goin' to hear a voice in the wind, an' the wild geese callin'. That's what we'll hear, 'cause we both listen for the same things."

"I don't want to hear that sweet-talk!" she said hotly. "With my husband fresh in the ground, you got no right to talk like that to me!" She clenched her fists in angry frustration, then calmed herself. "The Indian girl spoke to me this morning. Does she have a name?"

"*Hoo-wau-ne-kah*, The Little Elk. The boy's name's Jenner." Travis smiled. "Don't know his first. I thank you for keepin' 'em the night. When my business is finished this mornin', I'll be comin' after 'em."

His quiet reminder shocked her for she had momentarily forgotten Jethro Sweet's threat. She looked at Ben Travis, but his face was composed, serene. She wondered how he could be calm at a time like this. "Aren't you afraid?" She hadn't meant to ask this but it burst out unbidden.

"We're all afraid of somethin'," he said, and his eyes said a lot more. She wished that she had a veil; perhaps he would see less, read her less accurately.

He was looking past her and she turned her head to see what had caught his attention. The main settlement lay on the flats a mile away and a group of men were gathering before Sweet's store. With Clem Sweet leading them they began the procession that brought them toward the hill where Benjamin Travis waited.

He watched them until Clem Sweet was close enough to be seen clearly. Then he said, "You'd better go back to your camp." He gave Sabrina a gentle shove, but she remained rooted.

"I'm staying. Mr. Travis, I'm staying!" There was finality in her voice, lifting her beyond argument, beyond persuasion.

So they stood together, waiting, as Clem Sweet and the male population of Illinois Town came up the hill. Clem walked with a long, easy stride and the followers had to trot to keep up with him. Priam Thomas saw them angling up the hill and put the children in the wagon. He took his rifle and climbed the hill, arriving a moment before Clem and the others.

The crowd fanned out. Sweet thrust his hands into his waistband and said, "Ma'am, if you've a kiss for him, give it to him now while he's still alive."

Travis pursed his lips. "I guess I got that much comin'," he said and pulled Sabrina against him. She gasped at the pressure of his arms and raised her hands

112

in a gesture of defense as his lips touched hers. His kiss shocked her breathless and her hands pushed at him, but only for a moment. She relaxed and touched his neck, then she locked her arms around him and kissed him with an abandon that was almost pagan.

Travis released her finally, allowing her to step back. She looked at him steadily, as though she would forever remember that wild moment of unspeakable tenderness and frightening power. As never before she saw him as a man capable of consuming a woman's will, enslaving her, if not by force, then by love, which was infinitely worse. Instinctively her guard raised and she vowed never to let Ben Travis kiss her again. Danger was there.

Then Travis placed his deliberate attention on Clem Sweet. "It's Jethro I want," Travis said.

"You'll have to take me first," Clem said. "Jethro's a gentleman."

"Is he a coward, too?" Travis asked.

Clem did not grow angry. "Naw, he just don't let fellas like you bother him, Ben." Sweet stripped off his buckskin coat. "I'm goin' to bust you up proper, Ben. I'm goin' to stomp your guts loose."

"You won't do it jawin'," Travis said and hit him. He threw the punch unexpectedly, a blow that would have killed a normal man. Clem caught the fist flush in the mouth and reeled back, a tooth sheared completely off. When he spit it out his lips were covered with blood. For an instant he stared, unable to believe that any man would dare do this. Then he charged with a bellow of rage, his boots crushing grass.

Travis threw up his arms to weather Sweet's windmilling attack, but Clem broke through, butting Travis in the chest with his head. With a pained grunt, Travis went backward, his feet stomping for purchase. He struck Sweet a glancing blow over the left eye, opening a deep gash, but the huge man gave no indication that he had even been hit.

Sweet was a grappler; he tried to hug Benjamin Travis, but the tall man kept batting Sweet's arms away. Sweet lowered his head for another charge and Travis let him come on, but before Sweet could butt him, Travis brought his fist whistling up and Sweet's body arched backward. Sweet did not fall. He had the weight and the strength merely to plant his legs wide apart and become as unrootable as an old oak.

He did this now, watching Travis, panting, bleeding from nose and mouth. Slowly he raised his hand and wiped the blood off his face. He looked at his hand, then at Travis, still unmarked.

A wildness filled Clem Sweet's eyes and he growled like an animal, deep in his chest. "Stand and fight," he invited.

"You talk too blamed much," Travis said and made a mistake; he walked in on Clem Sweet.

With a triumphant roar, Clem grabbed Travis around the waist and applied pressure. Travis' back arched as he stiffened to resist this tremendous force, but Sweet's arms were giant-strong and Travis' face lost color as the breath was pinched intolerably. Sweet's heavy boots thrashed about, trying to stamp down on Travis' toes. With his hands on Sweet's face, Travis tried to break free but Sweet's mind ignored the fingers searching for his eyes and tightened his grip.

Holding the man thus, Sweet began to bring his head forward in short, sharp raps, striking Travis in the face. In this way he bloodied Travis' nose and raised livid bruises over the eyes. Then Benjamin Travis cupped both hands, drew his arms apart and slapped Clem Sweet over both ears.

With a sharp scream, Sweet broke his grip, bending double, hands clasped over his ears. The sudden concussion rendered him momentarily helpless and Benjamin Travis sank to one knee, drawing painfully for breath. Sweet was a man with a spike driven through his skull; the pain was sharply unbearable. Slowly Travis pulled himself erect and moved toward Clem. He struck him on the base of the skull with his fist, but lacked the power to put him down.

Sabrina, who stood by, shaken by the brutality of the fight, shouted, "Ben, watch out!"

Even with the warning, Ben Travis could not step back in time to avoid Clem Sweet's clutching arm. Sweet grabbed him by the ankle and threw Travis backward, then jumped on him, trying to crush his chest with his knees. Travis took the huge man's weight on his hip, but Sweet's out-thrust arms pinned his upper body flat.

Travis had his head jammed against one of his own marker stakes and with a sudden wrench, Clem pulled one free of the earth and swung it. Throwing up an arm, Benjamin Travis deflected the blow, but the forearm snapped and a distressed moan went up from the settlers. They had seen this kind of fight before, and invariably the first man who was crippled, lost.

Sabrina heard the bone snap and it felt as though someone had crushed her own body. She pressed both hands over her mouth and tears dimmed her vision. She looked quickly about for a weapon and saw Travis' axe lying ten feet away. In blind urgency she ran for it, snagging her long dress on another stake. She fell asprawl and forgetting the axe, tugged at the stake to uproot it. Benjamin Travis was gripping Clem's wrist, trying to keep his skull from being cracked while Clem's free hand pounded away at Travis' face.

The stakes were stout ash, two inch chunks, over two feet long. Sabrina swung blindly, catching Clem Sweet on the shoulder. He yelped in surprise, but the blow failed to knock him free of Travis. Sweet cursed her and divided his attention, trying to wrest the stake away from Sabrina. She clung to it like a dog at a rope end.

Travis cocked his fist, struck Sweet in the mouth, then grabbed the stake Clem held. He twisted, wrung it from his hand, then smashed him in the mouth with the butt end. Flesh ripped, teeth shattered; Sweet wasthrown to the ground and Travis came erect, his face gray with pain. His right arm hung crooked below the elbow and his breathing was an agonized sawing.

Clem was on all fours. Travis staggered toward him, the stake firmly gripped in his left hand. Sweet knew the rules and scrambled for another stake. He jerked one free and rolled as Travis swung, missing by a narrow margin.

116

Sweet aimed a blow for Travis' legs, hoping to break one, but Travis stayed out of reach until Sweet came to his feet. Both seemed eager to close, clubs swinging. Travis parried a downsweep, then jabbed Sweet with the butt end again. He caught the huge man in the eye, pulping the surrounding flesh. Sweet bellowed like a wounded bear and lunged against Travis, his face gushing blood. Travis hooked him under the chin with another short jab and then was in the clear. He swung a backhanded blow that caught Clem flush in the chest. His arms flailed the air as he reeled back, feet driving for traction. But he was on the downhill slope and fell, rolling thirty feet before stopping.

The crowd began a wild cheering and Sabrina rushed to Ben Travis, who brushed her aside. She felt a momentary stab of resentment at this brusqueness, then followed the direction of his eyes.

Clem Sweet was crawling slowly back up the hill.

The crowd saw this and murmured as they backed away. Even the stone-faced Shawnee Blanc, who had viewed the entire fight without expression, grunted, for all men admire bull courage.

Benjamin Travis waited with infinite patience and grudging respect. Clem Sweet fell often and his sobs of pain made strong men ill. One man said, "Jesus, how much can a man take?"

When Sweet reached the crown, Ben Travis said, "I don't want to, Clem."

Sweet shook his head like a bull. He looked at Travis and mumbled something through his smashed mouth. His remaining good eye was bloodshot but steady.

Almost blindly Sweet reached for Ben Travis' ankles. Without hesitation Travis swung the stake, snapping Clem's arm like a dry stick. Sweet growled and Travis hit him again, this time across the crown of the head, opening a long wound in the scalp. The blow drove Clem Sweet face-flat, but did not render him unconscious.

With his last strength Clem raised his bloody head and Travis brought the stake down again. In the quiet the sound was like a mallet striking an empty hogshead.

Sweet sank flat, then started to tip toward the downhill side. His lax arms and legs thrashed as he bounded over small hillocks, gaining momentum until he came to rest in the creek, one hand on the bank, the rest of him in the water.

Benjamin Travis looked at the male population of Illinois Town and said, "Go take care of him before he drowns. An' when you pack him to Jethro, tell Jethro there's a rifle ball waitin' should he ever walk up this hill."

They cheered, for an unpopular champion had been de-throned. Travis turned away from them, looked at Sabrina Kane and tried to walk to her. He took two steps and fell forward into Shawnee Blanc's waiting arms.

"Big man," Shawnee Blanc said and smiled. Sabrina was amazed at what it did to the Indian's savage face.

Priam Thomas broke up the crowd, sending them downhill. They gathered around Clem, fished him from the creek and bore him to the store where his brother waited on the porch. Sabrina was trying to get Shawnee

Blanc to place Travis on the ground. Thomas joined her when the others had gone.

"Goin' to have to set that," he said. "Consarn it, Shawnee Blanc, put him down!"

He picked up Travis' axe and split a stake four ways for splints. Sabrina kneeled on Travis' shoulders to hold him. Priam Thomas and Shawnee Blanc yanked quickly on the arm and Travis groaned loudly when the bones went together.

"Got to have somethin' to tie it with," Thomas said.

Sabrina lifted her dress and ripped at one of her petticoats. She looked at her father and colored as she wrapped Travis' arm. Thomas said. "Don't seem quite proper for a man to wear a woman's unmentionables on his arm. 'Specially when she hates him as much as you do."

"Oh, shut up! Why do you always have to be talkin' when you should be listenin'?"

Benjamin Travis moaned and tried to sit up, but Shawnee Blanc had to help him. He tried to grin and found it hurt too much. He looked at his splinted arm and there was regret in his voice when he said, "Damn, now I can't play my banjo."

"You can't build either," Sabrina snapped. "But you wouldn't think of that!" She had tears in her eyes and dashed them quickly away.

"What you cryin' about?" Travis asked. "I licked him, didn't I?"

"Oh — you don't know anything! You kiss a woman and get yourself half-killed and all you can think of is your blamed banjo."

"We'd best get him to the wagon," Thomas said. "Lend a hand there, Shawnee Blanc."

"Let him help himself! He's so all-fired independent!" She waved her hands. "Go on, an' take this heathen varmint with you." Priam Thomas shrugged and walked downhill with Shawnee Blanc. Travis made his feet with an effort and several loud groans. Sabrina fought down her sympathy for him.

"I'm going now," she said.

"I'm mighty bad hurt, Sabrina," Travis said. He took a few weaving steps. She looked at him, then came back quickly and put her arm around him, letting his weight come against her.

"Here, lean on me now," she said. "I swear, Ben Travis, if I wasn't here to look after you, you'd fall downhill and break the other arm." They walked slowly and Travis let her lead him. Once she slipped and nearly fell. Travis stopped himself in time for instinctively he reached out to support her. She said, "Well, you don't have to go limp!" She failed to see the veiled amusement in his eyes.

"Sure am sorry about the house, Sabrina," he said. "You'd have liked that house, you surely would've."

"I'll build the house myself," she said. "Lands sake, I want it done right."

He stopped and with his arm still around her, held her close. His face was now puffed and lopsided. One eye was completely closed and the blood from his nose was dry-caked to his chin. "I'm sorry about the kiss," he said, "but you was so all-fired pretty and since nobody's ever whipped Clem before, I thought —"

120

"Banjo playing! Kissing! Fighting!" She put her head against his chest for a moment, her eyes closed, remembering the feel of his lips, the single instant in time when he had made her a complete woman, with a woman's yearnings.

Then she pushed these thoughts aside, wondering why it had to be that a man like Ben Travis, with his laughter and light manner, was so desirable, yet so dangerous. She thought of Cadmus Kane with some shame, knowing now that their love had never been real; she felt that she had cheated him and since he was dead, could never make it up to him.

Benjamin Travis was the strongest willed man she had ever known and unfathomed danger lay in him because of this. A woman needed a laughing man, but she needed another kind of man, too, a steady man who could and would provide for her, yet make her feel alive, desired. There was too much of Able Kane in Travis. Able was not a laughing man; he found life too stern to be enjoyed. Yet he had that rock-solid will behind everything that he did. He, like Benjamin Travis, was a completely independent man, and no woman would ever change that. A woman shared only what *she* had with the Ben Travises and Able Kanes; they shared nothing, figuring that a roof and a dress and food were enough.

When they reached the wagon, Sabrina turned away from Travis. She said, "When you feel up to it, we can start work. Papa'll cut and notch. Shawnee Blanc and I'll set logs in place. You can do what you can."

Her voice was cool and distant, as though she spoke to a hired hand. A perplexed frown built across Benjamin Travis' brow. He watched her enter the wagon and open a trunk. She took out a carved clock and looked at it for several minutes. There were other things that she found cause to dawdle over.

Priam Thomas came up, glanced into the wagon, then pursed his lips. He spoke quietly to Travis. "Cadmus Kane's stuff. Some things is hard to let go of, boy. Especially a woman's notions. You got to understand."

"She sure soured toward me all of a sudden," Travis said.

"Uh," Thomas said. "That kiss you give her — it mean anythin'?"

"Not to her," Travis said. He closed out Priam Thomas by going to the water bucket to wash his face. The beating had more than torn his flesh and fractured his bones; its effect would remain with him for many years.

For the better part of the forenoon, Benjamin Travis sat in the camp, his face stolid, his complexion gray. Pain etched lines around his lips and eyes. Before noon he asked Priam Thomas for his razor and spent some time shaving. A short time later he was too sick to stand.

Little Elk wandered under the wagon and found Travis moaning. She studied the tall man with bewilderment, then ran toward the edge of the timber where Shawnee Blanc was setting figure four rabbit traps. They came back together, both hurrying.

Shawnee Blanc had his look, then ran toward the creek where the willows grew thickest. Little Elk puffed hard to keep up.

They burst through the protective thicket and Sabrina gave a short shriek of surprise before she saw who it was. "You crazy Injun, get out of here!"

She was bathing in knee-deep water, a bar of soap in one hand, a cloth in the other. She sat down quickly, letting the water cover her.

"*Peen-tee, Day-kan-ray!*" Little Elk danced up and down with agitation. "*Peen-tee!*"

"You come," Shawnee Blanc said. "Big one bad sick."

Little Elk splashed into the creek although the water reached over her waist. She grabbed Sabrina's hand and tried to tug her toward shore. "*Peen-tee!*"

"Shawnee Blanc, go back," Sabrina said. "Doggone you, mind! I've got no clothes on!"

The Indian turned and Sabrina waded ashore, carrying Little Elk with one arm. She deposited the little girl on the bank, then slipped into her pantaloons, not bothering to dry herself. Three petticoats and her dress followed, then with Little Elk pulling her, she ran toward the wagon.

Bushrod and the boy, Jenner, had heard Little Elk's excited cries and ran down the hillside toward the wagon. Breaking clear of the brush near the creek, Sabrina could see the wagon and Benjamin Travis writhing on the ground. Beneath the wagon bed another man's legs moved about. She shook loose from

Little Elk's hand and rounded the front corner of the wagon, stopping stock still when she saw Jethro Sweet.

He had a long rifle in his hands and there was a smear of blood on the octagon barrel. Benjamin Travis lay beneath the wagon, blood coursing down the side of his face. Sweat beads stood out boldly on his forehead as he watched Jethro with unwavering attention.

Travis said, "Get out of here, Sabrina. It's me he wants."

"Come out from under that wagon," Sweet invited. "I'll split your danged skull."

Little Elk and the two boys came up behind Sabrina. The girl clung to Sabrina's skirts and peered around at Jethro Sweet. But Jenner stared boldly.

Sweet said, "Get them brats out of here!"

"You get out of here," Sabrina said. Her legs began to tremble and she put out her hand and touched the wagon, thankful for the support. "You're real brave, sending your brother to do what you're afraid to do. If Ben Travis was on his feet you'd be running now!"

"But he ain't on his feet," Jethro said. "And you don't scare me none."

Suddenly Sabrina gained an insight into this hulking man: He was mouth and no heart; she sensed it. "You're yellow, Mr. Sweet. One of these days I'm going to prove it to the people here. Then they'll spit on you."

"You're a woman," Jethro said, "and I wouldn't harm a woman unless she acts like a man." He shifted his big feet and looked toward the hill crest. "Your pappy's out of callin' distance an' he left his rifle behind. Looks like I'm callin' the tunes here today, don't it?"

124

He poked at Benjamin Travis with the muzzle of the rifle, trying to reach his face, to cut him up. But Travis slid back out of reach and Sweet swore volubly, moving toward the side to get at him.

"You're a filthy animal," Sabrina said.

"Call me names," Sweet invited. "They don't mean anything to me."

Jenner, who had observed this with round eyes, suddenly whirled, darting around the back of the wagon and scrambled inside. Jethro flipped his head around and said, "Where the devil's he goin'? Call that kid back here!" He poked at Travis with the rifle barrel, but this time Travis caught the barrel and jerked. Sweet's flintlock had been cocked and the sudden pull caused him to set it off. Flame and ball passed within inches of Travis' side, spewing dirt as it plowed into the ground.

Jenner chose that time to scramble out of the wagon, dragging Benjamin Travis' rifle with him. Jethro Sweet saw it and took a step. Then he saw something else that made him stop, Shawnee Blanc emerging from the nearby brush. The Indian dropped his load of wood and ran forward, drawing his hatchet from his belt.

Sabrina grabbed the rifle away from Jenner and thrust it under the wagon to Travis, who quickly cocked it. Shawnee Blanc was drawing close, almost within throwing distance and Jethro Sweet knew it. He whirled to run and Travis shouted, "Do and I'll kill you!"

With Travis' rifle covering Sweet, Shawnee Blanc stopped, put his hatchet away, then unconcernedly walked back to where he had dropped the wood gathered it, and came into the camp as if nothing had happened.

Benjamin Travis was pulling himself from beneath the wagon. He grabbed the spokes of the rear wheel and hauled himself erect. The muzzle of his rifle was pointed at Jethro Sweet's chest. "I got somethin' to say," Ben Travis said, looking at Jethro. "Now you hear it good, 'cause I'll never repeat it. That hill is sure-fire death if you ever come near it. So's this camp. Shootin' you'll be real easy, Jethro. I do believe I'd enjoy it."

"I'll stay away from your damn hill," Sweet said. "An' don't ever come near my store. Not you or your damned tribe either!"

"Then get out of here," Travis said. He locked an arm around the wagon wheel to keep from falling and stood that way while Jethro stomped away.

Then Benjamin Travis closed his eyes and his face turned to chalk. "Ben! Ben, what's the matter?"

"I'm sick, Sabrina. Jenner, my gun — take it but be careful, it's cocked."

The boy scooted around Sabrina and tenderly took the rifle. Then Travis slipped to the ground and Sabrina saw that he had been afraid to drop the gun lest it go off and hurt one of them. Sweet's gun barrel had opened a deep cut on his forehead. The whiteness of exposed bone made her stomach rebel but she fought this down and sent Jenner after water. Little Elk and Bushrod crouched down beside her to watch while she bathed the cut.

Finally Benjamin Travis revived. He rubbed a hand over his face, focused his eyes with an effort, then turned his head to look at her. "He had me, Sabrina. Dog my cats if he didn't."

"Someone's comin'," Jenner said, and Sabrina looked toward the settlement. It was Ninian Lockwood and his oldest boy. Both were running. Priam Thomas, also summoned by the shot, stopped at the crest of the hill and then came on at a run. Others were approaching the camp. Sabrina recognized Shadrach Bond and his three oldest boys. They came into the camp together, then stood around, uncertain as to what to do.

Priam Thomas pushed his way through. He took one look at Travis' white face, and said, "Get him flat." He pushed Sabrina back. "I'll tend to this."

She turned to the back of the wagon where the others could not see her and put her head in her crossed arms until the shaking spell passed. The little Indian girl clutched her skirts, and Sabrina picked her up and held her.

"We'll give you a good Christian name. All right? Let's see, we'll call you 'Mary.' Does that suit you? Mary?" She knew the child could not understand, but it was good to talk, for it made her mind function again. She waited at the back of the wagon until she heard the others leave. Then she joined her father.

Priam Thomas had placed Travis back under the wagon out of the sun's reach. He said, "He's sick, but it figures. A man can't take that much punishment without somethin' happenin'."

"What'll we do?"

"He'll either get over it or die from it," Thomas said. "Just let him be. You ain't a doctor."

"What's the matter with you?" She snapped. "Don't you care?"

"Sounds like you do," Thomas said. "But there's a difference between a man an' a woman, Sabrina. A woman will do all the rantin' for both." He went to the wagon for his rifle, shouldered it, then added, "I'm goin' into the settlement. Maybe there's someone there who knows somethin' about medicine."

"Jethro Sweet warned us not to set foot near his store!"

"I ain't goin' there," Thomas said and struck out, following the creek bottom.

For an hour Sabrina bathed Benjamin Travis' face, trying to fight off his mounting fever. She bandaged the split scalp with torn muslin and she was thankful that the bleeding had stopped. Finally Priam Thomas came back with a dark, stringy-haired woman.

"This is Mrs. Menard," Thomas said. "She's half Cree and claims to know what ails him."

Sabrina looked at Mrs. Menard and felt a strong revulsion. The woman was dressed in rags and dried blood caked her hands and forearms, probably from a recent chicken killing. She had a blunt, brown face, dark eyes and an Indian's stony way of staring. The urge to object was on Sabrina's face and Priam Thomas read it.

"Best keep out of this. She's patched up a few in her time. Let her go ahead."

"*Parlez vous Francaise?*" Sabrina asked.

"*Oui.*"

128

"What's wrong with him?" Sabrina groped for her French. "*Ques que ce?*"

"*Du rien.* It is nothing," Mrs. Menard said. From a small bag which she carried suspended on a greasy cord around her neck, she took herbs and crushed them in a filthy palm, then put them in her mouth and chewed them until a soggy lump was ready to be spit out. Then she stoked the fire, heated water for another brew, and while it cooked, applied the cud of herbs to Travis' head. At Mrs. Menard's direction, Sabrina and Thomas supported Travis while she forced the concoction down his throat. He strangled, spit up, but in the end managed to drink most of it.

Then Mrs. Menard stepped back, smiling, her dark eyes glowing. "So he ees the one? Name of a cow, he ees strong." She looked at Sabrina, and seemed a little disappointed to find her with a flat stomach. "He weel give you many sons, that one."

Sabrina flushed and choked back a denial of any such alliance. Explanations would be worthless to Mrs. Menard, who was obeying a primitive impulse and believed every other woman would do the same.

"Will he live, Mrs. Menard?"

Mrs. Menard laughed and popped her cheek with her thumb. "*Oui*, he weel live. M'sieu Sweet, he weel also live. For awhile I theek I 'ave to cut off hees arm. Name of a name, eet's a wonder I don't 'ave to cut off hees head."

She turned and left without another word. Sabrina looked after her until she disappeared around the edge of a knoll.

129

Thomas said, "You think he will get over it?"

"I don't know," Sabrina said. She looked at Ben Travis and he seemed so waxen, so lifeless.

"Nothin' to do but wait," Thomas said.

"I'll wait," Sabrina said. "That's a woman's place; you always said that."

Thomas cleared his throat. "I've said a lot of things, and at a time like this I begin wonderin' how smart some of 'em were." He shifted his feet. "I'll stay around the rest of the day if you want."

"Never mind," she said. "Shawnee Blanc never goes far. The children'll be hungry soon."

She sat with Benjamin Travis and told herself that she only did this because he needed care. The heavy sweating had stopped and she brushed the hair from his battered face. In the stillness she fancied that she could hear his banjo as she had heard it that first day on the river. She closed her eyes and was surprised to find that his smile stood uppermost in her memory. His smile and the soft way he had of laughing, as though the whole world were a private joke that he alone understood. Cadmus Kane had had a smile like that. No, not like that. More of an apologetic smile, as though he were the butt of some joke and chose that way to accept it. Somewhere in life he had found it less difficult to laugh at himself than defend himself.

I never treated him very good, she thought. *Always telling him what to do, what I wanted to do.* She wondered if a woman could ever truly respect a man she could boss around? The difficulty lay in trusting a man enough to place personal freedom in his hands.

130

There was little difficulty with a man like Cadmus Kane; you knew before hand how it would be. But a man like Benjamin Travis — you'd only know when it was too late to turn back.

Shawnee Blanc filled the water buckets and chopped wood to last the night. Priam Thomas sat smoking his pipe. "He any better?"

"I don't know."

Thomas grunted. "You have trouble with your men, Sabrina."

"He's not my —"

"Don't say somethin' you'll regret," Thomas said quickly. "Sabrina, remember that if a woman has to turn hard to get what she wants, then what good is it? He fought for you. You was ready to fight for him. What does that mean, Sabrina?"

"I'd do the same for a sick dog!"

"About that kiss —"

"That was nothin'! His kind's kissed a lot of girls!"

Priam Thomas snorted. "What'd you expect him to be? You afraid of him or your damned notions about havin' your own way?"

"I'm not afraid of any man. I just won't be chained down, that's all!" She met her father's eyes with defiance, but her resolve melted and she stared at her folded hands. "I guess I like Ben well enough, but I wouldn't marry him on a bet. A woman'd naturally be swayed by all that sweet talk and banjo playin', but that goes just so far with me. It don't put a roof over my head or food on the table. I know his kind, Papa. When I needed him most he'd be drinkin' or out huntin'. So

131

I've made up my mind. There's nothin' between Ben Travis and me. And there never will be."

"All right," Priam Thomas said and turned away. He looked toward the bend in the creek and saw the population of Illinois Town approaching. "Sabrina," he said and then she saw them too.

"What is it?" she asked.

"Don't know," he said and sounded worried. She left Travis to stand by her father's side. Together they watched the people come on. Each man carried a shovel, an axe or a saw. They marched like an army and with the same determination.

CHAPTER
SIX

The population of Illinois Town crowded around Sabrina's wagon camp. Ninian Lockwood acted as spokesman. Leaning on his shovel, he said, "Ma'am, seein' as how your man done us all a good favor, we're goin' to have a house raisin' here an' now." He spoke to a man standing at his left. "Elias, take a hind wheel off'n that wagon to use for measurin' off his property."

Sabrina looked at her father, too surprised to say anything. Priam Thomas said, "As head of this family, I thank you one and all."

They cheered and he stepped back while they propped up the wagon to remove the wheel. One of the men cut a stick and tied it to a spoke. Another stick was cut to use as a short axle. With a man on each end they started off along the creek, rolling the wheel. Each time the stick struck the ground it gouged a mark. Lockwood shouted, "Five hundred and three to a mile and mark them off a goodly piece now!" He took Sabrina by the arm. "We all saw his stakes. You mind showin' us where he had things figured to go?"

"Why, I —"

"Go show him, dammit," Thomas growled. "I'll tend Ben an' the kids."

"The women'll do that," Lockwood said. He turned and waved his arm and led his citizen army up the hill.

During the rest of the day the sound of axes was loud in the woods. Teams of horses dragged logs to a crew of men who did nothing but shave two sides flat and notch ends. Lockwood wanted to erect a simple cabin, but Sabrina, instead of showing him the site and leaving to join the other women, stayed on to boss the activity, much to Lockwood's disgust. She insisted that a trench be dug to hold the base logs and that proper drainage and ventilation be provided to keep the underside of the cabin dry in wet weather, and from rotting in the summer. So a group of men dug the trench and giant cottonwood cuts were imbedded, then notched. Lockwood, who hated to agree to anything, did say grudgingly, "Cottonwood won't rot."

By the time darkness fell, the sill logs were in place and notched, carefully cut to hold the floor joists. The workmen came off the hill to the camp by the creek where a dozen bright fires announced the supper time.

Sabrina went to her wagon and found Benjamin Travis awake and enjoying himself. A young woman knelt by his pallet and carefully, lovingly, spooned mush into his mouth. Sabrina said, "He can feed himself, can't he?"

The young woman didn't bother to get up. "He seems so weak."

"No man is weak," Sabrina said. She looked more carefully at the girl and wished she hadn't. She had a smooth face and long flaxen hair. The bold eyes didn't ruin anything, either, Sabrina noticed before turning away.

A little later she asked her father, "Who's that tending Ben?"

"Patience Eddy," Thomas said around a mouth full of food. "Lives over yonder." He pointed toward the settlement.

"There's no need for her to baby him," she said. "He's not hurt so bad he can't feed himself."

"Well," Thomas said, "if you hadn't gone up on the hill and butted in men's business, you'd be feeding him."

"Huh!" Sabrina crossed her arms. "You want a job done right, do it yourself."

Thomas smiled. "I reckon the Eddy girl feels the same way."

The largest fire had been built near Sabrina's wagon and the women prepared a huge meal, enough for everyone. Each had carried food: corn meal, hamhock, bacon, a side of venison, preserves from wild plum, choke-berry jams; Sabrina could not recall when she had seen such a meal.

Sabrina filled her plate and moved toward the shelter that had been rigged for Ben Travis, but she saw that Patience Eddy was still there, although Travis was through eating. Sabrina turned away from the camp and saw Shawnee Blanc's shadow a few yards away.

The Indian grunted when she drew near. He said, "He your man." He offered his hatchet. "Cut off yellow hair's ears."

"Oh, shut your heathen mouth!" Sabrina said. Shawnee Blanc put away his hatchet and Sabrina

135

turned back toward the fire. A group of men gathered around Benjamin Travis and since Patience Eddy was a girl who knew her place, she joined the women. Sabrina's first impulse was to go to Travis, but she checked it. These people believed too much already. Any further demonstration of concern, no matter how innocent, would cement the opinion in their minds. And she didn't want that.

So she stayed with the women by the fire, her mind closed to their chatter. At least until Patience Eddy came over, her smile bright, her eyes challenging.

"Mr. Travis is such a brave man, isn't he?"

"So's a bull," Sabrina said. "But did you ever try to live with one?"

"Well, I do decl —" Patience began but Sabrina cut her off.

"I know what you want, and if it's Ben Travis, you can have him."

She had to get away from the bright eyes, the expressions of outright disapproval. So she left the women and stepped into the darkness. She could hear the men talking and her ears strained to pick up the thread of their conversation.

One of the men was saying — she thought it was Bond: "That sojer's comin' back one of these days, Ben. You really meant to build that shot house?"

"Seemed like a good thing," Travis said. "They'd boat the ore down from Fort Dearborn. We'll rig an oven to melt the iron and besides makin' shot, there's a heap of things we can make. Could be a man could make tools here, so's a man wouldn't have to cart everything from back East."

"Jethro's agin' it," someone else said.

"He's scared," Travis said. "If the soldiers build that fort up river, we'll have an outlet for trade goods. They'll need food an' furs, an' they'll pay in Spanish dollars or script. Once that happens, Jethro won't have his choke hold on Illinois Town. He can't fight 'em all an' he knows it."

"I guess," Lockwood said, "it comes to more'n the sawyer camp you mean to have, Ben. A man can't eat timbers. It's somethin' a man buys or trades for. The first barrel of flour you took in trade, or bale of plews, then you'd be in competition with the Sweets. Can't say's I blame 'em for kickin' up a fuss."

"A man can't hold onto somethin' forever," Travis said. "Times is changin'; I seen changes back East. Another ten years an' this country'll be fair to middlin' settled. We got to get ready for it. Get roads, a church, schools. Got to have business ready for movers when they really start comin', by the thousands."

The men laughed but they believed him. Shadrach Bond said, "You turned the first stone, Ben. You turned it when you whupped Clem Sweet. I doggies, that was a real chicken-flutter set-to. Somethin' I never seen the beat of before, an' never expect to again."

"You'll never see me doin' it again," Travis said. "I must have plumb lost my mind to have even thought of it."

"It was that kiss you give your woman," someone said. All the men hooted loudly at this and Sabrina's face colored deeply. Several of the women glanced knowingly at her, but the deeper shadows hid her face from their prying eyes.

"Now hold on there a bit," Travis began, but was shouted down.

"She sure is some fightin' rooster," a man said. "The way she lit into Clem when he was fixin' to club your brains out was a sight to see."

"She knows her mind, too," another said. "Half the time I can't make up my mind whether she's a purty man wearin' a dress or a woman lookin' fer man's pants that'll fit her."

Laughter beat against her ears in waves and she closed her eyes until it died off. Travis was saying, "Now hold on. Hold on there." Finally he had their attention. "Seems there's a thing or two to be straightened out here. First off, Miz Kane's a right proud woman with some mighty set notions of what a man ought to be. Seems that I don't hardly come to taw with all my fightin' an' fussin' around. Some of you figure I fought for her. Well, I'd have fought Clem if she hadn't been here at all." He looked at each of them. "I want you to understand that this home you're raisin' is her home; I got no claim on it at all. An' when you're through, she'll thank you kindly herself, a lot better'n I can do."

Priam Thomas, who was leaning against the wagon with his pipe, watched Sabrina while Benjamin Travis spoke. She stood absolutely motionless, her face inscrutable. There was a touch of sadness in her manner.

Thomas made his way to where she stood. "You damn fool," he said. "Go out there an' call him a liar."

"I can't," she said.

"Can't or won't?" he asked and left her.

The crowd around Travis was beginning to break up and Thomas knelt down. He said, "That was a fool speech you made."

"She wants it that way," he said. "She's made it mighty plain that I'm short weight."

"You're both fools," Thomas said. "What you goin' to do about it, Ben?"

"As soon as I'm able, I'll start my sawyer camp," Travis said. "I guess I can show her I ain't that worthless."

"She already knows that," Thomas insisted. "It's her own notions she's got to get rid of."

"It's up to her to do it then," Travis said. Patience Eddy came toward him and Thomas left.

Someone brought out a fiddle and commenced to play. Elias Kinney called the dances and for an hour the camp was alive with the sawing fiddle and capering feet. Ben Travis lay in his shelter and watched, irked because his broken arm prevented him from playing the banjo. He looked for Sabrina among the dancers and failed to find her. This annoyed Patience Eddy and she tried to make her smile brighter, her voice more animated.

A little later Travis saw Sabrina near the wagon with the three children, but she did not look his way and he did not call to her.

The next day Sabrina ate a hurried breakfast, hustled the children down to the creek with Shawnee Blanc, then went up the hill in time to meet the first settlers. She started the younger boys gathering stones for the fireplace while their elders mixed up a mud and grass mortar. She watched them work, the Seatons from England, the Pillefrews from Durham County, the McLeashes, the Donegals, all eager to give their skill and labor.

There were pins to be shaved for fastening door and window frames soon to be hewn and smoothed. She attended to every detail, at times driving Lockwood nearly out of his mind with her exactness. Wall logs were hauled up, wrestled into positions for the augur holes and pins. One by one the notched timbers were set up and by nightfall the wall was four logs high.

None of the settlers gathered around the wagon, for the day had been filled with hard work and they all dreamed of a supper and early bed. Returning to her own camp, Sabrina was surprised to find that Patience Eddy had already cooked the meal, fed the children, and was just sitting down to give Travis his supper.

Thomas and Shawnee Blanc were puffing pipes when Sabrina filled her plate. Thomas said, "The cabin's goin' up fine."

"I didn't see you bending your back," Sabrina said. She glanced at Shawnee Blanc and added, "You keep your opinions to yourself, you hear?"

"Me not woman, talk all time," Shawnee Blanc said.

Sabrina ate her meal in silence, then cleaned the pots, scrubbing angrily because Patience had used so many. Somehow it seemed that every woman had her own system, a way of doing things. Poverty, sickness, death; all these things were endurable, but another woman in her kitchen was something none could abide.

Patience finally went home and Sabrina climbed into the wagon and undressed. She could see Travis' lean-to and knew he was awake, but clamped her lips shut and vowed not to speak. For a time she lay awake, listening in case he spoke, but he never did.

It was some time before she could get to sleep.

The next day Benjamin Travis surprised everyone by walking around. He limped badly and his broken arm pained him considerable, but he took over the supervision from Sabrina Kane. By noon the walls were finished, the three rooms separated by log partitions. Door framing would be in by nightfall.

The house faced the river, with a door and two windows opening to the sweeping view of the valley, and St. Louis on the other side. The team of men putting up the fireplace was making rapid progress, and several boys carried small sticks for the slow fire necessary to dry the mortar gradually and prevent cracking.

Sabrina Kane avoided Ben Travis; he hadn't been sure at first, but now there was little doubt. Twice he tried to speak to her, but she found something to do elsewhere when she saw him approaching. After that he left her alone.

Pierre Menard had the skill and the sons to make the furniture, and to this task he applied himself. With stout poles he constructed a large, double bed, carefully notching the post to take the rails, and afterward pinned them solidly with ash pegs. The women wove a set of rope springs while others made a tick of canvas, stuffing it with dried grass until it was fat and comfortable.

With the cabin so near completion, Sabrina wanted to move in, but Lockwood would have none of it. The cabin would be finished by noon tomorrow, he promised. Then there would be a celebration and games.

That evening Sabrina left the hill early and was cooking supper when Patience Eddy showed up. When she saw Sabrina, a pout pulled the bow of her lips out of shape and she left before Ben Travis arrived.

Sabrina Kane, he noticed, seemed to be in unusually good spirits. Even Shawnee Blanc saw it when Sabrina gave him a second helping of stew.

The next morning the ridge pole, rafters and stringers went into place and shingles were laid. Pierre Menard and his sons completed the last of the furniture: four chairs to match the stout table they had built, and a bunk for each child with a ladder to reach the uppermost.

The inner and outer doors were hung and Sabrina poked the latch string through, saying, "It'll always be out."

Then she cried because everyone had been so kind.

Lockwood led them off the hill to the camp below where the women prepared a huge meal. Pierre Menard gathered some men around him and got a wrestling match going. Another produced a jug, which was passed around and soon emptied.

The French citizens cared very little for this strenuous sport, preferring something more in the line with their daily tasks. Since all of them owned and drove oxen, a prize of a live pig was offered for the best demonstration with the bullwhip.

A tall gangly youth of fourteen was chosen to hold the targets, which he did without fear, for anyone lacking the skill to hit an apple or potato held in the palm at ten feet was considered too inferior to be a man. Sabrina stood with her father on the sidelines, watching the Frenchmen step up with their whips.

The first elimination was simple. A potato was held at arm's length and each man was required to cut it with his whip. Only the top of the potato was touched, since none wanted to live with the disgrace of hitting the boy.

After this first round was over, Sabrina said, "I can use a live pig," and turned to the wagon.

Thomas grabbed her arm. "That's for men! Dang it all, what'll they say when a woman steps out there?"

"Woman or not, I want a chance at the pig." She jerked her arm free, made her way through the gathering of ladies and got her own whip from the wagon. Travis saw this and without attracting attention to himself, walked over to where Priam Thomas waited with his scowl.

"She'll make a talk of herself," Thomas grumbled.

"She's an independent woman," Travis admitted. "She may win the pig."

"To hell with the pig," Thomas said. "There's things a woman can do and things she can't. This is one she can't."

The target had grown smaller by the time Sabrina entered the contest. The men looked at each other uncomfortably and the women were buzzing with talk. Everyone, it seemed, suddenly became interested in the bullwhip cracking.

This was cutting a stick, which the young man held straight out. The men stepped aside for Sabrina, because she was a woman, but they would never get over it. She ran the whip through her hand, threw it behind her, then cast. The stick snapped and the men cheered, for skill was admirable regardless of sex.

For another hour the contest continued, and each time the target changed, more men were forced to drop out. Sabrina remained with two men, both burly Frenchmen who were enjoying themselves immensely. The sun had turned off hot and the shoulders of Sabrina's dress were damp with sweat.

The young man held up a branch from which hung three plum blossoms. The object was to cut only one blossom off, leaving the other two undisturbed. One of the Frenchmen made his cast and the crowd cheered when the blossom vanished in a shower of torn petals. Sabrina was next. She licked her lips, laid the whip out and cast, but her aim was faulty and she caught both clusters and was eliminated.

She turned and joined her father and Ben Travis. "Goodbye pig," she said.

144

"You lost the prize, but you've sure got people talkin' about you. You couldn't have done better if you'd appeared in public in your pettishirt."

Sabrina's glance whipped to Ben Travis. "Don't you have anything to say?"

"Well," he said, grinning, "it seems that I was goin' to say you handle a whip right smartly. Where'd you learn how?"

"My husband taught me," Sabrina said.

Thomas grunted. "He used to make more winnin' bets with a bullwhip than he made plowin' his farm."

"What I haven't figured out," Travis said, "is which is sharper: Sabrina's tongue when she gets her dander up, or the end of that bullwhip."

"Just hope you never find out," she said and put the whip back in the wagon.

That evening there was more dancing and Benjamin Travis joined in, much to Sabrina's disgust. Priam Thomas sidled up while the dance was in progress and said, "That Eddy girl's a handsome wench, ain't she?"

"I haven't noticed," Sabrina said.

"You ain't taken your eyes off her an' Ben all evenin'," Thomas said. Sabrina shot him a quick, mind-your-own-business glance and continued to watch Benjamin Travis make a fool of himself with Patience Eddy. Patience had a tall grace and when she danced her blonde braids whipped around gaily. Sabrina could hear her laughter above the throb of the music and returned her mocking smirk with a wooden stare as she whirled close.

145

"If that's what he wants," she said, "he's welcome to her."

Priam Thomas took the clay pipe from his mouth. "Hell, they're just dancin'!"

"Dancin' — kissin'; she's one step from the street!"

Priam took her arm. "Sabrina, that's no way —"

"Oh, leave me alone!" She turned quickly and went to the wagon where the three children peered over the tailgate, eyes bright with excitement in the flickering firelight.

"When can I dance, Ma?" Jenner asked. "When can I, huh?"

"There's more to life than dancin'," Sabrina said. "You'll find that out when you grow older." Sabrina lifted the little girl from the wagon and held her in her arms. "*Peen-tee-geen n'dau-nis*, Mary?"

The little Indian girl laughed and patted Sabrina's cheek.

"Whillikers," Jenner said, "you learn quick, Ma." He touched Mary on the arm. "*Mah-ne-me-nee?*" The little girl leaned back and gave him a hug. "Ma," Jenner said, "there's nothin' wrong with Injuns, is there?"

"No, Jenner," Sabrina said.

"You like Shawnee Blanc, don't you, Ma? Even when you call him a heathen Injun, you like him, don't you?"

"Yes," she said, smiling. "That's just an expression. He understands."

The dance ended with a burst of stamping and whooping. Someone produced a jug of Blue Ruin and passed it around. Sabrina turned her head in time to see Benjamin Travis hoist it for a long pull. Then he

146

turned and kissed Patience Eddy and everyone laughed. Sabrina pulled her eyes away and felt heat rise in her face. Jenner watched with curious eyes. "Whillikers, Ma — he kissed her!"

"If you grow up like that, I'll hide you proper!" Sabrina said. She put Mary back in the wagon. "Now get to sleep, all of you. Tomorrow night you'll have your own beds." She saw that they were covered well and went back to the fire. Priam Thomas was knocking the dottle from his pipe and he watched her approach. From her expression he knew that she had seen Ben Travis kiss the Eddy girl.

He said, "It was all in fun, Sabrina. Course, it don't matter no way what he does. He's nothing to you."

"That's right," she said. "If he wants to make a fool of himself, that's his own doing. I'm going to bed."

She turned back toward the wagon, then stopped suddenly. In the deep shadows stood five Indians, blankets pulled tightly around them. Their eyes were steady and bright and from beneath the blanket folds poked the muzzles of trade muskets and bow tips.

"Pa!" Sabrina spoke without taking her eyes from the Indians. Bright streaks of paint made weird slashes across their foreheads and cheeks.

Priam Thomas turned, saw them and spoke to a man standing nearby.

A gentle chain reaction flowed over the people. As they turned, their talk died, and as sounds faded, still others grew quiet. In another moment the music stopped because no one was paying the slightest attention to it. The dancers stood frozen, all facing the immovable Indians. A man's voice said, "Fetch me my rifle, Rachel."

Another said, "Let Ben handle it. He knows Injuns."

"Ben? Ben, where are you?"

Travis worked his way gently through the crowd. He stopped near Sabrina for she stood closest to them. "Put more wood on the fire and get a little light here," he said.

When the flames mounted and he had looked them over, he said, "Sac and Fox war party. *T shah-ko-zhah?*" He offered his hand, palm up.

"*Hoh! Neetchee.*" He spoke to the settlers without turning his head. "They say they're friends. Thomas, see that some food is brought up. You folks make way there by the fire."

Someone grumbled about sharing with Injuns, but Travis' command was obeyed. A lane opened to the fire and the Indians walked down it, glancing neither left nor right. When they were seated, Travis said, "*Wana mi-ke nita ko-dapi kon.*"

"*Iyo tiye oma wani yelo. O hunke sni o taye. Iki cize woan kon. Wana hena'la yelo. Iyo tike kiya waon. To ka hiyo wau welo. Mise ya tuwa cante.*"

With the speech out of the way, the Indian placed his rifle across his knees and the others followed suit. Then they accepted the offered food.

Ninian Lockwood asked, "What the tophet was all that about?"

"Figurin' it out myself," Travis said. "He says they've traveled under difficulties, meanin' a long way, prob'bly. Then he says, the poor are many. Could be they had a fracas an' got whupped."

"Fracas with who?" Elijah Blackwell asked this. He was a rangy man with a suspicious nature and little liking for Indians.

"Sioux probably," Travis said. "They talk Sioux an' from their trappin's they're from up-river. Maybe around Fort Dearborn way. He says he's a warrior but now it's all over, meanin' the fight. He claims to have looked for his enemies an' found 'em. The last was a brag: he depends on nobody's courage but his own."

There was no talking while the Indians ate, and if they felt any resentment at the stares, they hid it behind their unreadable faces. They accepted coffee and tobacco. Then Travis talked to them further. For thirty minutes a low, guttural conversation passed between them, uninterrupted. Finally Benjamin Travis straightened and said, "Folks, the way I get it is they been raidin' the Sioux territory an' been run out. They come south because the Sac and Fox has got friendly tribes down here. They figured the Sioux wouldn't chase 'em so far. Well, they're out of powder an' ball, and nearly out of grub." He looked around at the gathering. "You folks has been wantin' peace with the Injuns, then here's your chance. I'll invite 'em to stay for the night an' in the mornin' come back with some corn an' fixin's. Any of you that's got a dram of powder an' lead to spare, fetch it along."

"You goin' to put them Injuns up for the night?" Blackwell's voice was incredulous. "By Jupiter, I'm barrin' my door!"

"Bar it then," Travis said flatly. "I tell you, treat 'em right and you got no call to be fearful." He waved his hand. "Best be gettin' home now. Bring back somethin' in the mornin'."

There were some disgruntled comments but they departed. Sabrina and her father still stood near the wagon, watching the Indians lick their fingers and talk softly amongst themselves.

Benjamin Travis spoke a few words, then ignored them. The Indians rolled into their blankets to sleep. Travis took Sabrina's arm and led her to the tailgate. "Sleep inside tonight with the kids."

"Is there any danger? You said it was all right."

Travis spoke softly. "Was you alone in the woods they'd likely jump you for shot an' powder, but here they'd rather ask for it."

Thomas took his rifle, shot pouch and powder horn, and with blankets draped over his shoulder, went up the hillside and camped beneath the fruit trees where he could see the wagon.

"I'll sleep under the wagon," Travis said.

"You don't have to," Sabrina said. "I'm not afraid."

"I don't mean to argue; just get in the wagon."

"Too bad the Indians came," she said with acid sweetness. "You might have got yourself another kiss."

"May not be too late yet," he said and caught her to him before she understood his intent. She tried to block his face with her hands but his strength was great and he pressed his lips against hers. She realized fighting was useless; the desire to fight vanished. One part of her mind prayed that this moment would endure

150

forever while another part, a more sane part, filled her with self-contempt because her resolve had been so easily dissolved.

Travis released her gently and she slapped him with all her strength. His head rocked back and he looked at her without surprise, as if he had expected to pay this price.

"I'm not Patience Eddy!"

"That's true enough," Travis said. "She's a woman an' acts like one. Any yearnin's she's got toward a man ain't the bossy kind."

"That's what you men want, ain't it — some heifer to breed? Then go to her. She'll likely share her bed with you!" Sabrina whirled and climbed into the wagon. Travis stood there a moment; then he lay down beneath his shelter. A glance at the Indians assured him that they were quiet, but he drew his flintlock next to him before rolling in his blankets.

On the hillside, Priam Thomas remained vigilant. Farther to the left, the shadow shape of Shawnee Blanc was briefly outlined. Travis smiled and settled himself.

Throughout the night possibly the only souls in the entire settlement who slept soundly were the Sac and Fox Indians. Ben Travis woke often from his light sleep and at dawn found them still in their blankets. He rekindled the fire and put water on to boil.

Sabrina Kane climbed from the wagon and said, "That's a woman's job." She shouldered him aside unceremoniously and Travis smothered a smile.

"You still hatin' me this mornin', Sabrina?"

"No," she said calmly. "I don't think of you at all except as just another mouth to feed."

Priam Thomas came down from his hillside camp as the Indians began to stir. Shawnee Blanc carried in a load of dry firewood but said nothing to the Indians. They looked at him carefully and he went away.

The Sac and Fox warriors sat in a clannish knot while Sabrina cooked a kettle of pap. The sidemeat was roasted on a stick and Jenner was assigned the task of turning it constantly. The other two children scrambled from the wagon and ran to the creek. When the Sac and Fox warriors saw the little girl, they jabbered in low voices. Travis turned his head to better hear what they were saying, but when they saw this, talk ceased.

Sabrina fed the Indians first and for a treat, mixed a jug of switchel: molasses and water with a little vinegar added. The Indians grunted in pleasure and drank it all.

Soon the settlers began to gather. All were poor people, working hard to raise enough for their own needs, but everyone carried something for the Indians. Travis directed that a blanket be spread and the goods piled upon it, for he knew well the value of making a great show around Indians.

There was cornmeal, jerked venison, potatoes, coffee, some tobacco, a few spices, over two pounds of gunpowder, and enough musket balls of assorted sizes to carry them south to the land of the Shawnee, their friends.

The Sac and Fox leader rose and spoke with great dignity.

152

"Ayus' tan peza ta wakan. Appe'tu mita wa kon le'tu numwe'."

Travis translated. "He says you've given him holy medicine and that he considers this day his. *Hoh! Wa' yelo.*"

"Hoh! Neetchee."

They carefully divided, bundled the goods and then walked through the village and went south, following the Mississippi. Everyone watched them until they disappeared from sight. Blackwell said, "I'm sure glad they've gone. Makes a body nervous, havin' them heathen around."

"They're simple folks," Travis said. "The thing is, don't get excited aroun' Injuns. It don't take much to set 'em off."

Priam Thomas nudged him with his elbow and said, "Boat comin' down river, Ben."

Travis had his look. Everyone's attention turned to the river. The boat stood away from shore, drifting with the current. An oarsman at the stern leaned against his stout tiller and the boat changed course, angling toward shore.

One man stood in the prow, dressed in a blue coat and a leather hat with a bright red cockade. Lockwood said, "Sojers."

Oars were unlimbered and the man in the bow directed the landing opposite Sabrina's camp, where the population of Illinois Town waited. The soldiers were near enough now to be recognized. Travis said, "Well, dog my cats if it ain't Cap'n Pressly."

The boat was beached and Captain Pressly jumped to the ground, his small command following. A sergeant barked orders in a drill-field voice while Pressly waded across the creek. His blue coat was faced with red, the leather cap trimmed with a roach of bearskin, cloth band, cockade and feather. An epaulet graced his right shoulder, establishing his rank as captain in the 2nd Sublegion.

He came on, clutching his sword to keep it from thrashing his leg. When he saw Benjamin Travis he smiled and extended his gloved hand long before he was close enough to shake. Pressly's dark eyes made a quick survey of Travis' battered appearance, and he said, "Tangle with a bear, Ben?"

"Clem Sweet."

"Same thing," Pressly said. He nodded to acquaintances and then saw Sabrina. His eyes brightened and he hurriedly whipped off his hat, making a sweeping bow. "Your servant, Ma'am."

Travis introduced Sabrina and her father. Pressly murmured his good wishes, then turned directly to the business at hand. "Did a small party of Sac and Fox come through here last night?"

"You missed 'em by minutes, Cap'n," Travis said. "We fed 'em an' saw that they was outfitted. You after 'em?"

"No, no, nothing like that," Pressly said. He heard his sergeant approach and turned. "Hold the men at the boat. We'll depart shortly."

Pressly turned back to Travis. "There's an Indian war brewing, Ben. Black Hawk, the Sac and Fox chief, is getting onery. The Sioux don't like it and everyone seems to be gathering all their friendly relations around them."

"We're pretty far south," Travis said. "The Shawnees are friendly enough, Cap'n. Seems like we'd be gettin' het up over nothin' was we to board up for an Indian scare."

"These things are like a prairie fire," Pressly said. "Ben, the battle of Fallen Timbers wasn't so far back people don't remember it. We need a base farther south. I asked you once about building a shot tower here. You said you wanted to wait until your trouble with the Sweets was cleared up. From the looks of your face, I'd say it was cleared considerable. Are you ready now?"

"Yep," Travis said. "You figurin' to move troops here, Cap'n?"

"Possibly," Pressly admitted. "Providing that an adequate supply base is maintained here. We'll need a very large building, amply fortified, with a large storeroom and a barracks to house at least fifty soldiers and four officers."

"When?"

Pressly frowned. "Two months."

"All right," Travis said, "providin' the folks in Illinois Town can stock it. Payment in trade goods or script."

"Jethro Sweet will fight, Ben."

Travis grinned. "He's already started over my sawyer camp."

"Money is very short," Pressly said. "We need a dozen forts between here and Fort Washington, but there's no appropriation to pay for them. It's up to the people, Ben. The Sweets wouldn't go along with me, so my hands are tied." He waved his hands toward the river. "This land is yours. We can only ask you to build on it for us."

"You bring your sojers back in two months, Cap'n. We'll have a place for you."

"I thank you in the name of a poverty-ridden government," Pressly said. "But be careful of the Sweets, Ben. When you cut timber for a fort, they'll be pointing rifles at you. The day the fort goes up and we move in, they're finished in Illinois Town and they know it."

"It don't seem right," Lockwood said, "the Sweets havin' all the profits."

"We have no idea of their true wealth," Pressly said, "but it would be safe to estimate that they are worth many thousands of dollars." He smiled. "Ironic, isn't it? The people with the most will give the least. Yet you have little or nothing and are willing to give it all." He turned to look at the waiting sergeant, then offered his hand again to Ben Travis. "Good luck, all of you. I'll return in two months."

"Supposin' we want to get word to you," Travis said. "Can a man go up river to Fort Dearborn?"

"Not without a strong force of at least ten armed men," Pressly said. "This looks like a bad year, Ben. Blackhawk is going back on his treaty and the settlers are beginning to move toward him from the north. You ought to see Fort Dearborn, Ben. Quite a settlement around it now."

"I'll have to get up that way," Travis said.

"Wait until the Indians cool down or we put them in their place." He said his goodbyes and returned to the boat, which was shoved into the current immediately. The oars came out and the long, laborious task of pulling upstream began.

Benjamin Travis said, "I'll be startin' my sawyer camp in a few days. Once we get it goin' we'll start buildin' the cap'n's fort."

"Where?" Bond wanted to know. "Not on my land. I'm a farmer."

"There's plenty of land along here," Travis said. "We'll pick a spot when the time comes."

There was nothing more to be said and the settlers turned toward their homes. Benjamin Travis watched them go and Sabrina covertly observed Travis, for she felt that he had committed himself more deeply than a man should.

CHAPTER
SEVEN

That night Benjamin Travis, Shawnee Blanc and Priam Thomas moved Sabrina's belongings into the house where she spent frantic hours stowing them properly. The trunk holding Cadmus Kane's things came first. The hand-carved clock with the glass face and short pendulum case was placed on the mantle. She wound it, set it by guess and stood back, admiring the soft ticking.

"Cadmus gave that to me the day we were married," she said.

"Right handsome," Ben Travis said. "There ain't many men that'd give a woman fancy gee-gaws."

"He'd have done better buyin' a new plow," Thomas said.

"That's a man's thinking!" Sabrina snapped.

"It was also a man's thinkin' that bought you the clock," Travis said gently.

And this thought stopped her, and a chasm of doubt sprang up; for the first time she seriously questioned the validity of her own thinking.

"Better get on with the unpackin'," Travis reminded.

She turned toward the trunk. She removed several pieces of fine linen, but these were put aside, to be used only on the most special occasions. Several new quilts were spread on the beds, and from the bottom of the trunk, carefully wrapped, came the conch shell.

"That was the crownin' bit of foolishness," Priam Thomas said. "Cadmus wanted one chance to fling his *folle avoine* before he got married. He was gone three months, an' when he come back he had that dang-blessed thing." He shook his head as though some men's madness was beyond his understanding. "Sabrina gets a pleasure out of it. Got to keep it locked, though, 'cause that danged Shawnee Blanc thinks it's medicine. Was he to git his hands on it, he'd sit all day, just listenin' to it roar."

Sabrina placed the shell on the mantle.

The pots were hung, the fireplace lighted. Sabrina sat down at the table and folded her hands. Her cheeks were smooth and her eyes held a sparkle of deep pleasure. "This is what I've always wanted, my own home."

"Is this different," Travis asked, "than movin' into a home a man already has?"

Her glance came up quickly. "Yes, this is *mine*."

"I guess then it does make a difference," Travis said.

Sabrina said, "In the morning I'm going to hitch the team and break ground."

A few minutes later Benjamin Travis gathered his things, and with Shawnee Blanc to help him, carried them back to the timber's edge and there made his permanent camp. Somehow the house didn't seem the same to Sabrina after he had gone. The rooms were almost too big and needed a big man to fill them.

That night she turned restlessly on her new bed. In the other rooms she could hear her father and the children stirring as though her own restlessness was contagious.

The next morning, Sabrina held to the hope that Benjamin Travis would come down from his timber camp, and when he did not, she began to grow uneasy. Priam Thomas suspected that something vexed her when she sharply demanded that he wipe his feet before entering the house. During the meal she scolded the children, accused the fireplace of drawing badly, and complained mildly of small, inconsequential things. This cemented suspicion in Priam Thomas' mind. He did not have to be a genius to divine that Benjamin Travis' absence lay at the root.

The next day Sabrina worked outside and that evening she put the children to bed early instead of allowing them to play near the creek. After breakfast the following morning she found work facing the timber and shot frequent glances toward the crown of the hill. When the noon meal was over, she sent Bushrod, Mary and Jenner to the timber to play. An hour later she went after them and found them in Benjamin Travis' camp.

He was seated on a deadfall, telling them a story. Sabrina said, "Children, I've been looking everywhere for you."

"But, Ma," Jenner said, "you told us we co —"

"I'm not going to stand for any sass," Sabrina said firmly. She gave Jenner a push toward the cabin. "The cows both need milkin', and you keep your eye on

160

Mary and Bushrod, you hear? I don't want them strayin' off."

"Yes, Ma," Jenner said and took the two children down the hill toward the creek.

Then she fastened a sharp glance on Shawnee Blanc. "There's kindlin' to be chopped and wood to be fetched. You want your meals on time, then get your work done."

"Waugh!" Shawnee Blanc said and trotted away.

Sabrina looked at Benjamin Travis' camp and was surprised. Although handicapped by a broken arm, he had built a half-cabin, a three-sided log structure with a stout roof. He had even staked out his sawyer camp. He said, "You've been workin' too hard, Sabrina."

"Whistlin' don't make the plow go," she said. His eyes contained a suppressed amusement and for an awful moment she suspected that her reason for coming here was too obvious. She laced her fingers together — then unlaced them. "I came up to tell you that you're welcome to eat with us. I don't mind fixing for one more."

"That's kind of you," Ben Travis said and studied her face. She avoided a direct glance and could not help wondering if he was recalling a moment when he had held her in his arms and all her proud notions had faded to nothing.

"I have to get back," she said suddenly. "There's work to be done and if a body don't watch that heathen Injun he'll sneak off and hunt birds." This wasn't true and she knew it. Shawnee Blanc was a good man to

161

have around. He kept meat on the table, and never sat down when there was something to do.

Travis watched her go off the hill and then turned back to his own business. That evening he made his appearance at her door and found a place set for him. Priam Thomas gave him a knowing glance but said nothing, other than a grunted greeting. Shawnee Blanc took the plate from Sabrina, and went outside to some secret place of his own. Travis took his place at the table and from the open neck of his shirt, brought forth a deerskin poke filled with coins. Sabrina and her father watched as he stretched open the puckered mouth and emptied the contents on the table.

There was well over five hundred dollars.

"I figure the meals is worth a quarter," he said. "That's breakfast an' supper. I'll be too busy to eat dinner anyhow." He counted twelve Spanish dollars. "Here's a month in advance."

Since Sabrina had put Benjamin Travis down as a man who frittered away both time and energy, she could not quite credit him with sufficient vision to put money aside. He counted out eighty more dollars and pushed them toward her. "There's the money you paid Jacques Fountainbleau. I took it off him the night Thomas nigh scalped him."

"I — I don't think it's right to take it," Sabrina said. "He did bring us to Illinois."

"We'll take it and thank you for your trouble," Priam Thomas said. He scooped up the money and pressed it into Sabrina's hands. "Let's have no nonsense now.

162

That's enough to feed us for a year, until a crop comes in."

She put it in a copper jar setting on the mantle.

After the meal she expected Benjamin Travis to stay awhile, to tell the children a story, but he did not. He got up, thanked her briefly and went out the door. Sabrina put the children to bed, then sat before the fire in her rocking chair. Priam Thomas drew on his pipe, the soggy dottle bubbling noisily.

Thomas said, "Travis better watch himself or he'll end up with his back plumb broke from responsibilities."

"It's about time," Sabrina said. Her rocker squeaked as she moved it gently back and forth.

Thomas sighed. "He'll make a fine man for some woman. If you don't rag him to death first. He'll change; a man always gives to a woman in the end. I did to your ma. It's too bad they end up hatin' the woman for changin' 'em. He'd be a good man for you, Sabrina."

"If I wanted to get on my knees to him." She stood up. "I'm going to bed."

She was up before dawn and after breakfast began the never-ending chores of a pioneer woman. In the forenoon she washed clothes at the creek and when Thomas finished the lye box, shoveled it full of ashes and soaked it down to produce the ingredients for soap.

That evening Benjamin Travis put in his appearance promptly and after the meal, said, "Thomas, I'm ready to fall timber. I'm payin' fifty cents a day, sunup to sundown. Menard has agreed to that wage. So's Bond's oldest boys. I need another man."

"Fifty cents a day suits me to a tee," Thomas said and the bargain was sealed.

Then they talked about the farm that was to be Sabrina's. They agreed that a ten-acre patch near the cabin would do for the first year or two, but in the meantime, twenty additional acres of trees should be girdled, that is, the bark cut through in a ring so they would die. In four years they would be ready to chop down and the stumps pulled.

The children pestered Travis for a story, but he begged off, saying that he had to get up too early for foolishness. He looked at Sabrina Kane when he said this and went back to his camp.

The next morning Priam Thomas rose at dawn, ate his breakfast and walked to the timber. Sabrina went to the lean-to and while Jenner milked the cows, she hitched the horses to the plow, intending to break ground for her garden.

Illinois dirt might have been rich but breaking it for seed was back wrenching labor. The wooden plow cut a shallow furrow, and she had to stop every ten feet to clean the share and moldboard, for the earth had a maddening habit of clinging like glue. All day long Sabrina could hear the ring of axe, the rip of saw, the slough of adz, and now and then, the crackling crash of falling timber. And it was then that she hated Benjamin Travis for luring her father away with money. She needed a man, had to have a man, for there was work

164

that a woman could not do alone. She hated Travis for making such a simple thing so difficult.

Yet when Ben Travis appeared for supper she said nothing about her feelings. Travis was busy talking about the fort he planned to build. The site he selected was on the southern most end of Sabrina's property, near the Lockwood's. Eighty feet long and two and a half stories high; that's how big he had planned it. The front was to open onto the river; a quay could be built by the soldiers to make landing of supplies easier.

During this talk Sabrina moved from fireplace spider to the table, slowly, as though her back was too sore for flexibility. Benjamin Travis observed her covertly and finally got up, crossing to her. He took one of her hands and spread it palm up, exposing raw and blistered flesh.

He said, "Thomas, stay home tomorrow an' plow."

"I can do my own plowin'!" Sabrina snapped. "He wants to earn the money, then let him! He owes me nothing!"

"Stay home," Travis repeated.

"You've just got to boss people, don't you? You're not satisfied until you're telling them what's good for 'em." The children watched wide-eyed as Sabrina came up to Benjamin Travis and shook her finger at him. "You've got your own business; tend to it and leave mine alone!"

"Stubborn as all get out," Travis said, smiling slightly. "Afraid some man's goin' to run your life. You intend to plow tomorrow?"

"Yes, if it's any business of yours," Sabrina said.

Travis pursed his lips and gave this some thought. "Thomas, whose horses be those?"

"Mine," Thomas said flatly. "At least two of 'em are. The other two is yours."

"In the mornin'," Travis said, "I'm goin' to need three animals to skid logs down to the fort site. I pay twenty-five cents a day."

Thomas was pleased with this maneuvering. "You just rented my horses," he said and went to the fireplace for his pipe and tobacco.

For a moment Sabrina Kane was too furious to speak. "Oh, you're hateful, Ben Travis! How can I plow with one horse when it's all two can do to pull the darned thing?"

"You can't," Travis said. "When you cool down so's you can see sense, I'll send Thomas down to plow it. Until then you can break it with a hoe if you're so all-fired stubborn."

Sabrina bit her lip to keep from crying. "Oh, I hate him!" she said and went into her bedroom. Thomas smoked his pipe in silence, told the children an outlandish story about how he saved the life of General 'Light Horse Harry' Lee during the 1779 raid on the British at Paulas Hook. Bushrod was too young to understand much of it, and Mary understood none at all, yet they all watched Jenner, laughed when he laughed and found pleasure in the old man's gestures and his sound effects: cannons firing, musket balls whizzing by.

Finally Sabrina Kane came out of the bedroom and herded the children before her. "They've heard enough of those lies," she said, but in the softness of her voice was her own memories of childhood stories on Thomas' knee.

When dawn brightened the sky, Sabrina had not forgiven Benjamin Travis, although he had been right; her hands were too sore to plow. She decided that his being right didn't bother her, but his matter-of-fact regulation of her life caused her anger to rekindle. God, to be married to such a man! Nothing but orders: Fix the meal, wash the clothes, mend my shirt . . .

Thomas left for the sawyer camp and Sabrina found plenty to keep her busy. Because she liked light in the evenings, there were candles to be made and she got out the tin molds. Her thoughts turned to winter, which would be here only too soon. There was a wood supply to lay in and clothing to be made. Even the spinning was undone. When she finished with the candle-making she began to check supplies and found them sadly wanting.

Actually, Cadmus Kane should have begun his journey while the snow had still been on the ground, but since he had never been the kind of a man who did things on time, Sabrina could not bring herself to blame him for the insufficient supplies.

She would just have to buy enough to last out the winter; she had the money, eighty Spanish dollars.

The early summer heat was growing strong so she went into the bedroom, stripped off her dress, then three petticoats, and put her dress back on, using only her bloomers for a foundation. The sudden airiness made her smile and she wished she had a mirror so she could see herself without the bulky padding women always wore. When the weather turned hot a man could take off his shirt, but a woman had to swelter beneath a long, heavy skirt and three or four petticoats.

Well, she decided, I'll wear the dress, but what I have under it is my business.

So she wrapped the eighty dollars in a small cloth and struck out for the village. The insects were beginning to arrive by the millions and they swarmed out of the grass each time her feet disturbed it. Flies and grasshoppers were insistent pests that made her fling her arms constantly. The grasshoppers were particularly annoying for they got under her dress, clinging to her bare legs and she had to stop often to shake them out.

As she approached Jethro Sweet's trading store, her first boldness began to wear thin and she could only think of Jethro's warning: Keep your tribe away from my store.

Since Benjamin Travis' beating had severely crippled Clem, Jacques Fountainbleau had become the general handy man. He was sitting on the porch as she approached. A bandage still swathed his head while his once-severed ear rehealed. His facial cut had been crudely stitched and was now a horrible, half-healed scar. He stood up as Sabrina mounted the porch steps and held the door open so she could enter.

Fountainbleau hurried behind the counter. "Madame, may I be of service?" His tone said that he didn't intend to be.

168

"I'd like to speak to Mr. Sweet," Sabrina said, and because she was secretly proud of Ben Travis' victory, added, "Which ever one is able to stand."

"*Oui*," Fountainbleau said. He went into the back room where Jethro labored over his records. A moment later Jethro came out, his eyes dark. He looked quickly about as though he suspected a trick.

"I'm alone," Sabrina said and Jethro's face took on color. He was a vain man; this was apparent in his dress, and Sabrina was determined to play on his vanity. "I've come to talk business with you."

Sweet smiled. "I only discuss it with men," he said. "In your case, with Ben Travis. Tell him to come here and we'll talk about anythin' he wants to talk about."

"This doesn't concern him," Sabrina said. "I'll need a few things for the winter." She looked around at the bulging shelves. Jethro had enough staples to feed an army.

"What I have's for sale," Jethro said. "But your man'll have to come an' buy it for you." He paused. "Unless he's afraid to come off his hill."

"I don't think Ben Travis loses much sleep over you," Sabrina said. "Your brother, Clem, didn't scare him much either."

She told herself that she only wanted to sting Jethro's pride, but to be entirely honest, she could not resist the opportunity to brag a bit, especially to Ben Travis' enemies.

Jethro leaned his doubled fists on the counter. "Since you're a woman, I can't get at you like I would a man, but I can shut you out. You want somethin' on my shelves? Then send Ben Travis. I'll give him a real bargain: a bullet!"

"What are you trying to do, Mr. Sweet? Make two towns here?"

"There's only one: mine! Travis is stealin' from my traps. I'll allow no man to do that."

"And how do you intend to stop him?" Sabrina asked.

"Send him around and you'll see," Sweet said. "God, a man's got a right to protect what he's built! You tell Travis that I know what he's up to. I know the sojers was here the other day, an' if he builds them a tradin' post, I'll burn it to the ground!"

Sabrina's smile was scornful. "You're so brave. Why don't you go up the hill like your brother did? Are you afraid you'd be carried down?"

Jethro's face was mottled with anger. He snapped, "Frenchy, show her out!"

"I'll go by myself," Sabrina said and walked to the door. But there she paused. "Just how smart do you think you are? I can go to the Lockwoods or the Pillifrews; they'll buy for me. You'll never know the difference."

"I'd know," Jethro said. "You an' Travis is the only ones in the settlement that's got any money. If you want your friends closed out, just send them around."

"What are you going to do about the money Travis is paying in wages? How are you going to tell my dollars from his?"

"Travis' money's worthless here," Jethro said. "And he won't keep them working long after they find it out either."

"You're not very smart," Sabrina said. "I'll tell Travis you said that and he'll figure a way to beat you." She turned and walked off the porch. Fountainbleau was again in his chair, having gone around the back way to the front.

Sabrina walked back toward her own place, but she walked slowly. At Mrs. Pillifrew's cabin she saw Mrs. Bond and several other ladies talking and veered toward them. They turned as she approached and watched her oddly.

Mrs. Pillifrew was passing around her pewter snuff box and each lady took a pinch, sniffing it from between their fingers, or placing it on the back of the hand to inhale. Mrs. Pillifrew offered the snuff to Sabrina, who shook her head.

"I tried chewin' pa's tobacco once, but it made me sick."

"Seems that you'd use snuff," Mrs. Bond said. "Lands sake, you do things as good as most men."

"You look thinner, Sabrina," Mrs. Pillifrew said. "You ought to eat more grits and fat."

"It's just that I've shed a few petticoats in this weather," Sabrina said. The ladies stared at her for a moment.

Then Mrs. Bond said, "Well, I do declare. What won't you think of next?"

Suddenly Sabrina wished she had her petticoats back on for the temperature dropped a good twenty degrees. The ladies looked at each other as women do when they have plenty to say and wished one would leave so they could say it.

"I was tellin' Mrs. Pillifrew the other day," Mrs. Bond said, "that you ought to have younguns of your own an' stop takin' every stray that comes along."

"Perhaps I will someday," Sabrina said.

"Sakes alive, you *was* married. Was there somethin' the matter with your man?" This seemed to open a lively discussion and while the ladies began to talk all at once, Sabrina turned and walked away before they missed her.

At her own cabin she found Jenner and the two smaller children playing with Lockwood's youngest three, a boy and twin girls, age three.

For better than an hour Sabrina puttered around the cabin, listening to the rip of Travis' saws on the hill crest. Finally she went to the timber and sat down on a stump to watch the operation. Pierre Menard was doing the falling, limbing and bucking into sixteen foot lengths. One of Bond's boys handled the team, the first three-abreast harnessing she had ever seen. The Bond boy skidded the logs in pairs to the saw pit, where they were worked onto the ways, held in a large A frame and there ripped. A large pit had been dug and over it a stout scaffolding erected. Travis, taking the dirtiest job for himself, stayed in the pit, handling the huge two-man saw with one arm. Priam Thomas was on the top end, straddling the log to be ripped. The pit was a hot, dirty place. Travis was stripped to the waist, sawdust like tan snow on his back and in his hair. Sweat ran in streaks down his sides, and although he could only use one arm, he sawed for thirty minutes before pausing, and this was only walking to the other end to start another cut.

They squared each log, then ripped it into planks, four by twelves. Already a stack was growing on the downhill side of the saw pit. The work was slow, brutal, and Sabrina found it tiring to even watch. Travis never came out of the pit and her father glanced at her several times, but neither stopped nor spoke.

The view of the settlement from the sawyer camp was magnificent. She could even see St. Louis sprawled on the other shore. On the road leading into the settlement a horse drawn wagon came on slowly. She could see someone on the seat and two men walked beside the team. Then the wagon stopped at one of the French farm houses and Sabrina lost interest.

Toward evening she went back to the cabin. She gathered the children, saw that they were washed, and began the evening meal. Her father and Benjamin Travis came down after dark, washed at the creek with a lot of sputtering and water splashing, then came in and sat at the table.

Sabrina said nothing until their appetites were blunted and the children had scampered off to play. Then she sat down, crossed her arms and said, "I went to Jethro Sweet's store today. He refused to sell to me."

Priam Thomas had been crushing tobacco into his pipe. He stopped and looked at Sabrina. Travis, who sat at the table across from her, stopped exercising the fingers of his broken arm. Sabrina looked from one to the other, and said, "Well, why are you gawkin'? Didn't you hear what I said?"

"We heard," Priam Thomas said.

"What'd you expect?" Travis asked. "You know Jethro'n me's feudin'. You can't do business with that fella. Knew it the first time I ever talked to him."

"He says your money's no good. He means not to sell to those who're spending your wages."

"Figures," Travis said with no alarm. He looked at Sabrina. "Did Jethro say anythin' about me comin' to do your buyin'?"

"That's it exactly! They mean to lay for you. Him and Fountainbleau."

"They'll have a long wait," Travis said. "I'm too busy to go shoot the Sweets. Expect to lay the sill logs of the fort next week an' set the poles for the shot tower."

"He challenged you!" Sabrina said. "Are you going to let it lay?"

"Why not?" Travis said. "Sabrina, if I'd stop to fight every bear that's growled at me in the bushes, I'd be fightin' 'em yet."

For a moment Sabrina could only stare. Then she colored deeply. *What did I expect of him*, she wondered. *You took him for granted and that was a mistake*. She glanced at Ben Travis and found him studying her intently. For a moment she had the shocked notion that he knew what she was thinking.

Travis said, "If you're *askin'* me to go now —"

"I'm not askin' you anything!" Sabrina snapped.

"All right," Travis said, as if it didn't matter to him one way or the other. "You're so dead set on runnin' your own business, then go ahead an' run it."

174

The children came streaming into the house, all noise and energy. Sabrina got up from the table and put them to bed. She left the bedroom door ajar and Travis could hear her leading them in prayers.

Priam Thomas spoke softly. "She wanted to ask you, you fool. Did you have to make it impossible for her? You know how proud she is."

"That pride'll kill a man sooner or later," Travis said. "It's been my observation that if a man wants somethin' bad enough, he'll ask anyway."

"You don't know her," Thomas said. He scrubbed the back of his neck with his hand. "All that talk about Jethro not lettin' folks buy with your money worries me some, Ben. What you goin' to do about it?"

"I've been thinkin' on somethin'. Is Shawnee Blanc around?"

"He's never far," Thomas said. He turned his head and yelled, "Shawnee! You heathen, git in here!"

Shawnee Blanc appeared almost instantly. He stood just inside the door, the filthy blanket wrapped around him. Travis said, "Shawnee, can you get through Sac and Fox country?"

"Uh," Shawnee Blanc said. "Three, maybe four days."

"To the fort on the big water," Travis said. "Fort Dearborn."

"Uh, five day."

"Got somethin' I want you to do, Shawnee Blanc," Travis said. He went to the wood box and found a small shingle. He shaved it smooth with his knife, holding it down with his foot while he worked. Then he

175

gave it to Priam Thomas. "Cain't write with my arm," he said. "This is to Cap'n Pressly."

Thomas used a soft lead bullet, which left a nice legible mark on the pale wood. He looked at Travis for the words.

"Tell him we need two boat loads of supplies in two weeks. Sweet's closed us out. Tell him we got to have the goods by then or there never will be a fort."

Thomas finished the note and gave the shingle to Shawnee Blanc.

"Git," Travis said, "an' don't let them Sac and Fox get your hair."

"I go," Shawnee Blanc said and disappeared out the door as Sabrina came from the bedroom. She sent an inquiring glance after the Indian. Thomas got up to knock out his pipe and place it on the mantle.

"Where's Shawnee Blanc going?" she asked.

"Errand," Travis said. "He'll be back in a few days."

Thomas took his rifle from its place behind the door. "Goin' for a walk along the creek," he said. "Don't wait up for me."

He closed the door behind him.

Sabrina turned to the spider and the hanging coffee pot. She poured a cup and set it before Travis. "I'd be obliged if you'd send Pa home tomorrow to plow." Her voice was soft.

Benjamin Travis hid his smile behind the raised cup. "All right," he said. "Sabrina, you didn't choke on that, did you? Was it so hard to ask?"

"Yes," she said, "it was hard. I've been going over it all day, looking for a way. I'm not used to asking a man

176

for anything. You don't make it easier with your bossy ways, either."

"I expect I don't," Travis said. He finished his coffee and went out, going directly to his sawyer camp. He kept thinking about Priam Thomas and how hard he worked all day and how tired he was each night. And it struck Travis as strange that a man would take a walk when he wanted to go to bed. Priam Thomas was not the same man that Travis had first met on the bank of the Ohio. Since the fight with Jacques Fountainbleau, the old man moved with more definition, spoke with more assurance. He had discovered his own value, Travis decided, and picked up his rifle from the half-cabin before walking downhill to the settlement.

There were a few scattered lights among the settler's cabins. In Sweet's store, wall candles brightened the fleshed hide windows near the open door. Travis mounted the long porch without sound. From inside he could hear Jethro Sweet's bold rumble, and Priam Thomas talking back, but not to Sweet. There was a third man present, a deep-voiced man who spoke with great certainty.

Travis left the porch and went around the building to the rear entrance. The back of the store was one black shadow. Travis walked carefully to avoid tripping. He tried the door and found it barred. Then he reached up and slit one of the bullhide windows with his knife, carefully holding the stiff edges aside with his shoulder to keep it from making a crackling sound. With the knife between his teeth he went in, pulling himself up and over. Then he reached through and got his rifle.

Through a closed door he could hear Priam Thomas making threats against the Sweets and all their ancestors. He moved cautiously across this store room and lifted the latch string, feeling the bar on the other side give, free itself from the lock notch. He cracked the door and found himself facing the main room, dim now with candlelight. The shadow-shape of Jacques Fountainbleau stood near the counter and Travis looked past him to Sweet and Thomas.

The third man was bearded and heavy through the shoulders. He had a square face and a square way of standing when he talked to a man. There was a dumb animal patience in his eyes and in his voice, when he said, "Again I say I have no quarrel with you."

"You're his kin, ain't you?" Jethro asked this. He was holding Thomas' rifle and when Thomas turned his head slightly, candlelight fell on his face, and the bruised mouth where Jethro's fist had struck him.

The third man sighed. "Can't you understand, I have no quarrel." He looked at Thomas and there was neither pity nor understanding in the glance. "Tell this man about me, Priam. I've traveled hard and fast, and now that I'm here I'll brook no nonsense from any man."

"Git the hell out of here, Able," Priam said. "Consarn your hide, take a man's advice for once in your life. You're buttin' your nose in where it ain't wanted."

"I'll let Sabrina tell me that," Able Kane said. He took a wrinkled paper from his pocket and shook it in Priam Thomas' face. "A man handed me this nearly two months ago. Is this all there is left? Is this all a man leaves behind, passed from hand to hand like a common dollar?" He shook his head slowly like a man will when he tries hard to understand something beyond his power. "The woman owes me an explanation, Thomas. I've come to hear it."

"Get out of here," Jethro said. "Thomas an' me's got personal business to attend to. You're interferin'."

"He knows where she is," Able Kane said. "He'll come with me."

Travis stood along the ink black wall no more than twenty feet from them. Fountainbleau was three paces ahead, leaning on the counter, absorbed with this small drama. Ben Travis leaned his rifle against several stacked feed bags and moved up to Fountainbleau without making a sound. Suddenly he whipped his left arm around the Frenchman's throat, and when Fountainbleau made a strangling sound and began to fight, Travis raised a knee to the small of his back and bore him to the floor. Fountainbleau's thrashing feet upset some stacked goods, bringing it down with a clatter.

Jethro, startled, flipped his head toward the sound. With the deep shadows and the counter blocking his vision, he was blind. And he dared not leave Priam Thomas so he stood there stupidly while Ben Travis strangled Fountainbleau unconscious.

Able Kane turned his head toward the back of the room but made no move. He stood there completely isolated in mind and if the building had collapsed around him he would have waited until the dust

179

cleared, then returned to his original, small point. He was that kind of a man, tackling only one thing at a time and never putting it down until he was finished with it.

"Frenchy!" Jethro yelled. "What the hell you doin'? Damn you, answer me!"

"He can't," Travis said and stood up so that Jethro Sweet could see him. He had his rifle pointed with casual attention.

Able Kane asked, "Who is this man?"

Sweet grunted in surprise and candlelight flickered in the whites of his eyes. He held Thomas' rifle and the urge to raise it was strong, but the urge to go on living was stronger so he kept it pointed to the floor.

"I asked you," Able Kane repeated, "who that man —"

"Shut your mouth!" Jethro snapped.

Kane's face turned stony. "I take that talk from no —"

Jethro hit him, a back handed blow that lifted Kane off his feet and propelled him backward halfway to the door. Kane slowly raised a hand, wiped the blood from his mouth and started forward again, almost ponderously.

"For Christ's sake!" Thomas shouted. "This ain't Pennsylvania; he'll kill you!"

"I let no man lay hands on me," Kane said.

Thomas knew what he had to do and did it. He snatched his rifle from Jethro Sweet and said, "Let's get what Sabrina needs and get out of here before I have to kill somebody."

180

"Let's just get," Travis said. "Didn't mean to interfere, Jethro, but you can see I had to. Thomas acted plumb foolish." He came around the counter, nudging Priam Thomas. "Go on, I'll be right along."

"By Jingo, Sabrina needs goods!" He looked oddly at Travis. "Didn't you hear me? What's ailin' you, Ben?"

"Nothin'," Travis said. "Thomas, Jethro's goin' to forget this little misunderstandin', but if I let you take Sabrina's wants, there'd be some shootin' over it. Ain't that right, Jethro?"

"You goddamn bet!" Jethro said.

"Who is this man?" Kane asked.

"Shut up," Thomas said wearily. "Git outside and wait."

"Now I —"

Thomas whirled on him, a very angry man. "In the name of God, do as you're told, you damn fool!"

There was stunned disbelief on Able Kane's face. Travis said, "Hell, if he wants to keep Jethro company, let him." He moved past Thomas and stepped out the door, Thomas following close behind. Travis stepped off the porch and put fifty yards of darkness between himself and the store. He could hear Able Kane plodding along behind, his steps heavy and methodical.

Travis stopped and Thomas began to grumble. "It beats me all holler why you wouldn't help yourself, Ben. I was meanin' to pay for the goods, if that's what you were thinkin'."

"Wasn't that," Travis began but Able Kane pushed his big voice in, cutting him off.

"I'm not a man to stand for words. I don't know you, but I'll stand for no words. Ask Thomas, he's known me twenty years."

"What's there to know about you?" Travis asked. "A man can see it all in one look."

Kane swayed like a wind-rocked tree. His body was stiff with resentment. "You're hurt now," Kane said flatly, "but I'll remember what you said." He looked at Thomas. "Show me where Sabrina Kane lives, Thomas. I've come far for words with her."

"They'll wait until morning," Thomas said.

"I didn't come to be put off," Kane said. "It's my brother she married. It's me she'll answer to for his dyin'."

"Then she'll answer in the morning," Thomas said. "If she's awake when I get home I'll tell her you're here. If she's asleep, it'll wait until mornin'."

"Things have changed you," Kane said solemnly. "You were once a kind man, Thomas." He turned away, his heavy boots plodding with each step.

Thomas turned to watch him leave. "Never ever expected to see him again. He was close to his brother, Ben. And he wanted Sabrina for himself." He shook his head. "Don't like this, Ben. A couple of months ago I'd have welcomed Able; he's a steady man, like an ox. But now I don't need him. Sabrina don't need him."

"That's for her to decide," Travis said. "Thomas, in case you tell Sabrina about this, leave me plum to hell an' gone out of it. I wasn't at the Sweets, you understand? See that this fella don't shoot his mouth off, either."

182

Thomas frowned. "What's eatin' you, Ben? What you up to?"

"Sabrina's made it plain that she don't want my help."

"That's a woman's lie," Thomas said quickly. "If you wasn't so blind —"

"I know what she wants," Travis said, "but she's got to know without me convincin' her. Thomas, one of these days she's goin' to admit to herself that she really needs a man, but *she's* got to admit it. A man'll never talk her into believin' it."

"You're her man," Thomas insisted. "You been her man since you come here."

"What about Able Kane? He's got ideas along that line."

"You're her man," Thomas repeated.

Travis shook his head. "She'll have to show me. She'll have to make it plain, Thomas. Remember what I said. And stay home tomorrow to plow. She asked."

"All right," Thomas muttered. "Sure hope you know what you're doin'. She don't and I sure as hell don't."

Travis smiled and watched him amble off, grumbling to the night.

CHAPTER
EIGHT

Priam Thomas broke a lifetime habit by leaving his bed an hour before dawn, and before the first heralding light of day began to thin out the darkness he came off the hill from Benjamin Travis' sawyer camp, leading a horse. He hitched the team to the plow and was breaking his fourth furrow when Able Kane walked across the flats toward him.

In the daylight, Kane looked older than his thirty-two years. His face was lined, a mixture of too much trouble and never enough money, although he was a man of frugal habits. He had brown hair worn touching his collar and his cheeks were whiskered, although his chin was clean-shaven.

He stopped and looked at Sabrina's cabin. "Is she there?" Thomas nodded. "You could have told me last night, Thomas."

"I could have, but you'd just have stuck your nose in where you ain't wanted."

Intolerance made a flat shine in Kane's eyes. "I've always made you welcome in my home, Thomas." He looked again at Sabrina's doorway and this time she came out, looked toward her father, then remained absolutely motionless. Able Kane turned slowly and

184

walked with measured deliberation toward her. She waited in the doorway and when he approached, he took off his felt hat and held it in his hands.

When they went inside, Priam Thomas wrapped the reins around the plow handle and washed his hands at the creek before going inside. Able Kane was already seated at the table, and the children gave him cold, suspicious stares which he ignored with a stolidness that was more animal than human.

Thomas sat down and Jenner, who was at that age where he saw and heard everything he was not supposed to, said, "You hurt your face, Gran'pa?"

Sabrina turned from the fire and came over to examine her father's face in the light streaming through the open door. "What *did* happen to your face?"

Able Kane opened his mouth to speak, but Thomas said, "By God, this is my house, I'll tell it." He glanced at Sabrina. "I fell in the creek last night."

She meant to question him further but from his expression realized that he would say no more. She put the food on the table and began to eat. Able Kane, however, left his wooden knife and spoon lie.

"I'll speak of my brother now," he said.

Thomas spoke around a mouthful of food. "Speak, we're listenin'."

Kane frowned. "I'll thank you to stop eatin' when I talk of the dead." His glance went to Sabrina, intolerant, unforgiving. "You're not grievin', it seems. I suspected it when a man handed me this." He reached inside his shirt and tossed it on the table.

"I don't have black to wear," Sabrina said. "But you're wrong, Able; I miss him. And I'll never forget him."

Benjamin Travis chose that time to approach the cabin, whistling a bright French hunting song. He washed before entering, and took his place at the end of the table, a place reserved for the head of the family.

Able Kane's eyes were polished agates as he regarded Travis. "You're younger than I thought," he said.

Travis helped himself to the sidemeat and pap, and then gave Kane a quick glance. Bushrod was three and his spirits were almost uncontrollable. His nonsense infected Mary until they were both giggling. Sabrina would have interfered but Travis held up his hand and disciplined them with a fine blend of sternness and understanding.

Looking from Travis to Sabrina, then back to Travis, Able Kane said, "Are you properly wed?"

"Now see here —" Thomas began.

"I was not speaking to you," Kane said. He turned his attention back to Benjamin Travis. "Miz Kane is my sister-in-law, and it beholds me to look after her."

Travis exhibited some amusement. "Tell you, friend, I can't seem to make up my mind whether you're dumb or just a damn fool. Sabrina don't need lookin' after." He cut his sidemeat and took a spoonful of mush. "What's your business, besides pryin' into other people's?"

Placing his hands flat on the table, Able Kane said, "A man who sits at the head of the table rules a home. I'll ask you again. Be you and Sabrina properly wed?"

186

"I've heard enough of this," Sabrina snapped. She stood up and pointed to the door. "Get out, Able. This is my house and you're making yourself unwelcome here."

"I asked," he said, "because it's my right. I've my due comin'. The wagon belongs to me; Cadmus had nothing of his own."

"Then take the wagon and get out," Sabrina said. "What'd you come here for anyway?" She picked up the letter she had written. "You must have started from Pennsylvania before I wrote this. Why?"

Able Kane shook his head and moved to the door. "I'll come for the wagon later," he said and went out.

Thomas looked at Travis and warned him with his eyes not to speak. Sabrina wheeled away from the table, went into the bedroom and closed the door.

"Ain't there no give in the man?" Travis asked. "He gets his mind locked onto somethin' an' acts like nothin' can shake him loose."

"Tell you somethin'," Thomas said. "A few years back Able decided to marry Sabrina when she come twenty. She turned him down but it seems he's never got the notion out of his head. He can't seem to understand she meant it."

"Must have been hell married to his brother," Travis said.

"It was; I was there." Thomas scratched his whiskers. "Able owned everythin', the farm, the livestock. Cadmus worked for hand's wages. Fer a year we lived in the same house, with Able never sayin' nothin', just sittin' there, watchin' every move that went on. He never liked me none, but he put up with me 'cause I was Sabrina's pa. He's got his own set notions of what's right an' what's wrong. Nothin' can shake 'em. Some folks'd say Able Kane was an' upstandin' man. Never cheats anybody an' never gets cheated. Yesiree, a mighty predictable fella, Able is. A reg'lar pillar of the church, but somehow I never had a likin' fer pillars."

With that said Thomas went outside and began plowing again. Travis went back to his sawyer camp and by mid-morning his crew was snaking logs off the hill to be erected on the fort site. Four long poles were set upright and by noon the first part of the shot tower was completed; sawed planks were being hoisted to build the platform where a man would stand to dump the hot lead into the water tank which had yet to be built.

Sabrina's chores were endless. Occasionally she glanced out the door at her father and marveled at his labor. He plowed without pause and she tried to recall the time when he had worked this hard without being driven.

Then Mrs. Pillifrew and Mrs. Abram came for a visit. Sabrina was outside working a churn dasher. She wore a thin cotton dress because the day was hot and both these ladies frowned when the sun shone through the material, outlining Sabrina's legs.

"My," Mrs. Pillifrew said, "how nice you keep a place, Sabrina." Her eyes took in everything. She was a squat woman, old before her time. She had the annoying habit of brushing imaginary hair from her forehead.

"It was kind of you to come over," Sabrina said. She looked at the bundles each of the ladies carried, but made no inquiry.

"Lands, it was the least we could do after what Mr. Thomas did last night," Mrs. Abram said. She studied Sabrina's surprised expression. "You don't know?"

"No," Sabrina said and felt somewhat irked at her father's stubborn silence. Since his fight with Fountainbleau, strange forces had been released in the man and he had assumed a bull-headed rein over her and as yet she was unable to break it. He insisted upon conducting his affairs without consulting her and gave her no explanation for anything he did.

I can thank Ben Travis for teachin' him that, she thought.

"Well ain't that just like a man," Mrs. Pillifrew said. She bent forward and spoke confidentially. "He went to Jethro Sweet last night. Yes he did, Sabrina. I heard it from Mrs. Lockwood this morning. He went there for the goods you wanted. Land sake, but that was brave, wasn't it? He choked Mr. Fountainbleau nearly to death and stood right up to Jethro."

"Of course he didn't get the goods," Mrs. Abram said hurriedly, "but who cares about that? He showed Jethro he wasn't scared of him. I wish my Lige had that kind of git to him. We'd have better land. He'd tell the Sweets where to head in."

"I — I don't know what to say," Sabrina said. She understood now where her father picked up the facial bruises, but she found it hard to believe that he had faced Jethro Sweet and come back alive. Still, he had been acting strangely since he began associating with Benjamin Travis. She suddenly realized that she no longer knew her father. He had stepped out of the ring of predictability and was capable of new things.

Several other ladies began to arrive, all bearing something: flour, salt, spices, dried fruits, potatoes, vinegar; the very things Sabrina needed. She listened to their talk and put up with their judging glances. When they went away they'd have plenty to talk about and somehow she didn't care much whether they talked or not.

The talk drifted back to Priam Thomas and his heroics. A story repeated often enough seemed to grow and by the time the ladies left, Thomas was a one man army and only his innate kindness had stayed his hand and prevented him from burning the Sweet store to the ground.

Sabrina stood in the doorway and watched her father plow. She had to admit that he was plowing as straight a furrow as she had ever seen, and he gave no indication of pausing.

From someone in the village, Able Kane had borrowed an ox, and led the plodding beast toward Sabrina's cabin for his wagon. Watching them come on, she was surprised at how similar man and beast were; they both moved with an almost indestructible deliberation. Kane nodded to her before going around in back. A few minutes later he drove back toward the settlement, hunched on the seat, silent with his own solitary thoughts.

Ben Travis' entire crew was at the fort site, stacking lumber. They went back to the sawyer camp and when they didn't come down immediately, she walked through the heavy, mid-day heat to the timber. The huge ripsaw was silent, but she supposed this was because her father was not there to handle the top end. Yet the other men were there. She saw them at the fringe of the timber, squatting in the shade, eating.

Benjamin Travis was sitting near the saw pit; she saw his broad back above the slab pile. He was talking to someone and she walked toward him, supposing that he was with one of Shadrach Bond's boys. She came around the end of the slab pile and stopped.

Patience Eddy's laughter broke away to a fading giggle. She said, "Oh, I didn't see you, Sabrina."

Benjamin Travis turned his head quickly, a mild surprise in his eyes. Sabrina frowned and spoke to Patience Eddy. "I can see that you didn't." In a glance she saw the pewter bucket in which Patience had brought Travis' dinner. There was a piece of bread left, and some coffee. Travis had a cup in his hand.

"Patience thought I'd get hungry," he said. "You want to sit down?" He swept a place clean of sawdust.

"No," Sabrina said. "If you were hungry, you could have come down."

"I didn't mind bringin' it," Patience said quickly. She smiled at Ben Travis and touched his hand possessively. Sabrina puffed her cheeks in silent disgust.

"What did you want, Sabrina?" She thought she detected concealed humor in Travis' voice and this infuriated her.

"I didn't want anything," she said. The words sounded hollow and foolish and she regretted them immediately.

"You must have wanted somethin'," Travis said seriously. "It's pretty hot for a walk." His eyes dropped to her thin dress. "But then I guess you'd be cool enough." Patience Eddy cocked her head to one side and studied Sabrina, who colored deeply.

"I tell you I didn't want anything," Sabrina snapped. "I'm sorry I came up here and bothered you." She turned and went down the hill, her step quick and angry.

Occasionally during the afternoon Sabrina looked out and saw Travis with his men, working on the shot tower. The top platform was completed, along with the booms and tackle block for hauling up kettles full of hot lead. Some of the younger boys in the settlement were gathering rocks and mixing mortar for the large baking crucible where lead ore would be melted, mixed with arsenic for making rifle balls of all sizes.

Below the tower, Menard and his men fitted together planks for the water tank. When filled, the hot lead would be dropped and as soon as it hit the water, would explode into chilled, round pellets, which were then sorted as to caliber. In this manner one shot tower could serve an army, and for anyone planning a campaign, as Captain Pressly was doing, such a tower was a must.

When the sun went down the men quit. Thomas took the horse back to Travis' sawyer camp and met him at the cabin door. Both washed and took their place at the table, Travis at the head.

Sabrina said nothing. When she set the table she banged Travis' plate and cup. Even the children suspected that something was wrong for they refrained from their childish foolishness.

During the meal, Travis asked, "Get the plowin' done?"

"Two acres," Thomas said. "That enough, Sabrina?"

"Yes, thanks."

"Didn't do it for thanks," Thomas said pointedly. "I did it because it was man's work and a man had to do it." Sabrina snorted and turned to the fireplace. Thomas winked at Benjamin Travis. "You hear about my trouble last night, Ben?"

"Some. Beats me how it got around so fast."

"I mentioned it to Lockwood on my way home," Thomas said.

"You better stay away from Jethro," Travis advised. "Sabrina, you better not go back there either. We'll get supplies without goin' to the Sweets."

She faced him quickly. "Are you telling me what to do now?"

"No I ain't, but we got an uneasy peace with the Sweets. Lord knows Jethro'll come gunnin' when we start puttin' up the fort walls in a few days. Time enough then to fight him."

"I have no intention of crossin' them," Sabrina said. "They leave me alone, I'll leave them alone."

This was, Travis realized, the best assurance he would get from her and he accepted another cup of coffee. His arm was healing rapidly and he no longer wore it in a sling, although it was still splinted. He was beginning to get some use of the hand and to strengthen it, lifted the coffee cup although the effort caused him some discomfort.

The night was warmed by the leftover heat of the dead sun and Thomas took the children over to see the shot tower. Sabrina cleared the table and washed the dishes in a small wooden tub.

Finally she said, "Is there anything wrong with my meals?"

"Why, no. You're a good cook, Sabrina."

"A quarter is too much for two meals," she said. She kept her back to him, working as she talked. "It's been botherin' me, chargin' you so much."

He studied her back, his eyes bright with pleasure. But he kept it out of his voice. "I guess I could pay you less."

"I suppose you could," she said shortly and then said no more.

Travis finished his coffee and then pushed his chair back from the table. He turned his head when Able Kane's heavy footfalls approached the door. Kane paused, knocked, then entered, frowning briefly at Travis.

When Travis stood up, Able Kane said, "Don't leave on my account."

"I wasn't," Travis said and went out.

Kane stood uncertainly in the room's center, his hat aimlessly moved between his fingers.

"Are you hungry?" Sabrina asked.

The pause said he was, but his pride made him deny this. "I've had a sufficiency, thanks."

"Have some coffee," she said and filled a clean cup.

Kane sat with it between his big hands. "These were my mother's," he said. "Cadmus had no respect for things that didn't belong to him."

Quite angry, Sabrina whirled. "Do you want them, too? If you do, take them and git!"

Able Kane straightened, a flat surprise in his eyes. "I'd not take them," he said slowly. "It was my intention to offer you all I have, as I offered it once before."

"And what would you get in return?" Sabrina asked.

He dropped his eyes to the table top. "A man seeks a fair bargain in all things," he said. "I'd expect you to put aside your foolish notions and settle yourself to a wife's duties. I'd want sons to help me with my work. I'm not a mean man, Sabrina. You know I'd not harm you."

The simplicity of the man softened her resentment. "No," she said softly, "you're a good man, Able. But a good man isn't what I want. I — I don't know what I want, Able. But I'm sure it isn't you."

He nodded slowly, then rose, leaving the coffee untouched. "I'll wait," he said. "You'll come to your senses."

She stared after him long after he walked out the door. Then she heard her father and the children coming and made herself busy. After the children had been hustled off to bed, Thomas said, "Seen Able leavin'. What'd he want?"

"The same thing."

"Uh," Thomas said. "He don't change much, does he?"

"Neither do I," Sabrina said. "I gave him the same answer."

The next morning, when Benjamin Travis appeared for his breakfast, Sabrina handed him a cloth tied into a sack. "I made your dinner," she said matter-of-factly. "A quarter's too much for two meals."

She turned before he could thank her. When he and Thomas left for work, he could hear her in the lean-to, setting Jenner to his milking.

Halfway to the sawyer camp, Priam Thomas said, "You know why she made you that dinner, don't you?"

"Yes," Travis said. "Now I got to eat two."

All that day Travis and his men snaked logs off the hill to the fort and dropped them into place. Toward mid-afternoon the long walls were three logs high.

Then Pierre Menard, who was working on the shot tower, called and pointed to the river. Four boats worked their way out of the current, rowing toward the shore where Travis waited. He recognized Captain Pressly. Standing behind the captain was Shawnee Blanc, wearing a huge grin.

Travis' men left their work and splashed into the water, taking the ropes flung to them. Together they helped pull the four boats half on shore. Pressly hopped down and stood by Travis while the soldiers began unloading.

Two of the boats held ore to feed the furnace and shot tower. The other two were low with the weight of supplies.

196

"You made a quick trip, Cap'n," Travis said.

"I need this fort," Pressly said. "There was a pretty stiff Indian fight near Rock Island last week. That's Black Hawk's country and he means to defend it. The way the settlers are coming in, they'll be pushing the Sac and Fox south before spring. When that happens the whole river will be a battle ground."

"Seems that talkin' peace is a lot easier than fightin'," Travis said.

"Agreed. And there are men in Kaskaskia that are working on it," Pressly said. "There's a move on to get Illinois admitted to statehood, Ben. That'll be the day. We'll have government backing then and make a permanent peace." He turned and looked at the shot tower and building. "You're making time here. Any trouble from Jethro Sweet?"

"No," Travis said. "Don't expect any yet."

"How's that?"

"You want to rob a trap, Cap'n, then wait until somethin's caught. Jethro's sittin' on his porch, watchin'. When we shingle the roof, he'll make his fight. Was he to burn it then we'd have to build it all over and I guess he figures we wouldn't go to the trouble."

"Don't let him burn it," Pressly said. "Those supplies are all I can spare."

"How's about campin' some of your sojers here?" Travis asked. "We can't sleep with our eyes open all the time, Cap'n."

"I'll leave Sergeant Muldoon and ten men," Pressly said. "And I'll have a hard time explaining that when I get back."

When the boats were unloaded, Pressly shoved off, leaving Sergeant Muldoon and ten regulars behind.

For the next three days, Benjamin Travis worked his men endlessly, but the walls went up, the joists went into place, and the gable was fitted.

Sabrina began planting her garden, now that Shawnee Blanc was there to help her. She set out straight rows of corn, pumpkins, peas, beans and melons, knowing that she was planting late and that an early frost would kill everything. But she had little choice.

The supplies delivered by Captain Pressly were stored in the newly erected fort and guarded day and night by the soldiers. Instead of paying his men in Spanish dollars, Travis set up records, bought the supplies and paid his men in usable goods.

Jethro Sweet spent most of his time on the porch of his store, observing the activity and trying to think of some way to beat Benjamin Travis.

With the crops planted, the men in the settlement left field tending to their wives and began working at Travis' sawyer camp. In spite of the terrific amount of timber necessary to build the fort, Travis' pile of sawed lumber grew rapidly and women began to nag at their husbands for a plank floor.

This was something Benjamin Travis had never considered before, a woman's influence on the frontier. A man was content with a dirt floor and a rag candle, but a woman wanted things a little better. Left to the men, a home would never be much more than four walls and a roof that didn't leak. But with a woman

198

pushing him, a man acquired glass for the windows, hardware for the doors, and if the woman kept up long enough, sawed lumber to build a proper house.

Benjamin Travis became aware of this when men came to his camp for lumber, offering in trade crops, furs, labor, anything that had a swapping value.

To Sabrina, it seemed that life in Illinois Town had suddenly taken on a new tempo; everyone seemed to be building something, a new shed, a new house. Even Lige Abram put together a forge and suddenly became so busy that he worked from sunup to sundown. Able Kane, never a man to sit idle when there was something to be done, bought an ox and hired out his wagon to Benjamin Travis. All day long he moved through the village, hauling lumber down the hill and hauling grain or trade into the fort, where Sergeant Muldoon stored it and applied proper credit.

From her cabin, Sabrina watched this. Often her glance went to the timber's fringe where Travis had his saw camp. She was carrying water from the creek to the house when she looked up the hill and saw Patience Eddy going home, pewter bucket swinging gaily. A frown marred the smoothness of her forehead and her full lips pursed thoughtfully. That night she waited until Benjamin had finished his supper, then asked, "How was the dinner I made today?"

"Fine," he said.

"What did Patience Eddy bring you?"

"Hamhock," he said. When she turned away from him, Ben Travis slapped his hand on the table and

199

roared, "By Jingo, it's gettin' so's a fella has to justify everythin' he does!"

The children looked at him round-eyed. Priam Thomas raised his head sharply. Sabrina had been stirring something over the fire and now she flung the spoon into the pot and turned to him, her eyes angry. "I don't care what you do, Benjamin Travis! Is that clear?" She waved her arms. "If you want to sit and listen to her simper, then you go right ahead!"

"Now wait a min —" Priam Thomas began.

"Oh, shut your mouth!" She looked to be on the verge of tears. "You ought to look at yourself, Ben Travis; it's enough to make a body sick at the stomach. She leans like a sick cat against a hot brick and you like it."

"Didn't say I did and I didn't say I didn't," Travis said, wondering what the hell he was defending himself for. "It seems that you're gettin' in a plaguey hobble over somethin' you don't care about," Travis said seriously. He stood up carefully; she was the kind of a spitfire who'd go at a man with her fists and he knew it. "As a matter of fact now, I kind of like Patience. I ain't gettin' any younger and she's a sweet notioned little thing that I ought to marry up with before someone else gets the idea."

Sabrina's mouth became a surprised, shocked O and Travis went out without another word, leaving her with her fading anger.

Priam Thomas cleared his throat and said, "I'm about to speak an' if you tell me to shut my mouth once more I'll hide your bottom with a stave." He

200

spoke with such unexpected seriousness that she could only stare. "Seems to me you've drove Ben into somethin' by showin' him what a he-man you are."

"I've showed him he's a fool!"

"Ain't your business to show him anythin'," Thomas said. "Why don't you be honest with yourself, Sabrina? You want him here in this house, 'cause it's his house, his plannin' an' you know damn well he built it thinkin' of you. Why don't you swallow that foolish pride and go up to his camp?"

"I can't," she said softly, hopelessly. "I can't because he wouldn't want me to be like that." She clasped her hands together. "In Kaskaskia he spoke harsh to me, the night he brought Bushrod. Later you said that if he was to ever let it pass he wouldn't mention it again. He never has. That's the way I am; he knows that." She suddenly struck her fist against her palm. "Papa, we never could seem to meet. Now I guess it's too late. Ben ain't a man to go back once he's said somethin'."

"I guess you're right there," Thomas said. "Looks like your cake all turned to dough again while you was makin' up your mind about him." He picked up his rifle and started out.

"Where are you going?"

"Bond's. There's a meetin'."

"Meetin'? What about?"

"Makin' Illinois Town into a regular town with a mayor and someone to enforce the laws." He shouldered his rifle and struck off down the creek.

Sabrina heated water and called Jenner in for his bath. He was that age when 'boy' is synonymous with 'dirt' and protested strongly when the two had to be separated by soap and water. After he was hustled off to bed Sabrina popped Bushrod and Mary in the tub, scrubbed them clean and tucked them in. Afterward she took her own bath, cleaned up the spilled water, and went outside to sit on the stoop. Frogs sang bass along the creek and the katydids filled the night with their racket.

Someone passed through the patch of wild mint south of the cabin; she could smell the strong flavors and it reminded her of her childhood when she would walk through the tomato patch just to wake the strong flavors.

Steps approaching made her turn her head as Able Kane came from the darkness and squatted. "I've given you time," he said. "You can't say that I've been unfair."

"You're never unfair, Able."

"I'm willing to forget," Able Kane said. "Was you to wed me I'd never mention what's past. I'd be a good husband, Sabrina. Why don't you believe me?"

"I believe you," she said softly. "Able, I've never thought that you weren't good enough, but maybe I'm not. Like Pa says, I've got some foolish notions. I'd rag you, Able; I don't want to do that."

"We all have to learn our place," he said. "Think on it." He stood up and walked away.

. . . Learn her place . . . was that the answer? Why was it she had to change men? She had tried to change Cadmus and Ben Travis. And Travis had changed. The laughter was gone.

She got up and went into the bedroom and lay on the bed, staring at the dark ceiling. She heard her father come home very late; a few moments later the house was silent. Sabrina never knew when she drifted off, but Priam Thomas' coughing woke her before dawn.

He had already stoked the fire and she began breakfast. Without thinking she set a place for Benjamin Travis, but when she served the meal he had not yet arrived. Priam Thomas said, "He won't be down."

"Did he say that?"

"He didn't have to," Thomas said. Shawnee Blanc took his food outside and Thomas made a quick job of the grits and pork. Her father, she decided, was getting more like Ben Travis every day; when a thing was done neither believed in talking it to death afterward.

Thomas took his rifle and went up the hill to the sawyer camp, arriving a few minutes before the others. He found Travis alone and said, "You mean what you said last night, Ben?"

"I said it, didn't I?" He sounded angry.

"Yeah," Thomas muttered. "That's what's worryin' me."

He didn't have time to worry long, for the day began with Able Kane arriving with his wagon. A load of sawed lumber was loaded and Kane drove away. His frequent trips up and down the hill were wearing a road from the saw camp to the settlement.

Kane drove past Lockwood's place and on toward the Eddy's. Patience was in the yard, making soap. Kane stopped and said, "Here's the planks your pa wanted."

"He's in the field, I'll get him."

"Time's money," Kane said without humor.

Patience dried her hands and went around the side of the cabin, toward the ten acre corn patch. Able Kane sat on his load of lumber, his big hands on his knees, as patient as a statue. He watched a small band of Indians emerge from a thicket a hundred yards down stream and a small shiver of apprehension went through him. He turned for a look in the other direction and saw the Eddys working their field. He wondered if he should call to them but decided against it.

He could hear the Indians talking now, guttural mumblings as they approached the cabin. They saw him and raised a hand in friendly greeting, scattering somewhat upon entering the yard. All Indians possess a childlike curiosity and one dumped over the empty churn to examine it.

Able Kane said, "Here there," and got down from the wagon.

Another Indian peered into the smokehouse while yet another went into the lean-to barn and scattered harness on the floor.

"You get out of there," Kane said. "Mind what I say now; that's another man's property."

One of the Indians grinned and went inside the cabin. Able Kane stood flat-footed, wondering whether it was his place to follow, and decided that it was. He could smell the rankness of unwashed flesh and the rancid grease in the Indian's hair. The Indian was dipping his fingers into everything, and laughed when he found the brown sugar.

"I spoke," Kane said. "Put that down!"

The Indian neither understood nor wanted to. He dumped some of the sugar into a hide sack and began his rummaging all over again. Able Kane looked around the room and his glance fell on the long-barreled fusil leaning against the door. Without hesitation he picked up the gun and cocked it.

Surprised, the Indian turned. He had recognized the clicking hammer and now his eyes studied Kane with a flat expression. He took a step toward him, probably to leave, but Able Kane didn't wait to find out.

He pulled the trigger.

The Indian cried out, clapped a hand to the fountain on his breast and fell, upsetting the table and splintering a chair. For an instant Able Kane stared at the fallen man, then whirled to slam the door and shoot the oak bar home.

Immediately the Indians began battering the door with the butts of their trade muskets, rattling it against the frame, stretching the heavy hide hinges.

Then someone outside fired a shot and a body sagged against the door, scraping as it slid to the ground. The Indians departed in a shower of shrill yells. Another shot was fired, then another . . .

Working nearly a mile away, Ninian Lockwood heard the shot. He was in his field and he raised his head to see where it had come from. Then he saw the Eddys running toward their cabin, and the Indians trying to get in. There were two more shots; the Eddys fired them. Two Indians fell. He stood there as the powder-smoke rose in puffy clouds, slowly drifting away. When he saw the Indians break away from the Eddy place and start upstream, he launched into a run.

His own cabin was directly in their path.

Lockwood flung his hoe away and yelled for his wife to get the children inside.

And that was what Benjamin Travis heard, that one long, anguished yell. He came off the scaffolding with Thomas. "Trouble," Thomas said and pointed to Lockwood's cabin. The Indians were approaching it at a run and from where Travis stood, he knew they would beat Lockwood to the door.

"Get my gun!" Travis shouted and started downhill like a deer, running with great leaps and bounds. Behind him, Priam Thomas was shouting to the others, urging them to join Travis. An instant later all were running toward Lockwood's place, but the fight had already begun . . .

Lockwood's wife ran out and an Indian grabbed her, smashed her skull with his tomahawk, snatched the baby from her arms and broke its back across the chopping block. One of the Lockwood girls, a slender blonde of twelve, ran toward her mother, screaming. Another Indian lifted his trade musket and at point blank range put a ball through her chest. She fell back, hands flailing aimlessly while life died in her eyes.

Lockwood cried out like a wounded animal and jumped the nearest Indian. The oldest boy slammed the cabin door and barred it, then stood before it with a musket. He shot one Indian through the buttocks and sent him howling, but another threw a hatchet, catching him in the throat. He died there by the door.

Lockwood and the Indian struck at the same time with their knives, each inflicting a terrible wound. Lockwood took the Indian's knife hilt deep in the chest, then coughed blood in the Indian's face. Blood streamed from the copper-hued neck and Lockwood pulled his knife free. They began to circle each other, both seemingly unaware that each was mortally wounded. Someone racing down the hill with Ben Travis paused to fire a shot and an Indian fell, but Lockwood ignored everything but the enemy.

They closed again, knives slashing. He ripped out the Indian's left eye and took another slash in the breast. Yawning flesh gushed blood. Arms around each other they struck and swayed and struck again, neither trying to fend off the other.

Lockwood's knife had severed the cords of the Indian's arm and laid open his face from eye to chin. But the Indian rallied enough to plunge his knife outward as he fell. Ninian Lockwood collapsed on top of him, dead.

Only two Indians remained and they fled as Thomas and the others arrived. Suddenly Thomas let out a hoarse cry and pointed.

The two Indians were running toward Sabrina Kane's cabin. Travis snatched his rifle from Thomas' petrified hand and struck out as fast as he could run.

CHAPTER
NINE

Looking out her doorway, Sabrina Kane found herself the unwilling witness to the capsuled horror of Lockwood's murder, and the massacre of his wife and three children. The sudden savagery with which the Indians struck had a mesmerizing effect so that she was unable to move or call out. One moment they had been peacefully approaching the Eddy place, and in the next they were transformed into howling fury, leaving a trail of dead behind them. When the Indians ran toward her own cabin, sudden fear provided the stimulus to overcome her paralysis.

Whirling inside she slammed the door and bolted it. The children were in the bedroom, stuffing a rag doll, and she closed that door too, sorry now that she had never put a latch on it for then she could have poked the string through the hole and in that way bought a few more moments of time for them. After witnessing the slaughter at Lockwoods she could only ask that the end come swiftly.

Then the Indians were in her yard, yelling and whooping.

The children in the bedroom heard this and Jenner tried to open the door. Sabrina pulled against his small strength, keeping it shut. "Stay there!" she shouted. "Jenner, do you hear?"

"Yes, Ma."

"Pile something against it," she begged. "Hurry like a good boy!"

As the Indians began to hammer at her door she heard Jenner dragging the huge chest across the floor. The door rattled as the Indians vented their fury at it. Sabrina backed away and stood by the table. She was unarmed. Her father had taken the rifle with him when he went to Travis' sawyer camp because he had seen a deer there and had a yearning for fresh venison. Shawnee Blanc had gone out before daylight to hunt wild turkeys.

One of the Indians came around the side of the cabin to the side window and with his knife slit the fleshed hide. Sabrina ran for the fireplace, hefted a stout hunk of wood and threw it. Her aim was bad and it bounced off the window frame. Through the bedroom door she heard Bushrod crying and someone — probably Jenner — clamped a hand over his mouth and brought silence.

She picked up another piece of wood as the Indian pushed the hide out of the way and lifted head and shoulders inside. Her aim improved and she bounced it off his shoulder, wringing a sharp howl from him. But this was not enough to stop him.

He came through head first, breaking the fall to the floor with his hands. He had his knife between his teeth. As she bent for more wood the other Indian appeared in the window opening. Sabrina threw the chunk and caught him squarely on the forehead. He went limp, draped half in, half out.

The Indian on the floor came up with a swoop, knife in hand. His eyes fascinated Sabrina for they were a deep brown, two globes of emotionless glass. He had discarded his blanket and stood half-naked and sweat oily.

As he advanced, she retreated step by step until her shoulders came against the stone fireplace. She watched him as he stood there, a muscle twitching in his face. When he bounded forward she turned for the nearest weapon she could reach, a heavy copper pot.

With an unrealized strength she seized the descending knife wrist and miraculously kept the blade away from her throat. With her right hand she pounded the Indian across the head with the pot and it bonged loudly each time she hit him.

His breath was hot in her face and both began to breathe heavily. The knife cut her shoulder in one bright streak of pain and had she not pulled her head to one side, the blade would have taken her through the throat. The Indian's sweating arm was difficult to hang on to and because he possessed superior strength, she could not hope to overpower him. Her only thought was to misdirect the blade as long as she could.

Then she heard a long, wild scream from outside, and the body lying half in, half out the window was snatched away. Long, brown arms came through, then Shawnee Blanc was in the room, his penny-colored face wildly distorted with rage.

He seized the Indian around the neck and threw him as a child throws a toy. The Indian hit the table, went over it, taking a chair with him. He crashed to the floor and rolled, coming erect.

"*Maka'-pezu ta-win!*" Shawnee Blanc shouted and the Indian froze in a half risen position. "*Maka-ta e'ton-way yo. Lena' nita'wa ktelo!*"

Travis and the others stormed into the yard and his shoulder was smashing down the door. Pieces of the lock splintered and it banged open. He stopped, spread legged, as savage as the Indian; this showed in his eyes, the tightness of his skin over his cheeks.

Priam Thomas came in then, his face slack with fear. He looked at the frozen tableau: Sabrina clinging weakly to the mantle, the Indian in the half crouch, Shawnee Blanc standing over him, and the motionless Travis with his rifle pointed dead center.

"It's all right," Travis said. "You all right, Sabrina?"

"Yes," Sabrina said, surprised she had a voice.

From the bedroom, Jenner called, "Ma? Are you there, Ma?"

"Hush," Sabrina said. "Keep the children quiet like a good boy."

Travis asked, "How'd you get in, Shawnee Blanc?" Then he saw the ripped window hide.

"One more outside," Shawnee Blanc said.

"I'll take care of it," Thomas said and went out.

Shawnee Blanc went to the mantle and took down the conch shell. He held it out toward the Indian, who backed away, shaking his head violently. He began to jabber fearfully.

"*Maka'-pez'u ta-win,*" Shawnee Blanc said, pointing to Sabrina. "Big medicine."

Then Benjamin Travis began to understand what Shawnee Blanc was saying. The roar in the shell was big medicine to the savage mind. Thomas came back in since Menard and his two sons had shown up. Another voice, that of Able Kane, spoke. "Make way there. I say, stand aside." His shadow darkened the doorway as he stopped and looked around. He was panting from his run, and sweat coursed down his heavy cheeks. He looked at Sabrina but did not approach her.

Thomas said, "What's it all about, Ben?"

"Shawnee Blanc's tryin' to convince him that Sabrina's a medicine woman."

"Heathen gibberish," Kane said. "I killed one; I'll kill the others."

"Take this Injun outside," Travis said. "Hold 'em both but don't let harm come to 'em, you understand?"

This seemed to be a personal insult to Able Kane.

"After all the killin' —"

Travis whirled on him. "Get out! Goddamn you, get before I put a rifle ball twixt your eyes!"

Thomas had Kane by the arm, urging this ox-stubborn man toward the door. "Fetch that Injun, Shawnee," Thomas said and they went outside.

"The children are in the bedroom," Sabrina said. "They must be very frightened."

Travis had to shove back the trunk to get the door open. He picked up Bushrod and Mary with one arm. "Take 'em down to the creek an' play, Jenner, but don't go near the Lockwoods. There's been trouble."

212

When he set the two on the floor, Jenner took their hands, and led them outside. He crossed to where Sabrina stood and it seemed to him that if she moved away from the fireplace she would fall. She looked at him and reaction overwhelmed her. Tears began to run down her cheeks. He put his arms around her and held her until the weeping stopped.

Then he made her sit in the chair and in spite of her protests, unlaced her dress to bare her shoulder. The cut was shallow and he washed it carefully with warm water. She sat with her hands in her lap, her eyes focused on the far wall.

"I saw it happen, Ben. Lockwood, his wife, the baby —"

"They went quick," Travis said softly. "Sabrina, in Injun country, that's a blessin' sometimes."

She stood up and relaced her bodice, turning away from him while she did this.

"I've got to leave for a spell," he said. "You'll be all right."

"You're going to Lockwood's?"

He nodded.

"What about Lockwood's children, Ben?" Somehow she could not get them out of her mind.

"We'll find someone to care for 'em," he said.

"You'll need me," she told him and went with him to the door.

There was a crowd gathered around Ninian Lockwood's place as they walked toward it. The fight had attracted nearly everyone in the settlement. Even Jethro Sweet was there. He looked at Travis, then at

Thomas and Pierre Menard, who stood guard over the two Indian prisoners. Able Kane stood like a solid oak, and if he felt any sense of responsibility for this tragedy, he let none of it show on his face.

Travis touched Sabrina lightly on the arm and joined the men. Jethro Sweet said, "Ben, with trouble among us we ought to put our differences aside."

"You're right," Travis said, somewhat relieved.

The women were clustered around the door of Lockwood's cabin, stunned by the tragedy. They talked a lot, but none ventured inside. The massacre was too new, the shock too fresh in their minds for action. They were thinking how easily this could have happened to them.

Sabrina Kane pushed her way into the circle. Mrs. Bond saw the blood on her dress and it seemed to remind her that she might have been the victim as well as a witness. "My," she said, "what a terrible thing." She made a point of not looking at Mrs. Lockwood who lay near the door, covered with blankets. The three children lay near her, also covered.

"Has anyone seen to the children?" Sabrina asked. "Where are they?"

"Inside," Mrs. Pillifrew said. "I was goin' to 'em but I couldn't. I got six of my own. How could a woman look at 'em without seein' her own? I couldn't go to 'em, that's all. I just couldn't."

The women looked at each other uneasily. Mrs. Blackwell sniffed and said, "I expect we'll divide 'em up. Don't see how I can feed anymore though; I got five now." She looked at the blanket-covered body of

Mrs. Lockwood and began to cry. Mrs. Blackwell was a woman who found grief in many things.

"Excuse me," Sabrina said and pushed her aside to enter Lockwood's cabin. The house was square hewn logs, a low building with three windows. The chimney was made of rounded sticks thickly plastered with clay. The first room was a small catch-all and woodshed. The main room was kitchen, living space and bedroom for all the children. Around the walls hung clothing: Mrs. Lockwood's best bonnet, which no proper woman would ever be without, and a silver-gray cloak with a long, peaked hood. All the furniture was round-posted ash, the bottoms woven bark. Sabrina could feel the living that had taken place in this plain house. She could hear crying from the back bedroom.

She went in and saw them sitting on the bed. "I'm Sabrina Kane," she said and gathered them into her arms. For awhile they cried and through the healing power of tears, the tragedy of death lessened. Finally Sabrina said, "I have a nice home. I'd like you to come and live with me."

She led the four of them outside where the women waited. Mrs. Bond looked at Sabrina and said, "It's a shame; I've said it before. A dirty shame."

"A family ought to stay together," Sabrina said. "I'll take them to raise."

"I guess you know your own mind," Mrs. Pillifrew said. She edged away, as did the other ladies. They acted relieved and Sabrina could not blame them. These were hard times and mouths were hard enough to feed without asking for additional burdens. Yet she assumed the obligation, a woman alone. A woman without a man. She supposed it was the sight of them sitting on the bed, so completely lost, that had made her take them.

"You're so brave, Sabrina," Mrs. Blackwell said and blew her nose on her apron, glad to find a new subject for tears.

"Come along, children," Sabrina said. "I'll make you some hot switchel." She gathered them under outstretched arms like a mother hen shielding her chicks from the rain.

Able Kane saw this and detached himself from the men. He approached her and said, "You mean to care for them?"

"Someone has to," Sabrina said.

"I've said nothing about the three you have," he said with slow deliberation. "But I'll be wanting sons of my own, not some other man's." He made a blunt, excluding motion with his hands. "I'll not feed seven."

She looked into his eyes, into the inflexible soul of this man, then her eyes moved past Kane and found Benjamin Travis watching her. Between them passed a unity of thought, a mingling compassion. Sabrina looked away quickly, afraid she would cry again, for on his face there had been an intensity of emotion she had never seen in any other man. She thought, when a man looks at a woman like that, she's had everything.

Able Kane's voice brought her attention back to him. "I'm a man who thinks of the future. A man can raise two not his own, but no more."

The Eddys arrived then and Able Kane left her; he had more important matters to settle in his bull-dog way. James Eddy, the elder, immediately singled Kane out and shook a finger under his nose. "Goddamn, you didn't have to shoot one, did you?"

"Fine thanks," Kane said solidly, "I get for protecting your property."

"They meant no harm," Jethro Sweet rumbled. "Injuns come an' go here, Kane. We don't allow 'em to live here no more, but by golly there's no call to up and shoot one."

Able Kane looked at Sweet, his conscience unruffled. "I was upholdin' the law of God: Thou shall not steal. I did right."

And that, Travis decided it, settled the matter in Able Kane's mind. He was right. And that was supposed to make everything else right.

Jethro Sweet puffed his cheeks and drew on a little-used patience. He spoke with the spaced clarity of a man dealing with a dumb animal, as though he was constantly reminding himself of this basic difference. "Kane, you're responsible. You started 'em off. God, man, you ought to know anythin' will start 'em goin'!"

"I'm sorry about the Lockwood tribe," Able Kane said, "but I am blameless. This was Indian doing, not mine."

"That's what we aim to decide," Jethro Sweet said. "In the meantime we'll lock the Injuns up in my storeroom. We can deal with them in the mornin'."

Kane straightened. His glance on Jethro Sweet was like a fist knotted in a man's shirt front. "Don't speak to me of blame, friend. Or of fixin' blame on me. I have right on my side." He pointed to the Indian prisoners. "A rope waits for them, for they're the guilty ones."

"I don't think so," Benjamin Travis said. He kept his voice down for he was a man other men listened to without having to shout.

Slowly Able Kane turned to Travis. "Do you blame me for this?"

"Blamin' you for anythin' would be like spittin' at the moon. But don't lay it all at the Injuns' feet. Jethro, you'd be smart to turn 'em loose."

"I can't do that," Jethro said flatly. "Ben, you know —"

Travis cut him off with a wave of the hand. He spoke to Able Kane. "You think on it a bit and you'll see the Injuns was only doin' what they thought right. When you shot one they thought we'd declared war. I've known it to happen that way before. We got a knack of rilin' Indians. The killin's been done, on both sides. I say turn 'em loose."

"Now hold on, Ben," Jethro said. "You ain't on that hill now. You don't run things down here."

"That's right; I ain't," Travis said. "But everybody's got a say from now on, Jethro."

"Yeah? First I heard of it."

"That's the way it is," Travis said. "You can be stepped on, Jethro. Don't make us do that."

"Better not try," he threatened. He looked around at the faces and saw little friendliness there. Able Kane's cow-bland face now took on a new appeal to Jethro Sweet. He said, "Kane, you started this. What do you think?"

"Hang the murderers," Kane said. "Justice must be done."

"What of the one you murdered?" Menard said.

Kane revolved on his heel. Somehow it seemed that he could never turn his head like other men. He had to revolve his whole body as though he were so solid that he was without joints. "Speak that word to me again and I'll knock you down."

"All right, all right," Jethro said. "I'm for hangin' 'em now, but I'll go along with you until mornin'. You can have your say then, but after you make a mess of things, I'll straighten it out for you."

"Just see that nothin' happens to the prisoners," Travis warned.

"I don't want to be responsible," Jethro said. "I'll hold 'em, but that's all."

"We're makin' you responsible," Travis told him.

"What about me?" Kane asked.

"What the hell about you?" Menard asked and turned away. The crowd began to break up, leaving Able Kane standing like the hub of a wheel after all the spokes had fallen out. Menard and Thomas got shovels and stayed to bury the Lockwoods. Travis remained to help them.

The oldest Lockwood boy was Gamaliel, age ten. The twin girls were Prudence and Grace, as alike as two straws. The small boy's name was Pride. He was three. Sabrina had difficulty seating seven children at the table, but she heated some switchel and filled their cups. Thomas came in shortly after and stood by the fireplace. He looked at the solemn-faced children. "Seven. That's a sizeable family, Sabrina."

"I'll need two more beds," she said. "Jenner can share his with Gamaliel; we'll have to have one more for Pride and Bushrod. Prudence and Grace can share one. I guess Mary can sleep in the trunk lid. We'll move all that junk Cadmus left out and make room." Sabrina bit her lip and looked like a woman who has so much to do she doesn't know where to start. Or perhaps she was searching for something to do, Thomas decided. At a time like this it was best when a person had no time for thinking.

Able Kane knocked and entered. He looked at the children but made no comment. He had spoken once and to his way of thinking, his word was good enough to endure for eternity.

He got wood from Travis' sawyer camp and made beds and in the end they were just as solid and plain and right as he was. He carried them into the cabin as Sabrina straightened the place, hanging an old blanket over the torn window. Kane lingered as though he waited to be given a permanent invitation, but none came. Finally he turned without a word and went back to the settlement.

The children were fed first, then sent to bed. Sabrina cleared the table, reset it and sat across from her father. "How could it have happened?" she said softly. "What made Able shoot that Injun, Pa?"

He looked at her briefly. "You know Able. You tell me how." He paused to chew. "He made up his mind to stop 'em from messin' around Eddy's cabin. Once he'd done that, there was no turnin' him aside. He's that way."

"What's going to happen to the Indians in the morning?"

"Likely they'll be hung," Thomas said.

"But that's wrong! Pa, you know that's wrong."

"I guess it is, but it's whatever the vote decides."

"Vote!" She snorted. "A bunch of men who're mad can't vote right." She reached across the table and grabbed his arm. "Pa, you got to persuade them that the Injuns were only doing what they thought was right. They don't know no better. When they're hurt they strike back."

"I know all that," Thomas said. "Sabrina, the men folks had a meetin' the other night and decided we was fed up havin' Jethro tell us where to get off. Everybody's entitled to a share in the rulin'. You know that. That's why it'll be put to a vote tomorrow. Jethro'll get a chance to argue his point, and he's only again' us so he can keep what he's got. But we'll vote. If it goes again' the Injuns there's nothin' I can do. Either way we'll show Jethro that *we're* runnin' things, not him."

"But it isn't justice," Sabrina said. She got up and went to the door, looking out. When she came back to the table she said, "Wonder where Shawnee Blanc is? He didn't come for his meal."

"I ain't seen him since the trouble," Thomas said. "Come to think of it he disappeared right after we took the Injun out of this cabin."

"He'll show up," Sabrina said. "He's never missed a meal yet." She poured another cup of coffee for her

221

father and one for herself. "I guess Able'd think I was crazy, talkin' *for* the Injuns instead of against them. He'd argue that they tried to kill me, and I guess they did after I started throwing firewood."

"It's a plaguey mess," Thomas admitted. "But we got to have law here, Sabrina. Every man in Illinois Town's got to have his say. We're goin' to have a mayor and police magistrate; then when somethin' important's to be decided, all the folks'll get a chance to vote on it."

"Jethro won't stand for that," Sabrina said. "Ben Travis has enough trouble without heaping more on him. And Jethro'll blame him for everything."

"Ben knows that," Thomas said. "We got to do the right thing, Sabrina."

"Now you sound like Able Kane," she said and gathered the dishes.

Thomas packed his pipe and bent over the candle for his light. Between puffs he said, "Another day like this an' I'll be old before my time." He glanced at her through the smoke. "I seen that look you an' Ben was passin' back an' forth. You ain't forgettin' how he spoke out concernin' Patience, have you?"

"I haven't forgot," she said, then paused. "But I'll never have to ask Ben Travis how he feels about me."

"You goin' to bust up somethin' between him an' Patience?"

"He don't love her," she said. "But he spoke the words and I'll leave the answer up to him."

Thomas thought this over. "Was Ben to claim you, there'd be only one boss in the family. I guess I don't have to tell you who that'd be."

"I could stand that now," Sabrina said. "I need him."

Priam Thomas grunted and knocked the dottle from his pipe. "That don't sound good to me. You don't stand a man because you need him, Sabrina. You feel that way, then take Able Kane."

He went to bed shortly and Sabrina sat before the fire, trying to understand her feelings. She decided it was a tragedy when two proud, unbending people fell in love. One had to give; that was a certainty. She wondered if she could without losing her self respect.

Yet this was not her only concern. She could not ignore the plight of the two Indians. With her slight knowledge of the frontier she could understand the white man's feeling toward the Indian, and in the same token she thought she understood how the Indians felt. The two races were separated by language and culture. Now two men were to be convicted by a law beyond their ken, sentenced in a language completely alien to them. Right or wrong, Sabrina found she could not sit idle while this happened. The white man's justice was for white men; the Indian should be punished by his own law.

When Priam Thomas began to snore, Sabrina took her shawl, draped it around her shoulders and went out, walking rapidly toward the settlement. She was not worried about meeting anyone, for the Indian attack had sobered them to the extent that they would stay indoors for a few days.

Approaching Sweet's trading post, she carefully made her way around the back. At each of the two doors she paused, feeling for the latch strings, but since

Jethro was a distrustful man, he pulled them in each night. She found another door and explored it with her hands. When she touched the cold brass padlock she knew that the Indians were imprisoned there.

A man would have pried the lock off or broken it, but Sabrina looked for another way. The store room had one window, high off the ground. It was without hide to allow ventilation.

Moving about, she found an old wine cask and stood on it. Her fingertips barely curled over the window sill. The Indians heard her and muttered softly to themselves. She got down carefully and went to the well. She had to pull up the bucket slowly lest splashing water arouse someone inside the store. When the bucket sat on the stone curbing, she untied the rope. After three tries, she managed to throw one end of the rope through the high window and made the other end fast to a nearby tree.

In a moment the Indians were up and over. They dropped to the ground, saw her shadow shape standing there, and ran for the shelter of the timber a dozen yards behind the trading post.

Sabrina carefully put the rope back on the bucket and lowered it in the well. Then she turned to go back to her cabin, but stopped when she saw the blocky shape of Able Kane standing by the building corner.

Her first thought was to run, but she recognized the uselessness of such a move. Able came up to her with his slow, deliberate step. "I suspected as much," he said. "There's wickedness in you, Sabrina."

"And what's in you?" She tried to push past him, but he blocked her with an out-flung arm.

"I must speak out against you in the morning," he said. "Right's right. But in no way does it change my offer. I made it and I'll not go back on my word once it's given."

He let her go then and she hurried back to her cabin, badly shaken. She felt a strong sense of guilt and wondered if Able Kane had planted the seeds in her mind. But she told herself that her crime was less than his, less than the men who would hang the Indians.

Then she thought of Benjamin Travis and what he would say when Able Kane made his speech in the morning.

She lay beneath a blanket and trembled.

CHAPTER
TEN

Sabrina Kane woke hours before dawn and lay staring at the dark ceiling beams, wishing she could hold back the rising sun. Last night, letting the Indians escape had seemed such a good idea, but now she was filled with grave doubts. She did not understand the reason for her sense of guilt, but she knew that rationalization failed to dispel it. She felt forebodings, like the sticky heat before a storm, the crowded sensation she always got when serious trouble loomed, undefined, threatening. Finally she could endure the waiting no longer and got up, dressing quickly. She went into the main room to build up the fire.

She tried to be quiet, but Priam Thomas had evidently been sleeping lightly for he heard her and came from the lean-to a few minutes later. "You're up early," he said and yawned hugely.

"I couldn't sleep," she said, setting on the water for the coffee.

Thomas went to the door and stood there, watching the sky lighten to the east. Jenner came from the spare room, stretching and rubbing his eyes. "Get the others up," Sabrina said. "Breakfast in a few minutes."

In the distance a bell started its brass gong tolling and Sabrina lifted her head, a sudden fear quickening her heartbeat. "What's that?"

"Don't know," Thomas said and went outside to see. He looked toward the settlement, then came back inside, his manner hurried. "Somethin's wrong at the Sweets," he said and grabbed his rifle. He ran out before Sabrina could stop him and when she went to the door he was already moving rapidly down the creek toward the settlement.

"They found out," she said softly and turned back inside, her brow wrinkled with worry.

The Lockwood children came from the bedroom and took their places at the table. Sabrina dished the food, saw that they were all seated, then indicated with a nod that they could begin eating. She turned her head often toward the door, and kept pushing down the impulse to follow her father. But she was determined to wait. This was man's business now that she was through meddling in it.

Priam Thomas was too old for running, but the clanging bell had an urgency that caused him to ignore his age. A large crowd was gathering near Jethro Sweet's front porch. He saw Benjamin Travis near the rail and pushed his way through until he stood at Travis' side. They glanced at each other and when Thomas opened his mouth to speak, Travis shook his head slightly, holding Thomas silent.

Clem Sweet was there, the first public appearance he had made since the fight nearly a month before. His face was healing well, although he would carry hideous scars the rest of his life. His arm was still encased in bandage and splints and residual soreness caused him to limp a little. Fountainbleau stood near Clem and they watched the crowd carefully.

Jethro came through the front door with Able Kane. His raised hand brought the murmuring to a halt and he swept them with his eyes before speaking.

"The Injuns didn't break out. They was let out."

This was the kind of ammunition Jethro Sweet liked to load in his gun and while the crowd got over the shock of being thus peppered, he rocked back on his heels, again in command of the settlers.

Thomas nudged Travis and said, "Ben, you goin' to let him get away with that?"

"Let's hear him out," Travis said.

"Now listen to me," Sweet said. "You folks let Ben Travis an' Thomas fill you full of ideas about runnin' your own affairs. I just knew somethin' like this would happen, an' it did. Them Injuns has skedaddled and when they come back they'll bring an Injun war with 'em!"

"Indian war" was a phrase that always created a stir on any frontier and Jethro let the crowd mumble it over. The fact that the Indians were gone mattered little now. The uppermost thought in their minds was the repercussions when they returned.

"Who says them Injuns was let out?" Travis asked.

Jethro regarded Ben Travis, who was the focal point for all of his troubles. "I'll let Able Kane tell it."

And he told everything he had seen, told it in a flat, righteous voice that rang with truth. When he finished someone in the crowd shouted, "What you got to say to that, Travis?"

Another: "Yeah, Travis, let's hear your answer!"

A dozen voices took up the cry and Jethro Sweet smiled, positive now that he had them swung to his side. They quieted finally and Travis said, "Don't get worked into a sweat. Can't you see Jethro's tryin' to get you back to his side?"

"I can see we made a mistake listenin' to you an' Thomas," one man shouted.

Jethro seized this club and swung it. "You folks listen to what I got to say now. Troublemakers like Travis an' Thomas is full of fine ideas, but none of 'em work. They're always talkin' about every man for himself, but in a settlement like this it's no good. Pretty soon you'd be cuttin' each other's throats to get a little more'n the next man. With me runnin' things, an' you bringin' me your goods, you get along fine."

This made sense to the settlers. With Jethro running things a man always had credit, enough to eat, and a roof over his head. Travis' way might be better, but it was filled with hazards absorbed by Jethro and his trading company.

Ben Travis had heard enough. The people were with the Sweets now and there was nothing he could do about it. As he turned away, Jethro shouted, "Travis, this is a warnin'! Be gone by nightfall or I'll shoot you on sight!"

Travis was shoving his way through the worried crowd, Thomas right behind him. Once clear he said, "Go to the fort and tell Sergeant Muldoon to keep them sojers on constant guard. Likely Jethro will try an' take what we got. He does that and we're licked."

When Priam Thomas trotted away to take care of this, Travis walked past the Eddy place, and past Lockwood's to Sabrina's cabin. The children were splashing in the creek and the cabin door was open. He entered without knocking and found Sabrina alone.

She turned when his shadow darkened the doorway. "What was the meeting about?" She hoped the studied casualness in her voice didn't betray her.

"Ask Able Kane." The look in Travis' eyes tore at her control.

She looked at him steadily, the blood rushing into her face. "So he told. He said he would and he always does what he says."

"Why did you do it, Sabrina?"

Her shoulders sagged. "You know why, Ben. They would have hung them."

"It wasn't your business to meddle," he said.

"But you know it would have been wrong to punish them!"

He repeated, "It wasn't your business, Sabrina. You're a head-strong woman, but this time you've gone too blamed far. You done what Jethro wanted, showed that folks ain't fit to handle their own affairs."

"Oh, you're twisting everything around!"

"I ain't and you know it," Travis said evenly. "Sabrina, you did the wrong thing. Some things has got to run their course, even when it hurts. This was one, but you fixed it to suit yourself. You fixed it so's they believe Jethro now instead of Thomas or me."

230

"I didn't mean to do that!"

Travis studied her with veiled eyes. "It don't matter much now, Sabrina. Jethro give me 'til tonight to get out of Illinois Town, or there'll be shootin'. I don't want to kill anyone, Sabrina, not even the Sweets."

His words were a numbing shock. "You're leaving?"

"That's right. You got me in pretty deep, Sabrina. I'm goin' to get out before I drown."

She felt a new panic. "Where are you going?"

"Away from here," Travis said and went out. He walked up the hill to his sawyer camp and gathered his sleeping robes, rifle and accoutrements. He shouldered the sleeping gear and paused for a last look around. His banjo was lying in the corner of the half-cabin and he left it there. He went off the hill, heading for the Mississippi River.

He stopped at the Eddy cabin and said his brief goodbye to Patience. Leaving there he cut toward the river, but as he passed near the fort he met Priam Thomas.

Thomas looked him over, then said, "Ben, you ain't scared of the Sweets."

Travis shook his head. "Sabrina's gone too far, Thomas."

"It can be straightened out," Thomas said. "Hell, she's a woman, Ben. She acts with her emotions."

"Does that mean she ain't responsible?"

"You know what I mean. Where you headin'?"

"St. Louis," Travis said. "Maybe there's a fur party makin' up."

"That sounds mighty lonesome," Thomas said. "I couldn't persuade you to cool off a day or two first, could I?"

"No," Travis said.

"Well, I ain't goin' to argue you out of it," Thomas said. "Right now I'd like to throw in with you. When Jethro finds out you've pulled foot, he'll think you was scared. They'll make it uncomfortable for me, you can bet on it."

"I'll be in St. Louis a few days," Travis said. "Might be I'll see you there?"

"You might," Thomas agreed. "This kinda spoils things for you an' Patience, don't it?"

"You ain't that much of a fool," Travis said and walked on. Thomas watched him for a moment, then hurried to the cabin, puzzled and yet wondering why.

Sabrina was in the doorway and from her expression he knew that she had been watching as Travis headed for the river. Thomas said, "You done it good this time."

"I didn't mean for it to work out that way! Will he come back?"

"Be a fool if he did; he's been showed he wasn't needed enough times." Thomas moved past her to go inside. He set the rifle down.

Sabrina bit her lip. "What have I done, Pa?"

"I'll try an' make it simple so's even you can understand it," Thomas said. He filled his clay pipe and lighted it. "First off, we was all set to take control away from the Sweets without any shootin'. We closed him out, or soon would've with Ben's fort, and we was goin' to vote the Injuns free. I say that 'cause the Sweets would have been with Able for a hangin' and since folks is so all-fired contrary, they'd voted to turn 'em loose just to be onery about it."

"How was I to know that?" Sabrina cried. "Pa, why didn't somebody say something?"

"Jumpin' Jesus, you expect a man to go around explainin' to a woman all the time?" He scowled. "Well, it don't matter now. You took folks' good intent away from 'em. Took it away an' made 'em look like a bunch of fools that didn't know what they was doin'."

"But I thought —"

"You didn't think!" Thomas smashed his hand on the table. "Jesus God, don't you have any faith in Ben Travis?"

"Yes, but —"

"Yes, but what?" He snorted and seemed too disgusted to go on. Finally he said, "Sabrina, you got the idea in your head that you've got to run things, that a man'll shut you out. Goddammit, this is man's business and you'd better understand it. There's things men do and there's things women do. You better get it straight which is which!"

"Don't shout and swear at me!"

"I'll shout and swear all I damn please! You want to know why Travis left? Because he don't trust you no more. Nobody can trust you." He puffed his cheeks and calmed himself. "But by Jehoshaphat, things is going to be different or I'll get a board and hide your hind end for you!"

"Pa!"

"That's right. I'm your pa and I'll do what I should have done a long time ago. Now git to your woman's work and stay there." He swung to the door. "I'm goin' to Ben's sawyer camp, if it's any business of yours."

Thomas left her standing there, open mouthed. She could not actually credit her father with such a firm stand, yet she knew instinctively that he had meant every word he had said. Somehow this little man had gradually developed into a big man, the head of the house, and Sabrina knew that never again would she have the ruling hand over him.

And she felt no resentment, for after twenty years Priam Thomas was now the father she had always wanted.

She tried to go about her chores but found them impossible, even the simple tasks. All she could think of was Benjamin Travis and the complete, unforgivable disgust he must feel toward her. She relived the moments they had spent together, even the ones when she had been angry with him, but now she knew that the anger had actually been at herself.

The children came in at mid-morning, hungry, and she gave them each a baking powder biscuit and sent them back to the creek to play. At noon Priam Thomas came down from the camp and entered the cabin. He laid Benjamin Travis' banjo on the table without a word.

When Sabrina saw it, she had only one thought. "He's back!"

"He ain't back," Thomas said. "I'd say he outgrew the use for it. You done that to him, Sabrina; you took away his laughter."

"Oh, Pa!" She sat down and crossed her arms, biting her lip to keep back the tears.

"I'm goin' over to the fort," Thomas said and went out.

Sabrina touched the banjo and one string twanged, a weird, off-key note. She could see where his fingers had worn the varnish off the neck and polished the brass frets. How many wonderful hours had come from this homely instrument she could only guess. How many hearts had he lifted and how many people had he made forget, even for a little while, their troubles and cares? This was Benjamin Travis' great gift; she understood now. And she had taken that from him simply because she couldn't put aside her foolish fears.

Quickly she raised her head, the crying stilled. She could see clearly all the times Ben Travis had had his way, forcing her to suppress her own will, but she knew no resentment and for a moment she could not understand why. Then she saw clearly, for his way was hers; it was made so by love and understanding.

She went outside to wash her face. The children were making mud pies along the creek bank and when they saw her, came up. Jenner said, "You been cryin', Ma?"

"Just smoke in my eyes," Sabrina said. She dried her face on her apron and spoke to the oldest Lockwood boy. "Take good care of the children now, Gamaliel. I'll be back before dark."

She went to the lean-to and took the coiled whip off the peg, then walked rapidly through the tall grass and swirling insects towards Jethro Sweet's trading post.

Sweet was on the porch, his feet on the railing, sleeping in the sun. He opened his eyes when Sabrina came up the porch steps. She had allowed the whip to uncoil and was dragging it through the dust behind her.

"Mr. Sweet," she said, "I once called you yellow, and I said I'd prove it someday. That day's arrived."

Sweet's eyes narrowed. "A man wouldn't talk to me that way."

"Able Kane'll be willing to answer for anything I say," Sabrina said. "He spoke for me and he's not a man to go back on his word."

"I'll ask him about it," Jethro promised. His eyes dropped to the whip and remained there for a moment. "There's no need to give me your tongue," he said and wiped a sudden sweat from his face. "You flourish that whip and I'll treat you like I'd treat a man."

"You're a hog," Sabrina said. "Get out of the settlement and stay out. We don't need your kind here."

"Move me," Sweet invited.

She understood what he intended to do — get close, which was the only defense against a bullwhip. A good whip-cracker had to strike with the tip only for maximum damage. As soon as he wrapped it around a man's arm or body, he was done; the whip could then be seized and taken away.

When Sabrina backed up a step, Jethro knew he was not going to get away with his plan and tried to leave the chair. But he was a second late and the tip caught him on the chest, knocking him backward. A fourteen foot bullwhip was a weapon capable of breaking one inch pine boards and when Jethro came to his knees he was bleeding where the forked tip had taken away skin. He acted like a man who had been mule-kicked.

Sabrina shagged the whip backward as Jethro surged to his feet, his face white with rage. She cast again, catching him on the hairline. Hair and blood flew and he backpedaled rapidly, bellowing for his brother and Fountainbleau to come and help him. Jethro backed against the porch railing, lost his balance and went over, arms flailing. He fell flat on his back in the dust.

Clem, attracted by Jethro's shouting, sprang to the open door as Sabrina swung around, snapping the whip. She caught Clem just above the open collar and he yelped, disappearing inside and slamming the door. She heard the bar fall into place and left the porch to stalk Jethro.

The settlers who lived close in came to their doorways to see what all the screaming was about and Sabrina ripped open the seat of Jethro's trousers, drawing a bloody line across his bared buttocks. He let out a helpless bleat of rage and flailed his hands, trying to catch the whip. But he would have had more success trying to snare a striking rattler.

There was little else left for Jethro but running, which he did.

Sabrina hooked him around the ankle, tripping him, but she used care not to let the whip end wrap more than twice; she had to free it before Jethro could grab it. Sweet kicked free and Sabrina stripped him twice across the back as he scrambled to his feet.

She went after him with a vengeance and a crowd gathered on the run. Her long skirts hampered her and five times she was forced to trip Jethro in order to slow him down and keep him just within whip range. Each time he tried to break away, she laid it on, driving him toward the river.

He was a wild man, raging and frothing at the mouth, his eyes glazed. Once, when he tried to grab the whip she opened the back of his hand. His shirt and fine coat were in tatters, his trousers sagging folds of cloth around his buckled shoes.

Half the settlement was behind her now, cheering and cat-calling. Sweet went into the water and she waded in, driving him out until the water was to his armpits. The whip snapped, spraying water. He went deeper until it touched his chin and there Sabrina held him, daring him to come to the shore.

"We drown rats," she said, "and you remember that."

Then she turned and coiling the whip as she walked, returned to Sweet's trading post. At the bottom porch step she faced the barred door. Her entreaties to Clem to come out harvested no response and after waiting five minutes, she turned toward her own cabin.

Her exertions left her shaken and sweat-drenched, but somehow she thought that Benjamin Travis would think more kindly of her when he heard. And she knew he would hear. Everyone would know within a month for this was what men liked to talk about and Jethro

Sweet would have to live with it; he would never be able to live it down.

But there'll be killing over it, she thought, and knew that Able Kane was not up to it.

She saw him leaving Lockwood's place and he waited for her approach. His face was a thundercloud and she suspected that he had witnessed from a distance the whole thing. Kane waited near the door and when she gave no indication of stopping, he said, "Would you pass me by without a word, woman?"

She stopped and turned to face him. "Did you see it?"

"A shameful thing," Able said flatly.

"I told him you'd answer for anything I did," Sabrina said.

The ox-like expression melted and his face filled with blood until she thought the veins on his forehead would burst. "You what? By Jerusalem, do you want my death?" He beat his hands against his thighs like a young rooster trying his wings. His feet stamped up and down in the dust, raising a tan cloud to his knees. "No," he said, and again, "No! I take back my words to you. I'd not have you for a wife."

"How can you take them back?" Sabrina said. "Able, you're a man who never goes back, once his mind's set."

"I'll not fight for you," he said and turned inside the cabin for his few belongings. Sabrina watched him without expression while he threw them into the wagon and mounted. He looked at her before driving out.

"Keep the cups," he said. "They'd break before I got home."

And then he was going, the oxen moving with a slow, plodding pace. Sabrina stood there for ten minutes while Able Kane drove past the settlement onto the rough wagon-road south. He'll get there, she decided. The ox will get him there, and that's all he cares about now.

She walked on to her own cabin and found her father waiting anxiously. "Have you gone crazy?" he shouted. "I was at Bond's when I heard about it." He mopped his face with his hand. "My God, Jethro can't take that and ever hold up his head again." He took a deep breath and seemed to be calmed by it. "Where was Able Kane goin'? I seen him drive out of the settlement."

"Back to Pennsylvania," Sabrina said calmly.

"Huh?" Thomas' eyes opened wide.

"I told Able that he'd have to settle with Jethro for what I did," Sabrina said.

He turned his back to her, overcome by the contortions of woman's logic. "I see it all now. You done this a-purpose, figurin' Able'd back down." He turned on her suddenly. "You schemed up this whole thing so's Ben'd have to come back; if I took it up with Jethro I'd be dead."

She tipped her head forward so he could not see the guilt in her eyes. "What other way was there for me, Pa? I couldn't let him go."

Thomas sighed, not the first man defeated by a woman's reasoning. "I guess you couldn't do anything else. But he'll hate you for this, Sabrina. He'll come back and fight for you, but you'll lose him." He waved his hand and picked up his rifle. "He told me once that your pride would get a man killed someday. Looks like he was right. Well, there ain't much time if I mean to cross the river and fetch him back tonight."

He went out, trotting toward the river ferry crossing.

The French ferryman was asleep on his raft and Thomas woke him rudely. The fare to the other shore was a Spanish dollar, which Thomas didn't have. So he pointed his rifle at the ferryman and sat near the raft's stern, covering the cursing Frenchman as he oared across the river.

Thomas squinted at the sky and saw that not much of the day remained. "You wait for me on this side," Thomas said softly. "An' if you ain't here when I get back, I'll swim across an' take your pelt." This was his first bluff in years and he hoped he sounded convincing.

He wheeled and struck out for the town on the low bluffs. The distance was less than a mile but his wind was sadly taxed. He came to the end of the single street and had a close look at this much discussed Babylon. The town was a wild, sprawling place with sin as common as dirt in the street. Three large trading posts belonging to the fur companies made up the hub from which the deadfalls and other rough buildings radiated. Thomas pushed his way through one dive after another, punctuating these excursions by brief pauses along the street edge. He watched bearded men move in waves from place to place, men who preferred to be alone with their animal-wild thoughts. Moccasined feet shuffled, bringing up the street's dust like thick fog. One man, very drunk, stood in the middle of the thoroughfare, swinging his fists at all who passed within range until another man knocked him asprawl with his rifle barrel. Somewhere a woman laughed in screeching gales and a gun exploded near the edge of town.

For better than an hour Thomas scoured the town until he found Benjamin Travis in the trading post bar. The tall man was sitting in a corner with a tot of rum, telling a story about a Cree buck who had been chased up a tree by a bear. When Travis saw Thomas he broke off his story and came to the bar where Thomas waited.

Thomas' face was dead serious. "You've got to come back, Ben."

"What's she into now?" He seemed slightly amused, as though all this followed a pattern whose future he could predict with certainty. Thomas was slightly annoyed because he didn't understand this part at all.

"Bad trouble. She took a blacksnake to Jethro and drove him plumb in the river."

Travis' laughter was magnificent. He finished his rum and set the mug on the bar. "What's Able Kane goin' to do about it, Thomas? He wants a woman bad enough he's got to take the bad with the good."

"He lit out for home," Thomas said.

Travis grunted. "Thought he talked a mite definite for a bold man. Suppose I don't come back, Thomas? What then?"

"Then I got to stand up to Sweet, an' I'm no match for him, Ben; I know it. You know it."

"If I go back," Travis said, "it'll be on her account, Thomas."

"Sure, sure, forget about me, Ben." Thomas spoke like a man who meant what he said.

Travis regarded him carefully. "That's some different tune than the one you sang when I first met up with you, Thomas. Seems that all you could think about was yourself."

"Things change, Ben; I ain't sorry they have either." He took Travis' arm. "Damn it all, man, she's your woman. Them soft, giggly things ain't for a he-cat like you! God, man, she's all woman and you're all man. What a shame it's to be wasted."

"How does she feel about this?" He was serious now.

"She done this to make you come back," Thomas said. "Ain't that enough?" He watched Travis and then Travis began to grin. Suddenly Thomas smacked his hand against the bar top. "I'm a real jackass; I see it all, clear as day. Damn you, Ben, you left hopin' to force her into changin' her mind. Seems that somethin' was funny when you told me you'd be here. That ain't your way, Ben, tellin' folks what you're about to do. You just wanted to be sure I knew where to reach you."

"Seems like I did," Travis said and went to the corner for his plunder. Thomas joined him at the door and they went out together. The night was growing deeper as they walked down the street toward the river. A fresh wind was coming up and overhead, a full moon began to shed light.

Thomas' threat had evidently impressed the ferryman for when they came to the river they found him still there, but in hot argument with two men determined to reach the opposite shore. Thomas said. "She's taken," and stepped aboard.

The two men were armed and inclined to argue, but Benjamin Travis said softly, "I wouldn't," and they sat down to wait for the return trip.

The ferryman poled them across and Thomas fidgeted nervously. When they reached the Illinois shore, Thomas said. "Pay him two dollars, Ben."

Travis tossed the ferryman two coins.

Thomas was all for going directly to Sabrina's cabin, but Travis shook his head and angled through the old French part of the town toward Sweet's trading post. Thomas said, "This ain't smart, Ben."

"A man's got a right to know what's comin'," Travis said and did not speak again until he approached Sweet's porch. There were no lights and he knew that his approach had been observed. He stopped at the base of the porch steps and said, "Jethro, let's have a talk."

From somewhere inside, Jethro said, "No shootin', Ben."

"Just talk," Travis said. A moment later Jethro appeared. He stepped quickly through the door, but stood to one side where the night made him nearly invisible. "I'm back," Travis said. "Likely I'll stay this time."

"I said you wouldn't, Ben. We'll have to settle our trouble."

"That's right," Travis said. "Jethro, remember you wanted it this way. The town's big enough for both of us. It's you that decided it wasn't."

244

"Tryin' to crawfish out, Ben?"

"No, but I don't like killin' a man, Jethro. There ought to be another way."

"There ain't," Sweet said. "There'll be three of us, Ben. Clem's got a score to settle. So's Fountainbleau."

"Too bad," Travis said and turned away. He noticed then that Priam Thomas had had Jethro covered during the conversation. As they moved along, Travis said, "Don't you trust him, Thomas?"

"Not by a jugful."

They walked through the new moonlight to Sabrina's cabin and found her sitting before the fire. She turned when she heard their steps and Travis went in first, standing just inside the door, his tall shape throwing a huge shadow against the wall.

Sabrina stood up slowly, her eyes never leaving his face. Travis said, "You got yourself into something this time, Sabrina."

"I know, Ben. I'm sorry."

"Are you?" Travis unshouldered his parflesche and set his rifle against the wall. Thomas slipped into the room for his pipe and went out again without a word. He closed the door behind him.

Travis looked at Sabrina and said, "I'll fight Jethro and his tribe because I have to, but there's somethin' I want you to get straight. You're my woman, Sabrina."

"I'm your woman," she said. "I'll never deny that, Ben."

"An' there won't be any hell raisin' about who's got the pants in the family. You understand that?"

"Yes, Ben." She spoke in a near whisper.

Travis smiled slightly. "Then are you goin' to come over here like you're supposed to, or do I have to come an' get you?"

"Oh, Ben," she said and ran to him. He gathered her against him and kissed her and she hurt him with her tight-locked arms. "Ben, Ben, I was so alone when you left. So terribly alone."

He held her for a moment, then dropped his arm away from her. "There's some business with Jethro that won't wait," he said and turned to the wall and his rifle.

"Ben! Ben, be careful." She was worried to the point of tears. "If I lost you, Ben, I'd die."

"It's my habit to be careful," he told her and stepped outside.

Priam Thomas was there, leaning against the wall with his pipe. Travis touched his rifle and asked, "That shoot straight?"

"Wherever you point it," Thomas said.

"I know where to point it," Travis said and took it. He slung his own rifle over his shoulder, muzzle down, and walked along the creek, carrying Thomas' gun. He walked with an easy, determined stride, his moccasins swishing through the grass. Around him the bullfrogs sang and the night was full of false peace.

CHAPTER
ELEVEN

The moonlight was strong and pure and while walking through the settlement, Benjamin Travis could see people moving about. As he passed Shadrach Bond's place, Bond saw him and yelled, "Travis, I thought you'd skipped out!"

Bond's bellow carried clear across the settlement and others looked out of their cabin doors. Travis switched his eyes to the Sweet's trading post, sure they had heard Bond's call. It was all right to let the coon know you were getting the dogs, he figured, but there was no use being too loud about it.

To prevent further shouting he walked over to Bond.

"Your woman got us in good this time," Bond said disgustedly. "That Injun she's had hangin' around's skipped out. We figure he's gone to bring back his friends."

"Shawnee Blanc?"

"That's who I'm talkin' about," Bond said. "None of them redskins can be trusted." He waved his hand to the north. "Forty miles up river is solid Injun country. Your woman turned 'em loose last night and that redskin of hers joined up with 'em. They've had time to gather a party an' head back. If there's trouble, it'll be

247

on her head. You tell her that." He noticed then that Ben Travis carried two rifles. "Seems that you're gettin' ready too."

"Not for the same thing," Travis said and walked on.

Bond's talk bothered him, not that he ever believed Shawnee Blanc would betray Sabrina; he had lived too long among the whites. Yet the speculation on the settlers' part was bad. A man that talked long enough usually ended up doing something foolish.

When he neared the trading post he paused beneath a tree where the night hid him completely. He decided that there would be no need to scout around in back, for Sweet would have it guarded. Probably Fountainbleau, Travis decided. That left two, possibly one if Clem counted himself out because of his condition. Yet this was something a man couldn't count on; he had a score to settle, too.

Travis listened carefully and heard nothing except a chorus of bullfrogs down on the river bank. A few locusts sang to the night, and somewhere an owl hooted, but other than that, complete silence.

The porch was bathed in moonlight and there was no alternative but to walk through it, in plain sight. Travis held his breath covering the last ten yards, then lifted his foot to step up on the near end. He was careful not to let either gun barrel strike wood and set up an alarm.

Ducking under the railing, Benjamin Travis stood up, drawing breath through his open mouth. The corner logs projected past the wall and he stepped into the shadowed ell thus formed, his head cocked to one side like a dog picking up remote and subtle sounds. For several minutes he stood there before stepping past, moving on tiptoe toward the open front door. He had taken several steps when he heard the whisper of buckskin behind him and whirled, shouldering Priam Thomas' rifle.

Before he fired he had an instant's impression of Clem Sweet, a huge shadow stepping away from the end logs. Travis realized that while he had stood on one side, Sweet had been standing on the other, within touching distance. Sweet was lifting his rifle one handed and they fired together, their shots nearly blending. Travis heard Sweet's bullet slam into the wall by his shoulder. Chips of wood and bark stung his face. Then Clem dropped his rifle as his right leg collapsed beneath his weight. He spun around, went over the porch railing and fell to the yard below where he cursed and clutched his thigh.

A surprised shout went up from one of the settlers, as they began running toward Sweets.

Inside the building a man's feet trounced the planks, racing for the front door. Travis put Thomas' rifle aside and unslung his own, cocking as Jacques Fountainbleau made an untimely exit.

With a curse, Fountainbleau threw up his fusil. Travis shot from the hip and the bullet took the Frenchman in the shoulder, spinning him half around. Then he reeled against the wall and sagged to a sitting position, cursing, trying to staunch the flow of blood.

Travis lifted his powderhorn, caught the stopper between his teeth and poured a hefty, unmeasured charge down the bore. From the patchbox in the buttstock he took a greased buckskin patch, placed this over the muzzle, then centered a ball. A shove with the wiping stick, a touch of powder to the pan, and he was ready to stalk game.

"Jethro! Jethro, there's two down! You're the last!"

The people running toward the trading post heard this. Lights began to wink on in doorways like distant stars and women stood in them, peering through the night for their men. Inside, Jethro shifted position and in his haste, knocked over a pile of trade goods.

"Ben? Ben, is Clem dead?"

"No," Travis said. "How you want it, Jethro? Come to me or have me come in an' get you?"

"Let's talk it over, Ben!"

"Talk's done. Shootin' now."

"We can talk, Ben. I ain't a hard man to get along with."

"You have been up until now," Travis said. "You want to talk, come on out."

The people of Illinois Town were now a solid packed ring around Sweet's porch. Travis glanced at them, then said, "Jethro, I won't wait."

"All right," Sweet said and his heavy shoes made clacking sounds on the floor. He appeared in the doorway with his rifle, slowly he set it aside as though he only half trusted Travis. "I'm tired of fighting you, Ben."

That was all; he had said it and there was no turning back.

Travis put his rifle up. "The town's big enough for both of us, Jethro. I said that once."

Sweet nodded, his glance searching for his brother. Fountainbleau still moaned by the wall, but Jethro cared nothing for him. He saw Clem in the dust and took a step toward him, halting when Travis spoke.

"These folks want to hear you say it, Jethro."

"There'll be no more trouble," Jethro said. This hurt him, but the worse hurt was yet to come.

"What about their credits?" Travis asked.

"I'll pay 'em off in money," Sweet said. "Is that enough, Ben?"

"That's all any man can ask," Travis said.

Jethro went to his brother and lifted him. Travis turned and left the porch. He found Priam Thomas in the crowd and gave him back his rifle. The others stood in silence, watching Jethro tend his brother. Somehow they all seemed a little disappointed for the end of an era should be sharply defined but this ended in softly spoken words of quiet agreement.

Travis said, "You ready to go home, Thomas?"

"Nothin' to do around here," Thomas said and they pushed their way through the crowd.

Sabrina Kane could not recall a time in her life when the minutes had moved so slowly and each moment had held so much doubt. For what seemed hours she waited by her fire, and when she heard the first burst of shooting, instead of finding relief, she found a cold clamp of fear constricting her mind.

She closed her eyes and prayed.

When she heard the next shots, muffled and seemingly far distant, she whirled to the door and stepped outside, stopping there. From across the flats to the settlement she could hear people calling to one another, converging on Sweet's trading post. She knew fear and doubt, but endured the waiting with the forced patience women assume during times of crises. When she could stand it no longer she turned and made herself a cup of coffee. She cooled it with a dash of water.

In the bedroom the youngest Lockwood child whimpered in his sleep. Jenner said something soothing and Pride Lockwood was quiet. She thought, Jenner's such a good boy, such a little man.

When she finished the coffee she put the cup on the table. The open door was an invitation and she stepped to it, looking again toward the center of the settlement.

All seemed quiet and dark around the trading post. There were no sounds save the bullfrogs along the river. Suddenly they stopped croaking. This drew her attention.

On the moonslick river, war canoes nudged into the bank and Indians sloshed ashore, feathered Sac and Fox warriors. The sight held her and she watched them come on toward her cabin, flitting in and out of the shadows near the trees.

Finally her survival instinct awoke and she whirled inside, slamming the door and sliding the bar in place. The Indians yelled, breaking into a run. Sabrina looked around for a weapon, the blood-freezing sound in her ears. She snatched up the fireplace tongs and waited, her heart pounding.

The bedroom door opened and Jenner came out, wide-eyed.

"Go back inside and close the door," Sabrina said. "Mind me now!"

Several of the Indians pounded against the door with their bows. A drum commenced to throb and a wild singing filled the night with a pagan flavor.

A voice she recognized as Shawnee Blanc's shouted, "*Maka'-pezu' ta-wan! Naya' pe cin do, Maka'-pezu' ta-wan!*"

Sabrina leaned against the door, feeling the vibration of their pounding go through her. Jenner opened the bedroom door a crack, looked at her, and came out.

"Is that Shawnee Blanc, Ma?"

" . . . *Hina' pa yo, Maka'-pezu' ta-wan! Hina' pa yo! . . .*"

"Yes, that's Shawnee Blanc." She closed her eyes.

"He wouldn't hurt you, Ma. Not Shawnee —"

"He brought the red beasties down on us," Sabrina said. "Hush now."

" . . . *Pezu' ta wakan Kola' wa' yelo! . . .*"

The pounding continued. Sabrina clapped her hands over her ears to shut out the sounds.

Then she heard another voice, that of Benjamin Travis, shouting, "*Kola! Tan-yan!*"

The Indians turned away from her door; she could hear them. There was a rapid conversation between Shawnee Blanc and Travis, and then Travis stepped to the door. "Sabrina? Open the door, Sabrina."

She slid the bar mechanically and opened the door. Travis pushed it wide and pulled her outside. She wanted to put her arms around him, to have him hold her, but he fended her off. "Not now, Sabrina." He looked at Priam Thomas, who stood nervously to one side. "Thomas, go inside and get that danged shell of Sabrina's."

The Indians were building up a huge fire and the drums increased their tempo. The dancing began and along the fringe of light the suspicious population of Illinois Town gathered, rifles ready.

"Shawnee Blanc brought 'em here to see you, Sabrina," Travis was saying. "That conch shell is big medicine an' Shawnee's a big man, since he discovered it." He looked around at the settlers. "Sure hope no one gets nervous and fires into this flock. They're peaceful and as long as you're big medicine, there won't be any trouble."

Thomas came out with the sea shell and Travis indicated the crowd with a nod. "Spread it around that there'll be no trouble started."

"I'll do that," Thomas said. "You intend to let 'em howl an' jig all night?"

"There ain't much a man can do to put a stop to it," Travis said. "They've come here to see the medicine. Wouldn't be smart to run 'em off."

"Guess you're right," Thomas said and began working his way through the settlers, talking, getting their nods.

Sabrina watched the festivities. Shawnee Blanc was dancing like a man possessed. "Seems strange," she said, "that they'd think a sea shell was medicine."

254

"It don't matter what they believe," Travis said. "Without that shell we'd be fightin' a no-give, no-take war. Shawnee Blanc's done us a heap-big favor, fetchin' 'em back. They don't give a whoop for these settlers, but because we're with you, they'll make peace. Without you they'd be shootin' fire arrows right now." He gave her a small push. "Git out there and show 'em the shell. Make it real mysterious."

She looked at the Indians somewhat fearfully, then stepped among them, bringing the dancing to a sudden halt. The drumming ceased with an abruptness that hurt the ears. A deep quiet settled around the huge fire.

Then the leader stepped forward and spoke: "*Kowa' kipe 'sni, pezu ta wa-kan. Wan-ma yanko yo, nawa zinye ta-han waon'.*"

Travis spoke quietly, but with great urgency. "Look pleased, Sabrina. He just paid you the highest honor an Injun knows how; he made you big medicine, like the wind and the sun. His tribe's swore to protect you."

Shawnee Blanc's eyes were bright buttons of pleasure. Several Indians went to the canoes and returned laden with fine pelts, blankets and clothing highly decorated with animal bones and trade beads. These were piled at Sabrina's feet. Then the Sac and Fox chief spoke again: "*Pezu ta wa-kan, kohan' wakta' waon yelo'. Bluha' honpi huwo' pezu ta wakan.*"

"He say all gifts for you," Shawnee Blanc translated. "Now he want see big-wind-in-hand. All want hear, Mother-of-Wind."

Sabrina held the shell up and the Sac and Fox chief approached it cautiously. He bent forward until his ear

255

nearly touched and on his face appeared the most amazed expression. The citizens of Illinois Town stood silently, watching.

They were not convinced that these Indians meant peace.

In the order of their rank, one by one, the Sac and Fox warriors came up to Sabrina and placed their ear against the shell. The last few were little more than boys trying to be brave in the face of the demon contained in the sea shell. Yet they dared not expose this fear to their elders.

After all had partaken in the 'medicine,' the leader spoke briefly, waving his arms high as he punctuated his speech with stamping feet. Then as suddenly as they had come, they turned to the river and their canoes. In a moment they were in the water, paddles dipping, pulling upstream.

Shawnee Blanc remained behind for he had discovered the medicine woman; he had a divine duty to perform, a voluntary slavery. And he seemed pleased with his lot.

Travis spoke to Priam Thomas. "There goes Cap'n Pressly's Indian war. An' you can spread it around that it was Sabrina's doin', too."

Some of the settlers acted as though they had been cheated out of a good fight, but the majority were grateful there had been no trouble. Thomas went among them, saying his goodnights and when the last were walking through the grass toward home, turned to Ben Travis and his daughter.

"I expect I've lost my home," he said.

"In-laws don't mix," Travis said. "Even a beaver pup leaves his ma an' pa."

"Well," Thomas said. "I ain't broke up about it." He grinned and turned aside, walking toward Bond's place, where he expected to talk his way into a bed in the lean-to.

Sabrina went into the cabin, shooed Jenner back into the bedroom and closed the door. Travis said, "Was I you I'd fetch that Injun stuff inside."

"You're the man around here."

"Uh," Travis said and made several trips to the lean-to.

When he came back in and closed the door, Sabrina was sitting by the fire, combing her hair. She wore a long, cotton nightgown that covered her feet. Benjamin Travis was filled with a sudden and confusing idleness. He said, "You're not sorry, Sabrina? I mean about the bargain."

She looked at him. "No, I'm not sorry," she said, but her tone betrayed her. She was sorry. Sorry that she had ragged him into being something that he was never intended to be. Sorry that she had not been woman enough to accept him as he had been, reckless, laughing, strong in his wild way. Yet she could speak of none of this or tell him that she didn't want to run anything, that she was glad to sew and cook and have his children. She suspected that he wouldn't want to hear it.

In the firelight his face seemed aged and she knew beyond a doubt that she had put this gravity in his cheeks. She felt this tug of guilt and said, "Ben, I've never told you, but I love you."

The words sounded flat and without meaning; tardiness made them that way. Suddenly she could no longer bear to look at her own creation and she turned her back to him, near tears. How foolish now was her belief that he would ever crush her spirit by domination. He was too strong a man, one who knew his strength and never needed to test it on others.

Travis regarded her thoughtfully, and man-like, assumed this moment of clumsiness to be of his own making. He was unlettered, a spontaneous man, and because of this, turned to the only avenue of expression open to him, the banjo leaning against the wall.

He picked it up, struck a gay chord, then smiling, said, "You want me to play you a tune, Sabrina?"

She whirled, tears of happiness dimming her vision. He hadn't changed!

Then she ran to him and he folded her in his arms. She bumped the banjo and it gave out a pitiful twang. Laughter bubbled in her, and she stepped away from him, her face animated, her eyes glistening with pleasure. "Play me a song, Ben. Play one every night we live. Don't ever let me forget what it is to live, Ben, not even for a moment."

Will Cook is the author of numerous outstanding Western novels as well as historical frontier fiction. He was born in Richmond, Indiana, but was raised by an aunt and uncle in Cambridge, Illinois. He joined the U.S. Cavalry at the age of sixteen but was disillusioned because horses were being eliminated through mechanization. He transferred to the U.S. Army Air Force in which he served in the South Pacific during the Second World War. Cook turned to writing in 1951 and contributed a number of outstanding short stories to *Dime Western* and other pulp magazines as well as fiction for major smooth-paper magazines such as *The Saturday Evening Post*. It was in the *Post* that his best-known novel, *Comanche Captives*, was serialized. It was later filmed as *Two Rode Together* (Columbia, 1961), directed by John Ford and starring James Stewart and Richard Widmark. Sometimes in his short stories Cook would introduce characters who would later be featured in novels, such as Charlie Boomhauer who first appeared in "Lawmen Die Sudden" in *Big-Book Western* in 1953 and is later to be found in *Badman's Holiday* (1958) and *The Wind River Kid* (1958). Along with his steady productivity, Cook maintained an enviable quality. His novels range widely in time and place, from the Illinois frontier of 1811 to southwest Texas in 1905, but each is peopled with credible and interestering characters whose interactions form the backbone of the narrative. Most of his novels deal with more or less traditional Western themes — range wars, reformed outlaws, cattle rustling, Indian fighting — but there are also romantic novels such as *Sabrina Kane* (1956) and exercises in historical realism such as *Elizabeth, By Name* (1958). Indeed, his fiction is known for its strong heroines. Another common feature is Cook's compassion for his characters, who must be able to survive in a wild and violent land. His protagonists make mistakes, hurt people they care for, and sometimes succumb to ignoble impulses, but this all provides an added dimension to the artistry of his work.